DEATH'S LEGACY

DENNIS K. CROSBY

FROM THE TINY ACORN ...
GROWS THE MIGHTY OAK

This is a work of fiction. References to real people, events, establishments, organizations, or locales are intended only to provide a sense of authenticity and are used fictitiously. All other characters, and all incidents and dialogue are drawn from the author's imagination and are not to be construed as real.

Death's Legacy

www.acornpublishingllc.com

Cover design by Damonza
Interior design and formatting by Debra Cranfield Kennedy

ISBN-13: 978-1-952112-15-7 (hardcover)
ISBN-13: 978-1-952112-14-0 (paperback)
Library of Congress Control Number: 2020918955

For my grandson, Robert James Crosby

◆　　◆　　◆

CHAPTER ONE

THE WORLD WAS CHANGING AROUND HER. SHE'D BEEN SO HELL bent on hiding that she couldn't see it, but she could feel it. She *felt* so much these days that hanging out on the sidelines was no longer an option. There were no signs or omens in the skies above, no messages from psychics or hidden meanings in tea leaves, and certainly no prophetic dreams of impending doom. But with everything she was feeling, Kassidy Simmons was certain someone would die, and soon.

Someone other than the woman lying lifeless at her feet.

What the fuck?

She hadn't wanted to take this case. Things in her life were spinning out of control, and she needed a break. But it was for her, that damned London Jaymes, a private investigator out of Chicago Kassidy had met years ago on a case. Kassidy had a difficult time saying no to her, hated disappointing her.

It pained her that she'd have to share this news.

Kassidy absently checked for a pulse, knowing there'd be none. After all, she sensed death as clearly as she felt the emotions of those around her. The bright red glow surrounding the motionless body spoke volumes. She searched for signs of violence. A stab wound, gunshot, any evidence of being choked or beaten . . . but there was nothing. Like so many others in town.

Lately, every news report in St. John seemed to be about one unexpected death or another. Having just spoken to Karen Dodd last night to confirm her identity and location, Kassidy had expected to close this case and get back to brooding. Instead, she'd found Karen dead in the living room of a house she shared with her boyfriend.

Karen Dodd, twenty-three-year-old medical coder from Chicago, had skipped out on some child support payments. Her luck had been about to change, following the recent death of her grandmother. Karen was to receive a substantial inheritance that would have made her square with her ex and potentially put her on track to pursue other goals.

An aneurism put a stop to that.

The weight of the recent deaths in St. John made Kassidy's heart heavy. It was as if she knew she needed to act but didn't have a clue how to curtail the tragedies. Could this death have been prevented? Arriving sooner wouldn't have helped this poor woman, yet Kassidy felt responsible. The sensation nipped at her like a young puppy at her heel. Her body vibrated, and her vision blurred as the anxiety overwhelmed her. *What's happening to me?*

Shakily, she backed into a bookcase, causing an avalanche of novels to topple over. "Shit," she whispered.

"Babe," said a voice from upstairs, "you okay?"

Kassidy's stomach churned. She's almost forgotten about the boyfriend upstairs. He needed to stay up there a little longer. His presence would only hinder her efforts at discovering what happened.

"Mm-hmm," she responded lazily. "Just some books, no worries."

She prayed the distance would mask her voice. The shower was running upstairs—hopefully, that would help. *Please let that help.* Kassidy closed her eyes, took a deep breath, and slowly released it. Sometimes this technique worked. Bourbon and Vicodin worked better.

She craved both now.

Opening her eyes, she retrieved her phone to call London. It took a second to find the number, and as she pressed the send button, a rush of air filled the room and a gray cloud seeped in under the front door. Kassidy silenced her phone and remained still as the gray cloud took form.

The vapor coalesced, dispersed, and there stood a dark-haired woman in a charcoal-gray pantsuit. *A Reaper.* "Apparently there's a dress code now," Kassidy whispered to herself. The Reaper knelt, looked over the body of Karen Dodd, then plunged her hand into the dead woman's chest. It phased through, harmlessly, and when she retracted her hand, she held a small glowing orb.

What the fuck?

The Reaper opened her mouth and ingested it. Kassidy fought the impulse to lunge forward and attack. This wasn't supposed to happen. Reapers were supposed to usher souls to the afterlife, not ingest them and damn them to an eternity of nothingness. Glaring at the suited woman, Kassidy's jaw tightened, and she gritted her teeth as her anger intensified. She no longer cared about remaining invisible. Hiding from the Reaper world was inconsequential in light of what had just happened. Besides, there was only one. Kassidy could dispatch the Reaper quickly before the others were alerted. She wanted answers and possibly, even more important right now, vengeance for Karen Dodd.

She rushed the Reaper.

Kassidy made herself visible seconds before pinning her against the wall. Her left forearm pressed against the Reaper's neck and her right hand vanished into a cloud of smoke, only to be replaced with a sickle which she pressed against the intruder's abdomen. She saw surprise in the Reaper's eyes. Eyes that had gone from silver to light green.

"Who the hell are you?" the Reaper asked.

"You're not in a position to ask questions, bitch," Kassidy spat back. "You need to explain why you just ingested that woman's soul right fucking now!"

The Reaper struggled.

"Answer me, damn you!"

The Reaper's eyes turned silver again, and she dematerialized. Spinning, scanning the room, Kassidy was frantic, unfocused, and unprepared when the Reaper suddenly reappeared and punched her in the face. The force of the blow shoved Kassidy into the bookcase, causing more books to tumble down.

"Karen?"

The voice upstairs refocused Kassidy. The Reaper dematerialized into gray vapor and exited the home. Kassidy wanted to follow, but adrenaline shot through her body like a geyser. She collapsed to one knee, clutched her chest, and gasped.

This isn't me. These aren't my emotions.

From a darkened corner, Kassidy watched as Karen's boyfriend rushed into the living room, screaming Karen's name. Visibly trembling, he shook the young woman, trying to awaken her. Awareness filled Kassidy. His awareness. Awareness that Karen Dodd was gone forever.

Pushing aside the feelings of the man in the living room, Kassidy willed herself to dematerialize into vapor, and she vanished.

◆　◆　◆

Kassidy materialized in the kitchen of her townhome and leaned against the countertop. Her head spun. She needed to process everything she'd just seen. She needed to contact London and let her know the case was over and her missing person was dead. She needed to get rid of the headache before it evolved.

She needed a drink.

Something odd was going on with her, and given the path her life had taken, that statement itself was strange. Kassidy was an empath, and not one of the new age, patchouli-reeking, "I can really feel your aura" types. No, a true empath, Kassidy's abilities only manifested in the presence of others. She sensed their emotions. The stronger the feelings, the more intensely she experienced them, and often, the more they overwhelmed her. She used to be able to mitigate the strength of the emotions she absorbed, reducing their negative effects on her mind and body. Back then they would mostly manifest as a migraine or neck tension. With some calming techniques she'd read about, she was able to manage the discomfort. In recent years, though, that had become increasingly difficult. When no amount of focus would help, Kassidy turned to Vicodin, then to bourbon.

The last few months she combined the two.

That The headache starting behind her left eye was not unusual. Since the increase in sensitivity to emotion, it didn't take much these days for the pain to begin. But it was ten in the morning, and there was no one else around. Lynn had left long before.

As usual, she had not been happy.

Kassidy loved Lynn, she truly did. Lynn was the kind of partner people dreamed of. Smart, funny, gorgeous, organized— she had her shit together.

Kassidy often wondered what Lynn saw in her, because in Kassidy's mind, she was a grade-A fuckup.

"Dammit Kass! Focus!"

Kassidy was finding it increasingly difficult to manage her thoughts. While normally task oriented, especially when working a missing persons case, recently her mind drifted toward other issues. Principle among them, her disintegrating relationship with Lynn.

After three years, things were shifting. The passion they had once shared was stale as week-old bread. With bread, though, you could pop it in the toaster and salvage something. Add a little butter and jelly, and you were good to go. Kassidy and Lynn had tried something similar. Their "toaster" had been a week away in Lake Tahoe. The plane ride had been fun, as had the drive from the airport to the house they had rented overlooking the lake. Even the first night or two had been exciting. But toasted or not, stale bread was still stale bread. Maybe Lynn finally realized she could do better. Maybe she was laying the foundation for a breakup.

These thoughts swirled in Kassidy's brain daily, particularly after sensing the cooler temperatures that manifested around Lynn. Kassidy still felt love from Lynn when they were near each other, but with a chill to it. She likened it to a fall afternoon in her hometown of Oak Park, Illinois. Comfort existed in the coolness, in the promise of the beauty of falling leaves, bonfires, and an occasional storm. The bad side to that was, of course, the inevitability of impending frigid winds, the snow, the ice, the longing for warmth. Winter lurked around the corner, and Kassidy had no idea how to stop it.

If she were being honest, she wasn't sure she wanted to.

Yet another reason to drink and pop a pill.

With that volatile cocktail, Kassidy could avoid tapping into Lynn's feelings—any feelings, for that matter. She could have some peace and feel normal, even if only for a short time. The problem was the voice on the inside, the voice that told her, dared her, to open herself up to Lynn's feelings.

Every so often Kassidy would skip her med cocktail to sense Lynn's emotions. Each time, she was so devastated by the conflict and ambiguity in Lynn that she couldn't help but drink. Then she'd add that extra spice, and voilà, Vicodin was a sleeping pill. For a long time, her dreams offered her refuge. Today, it was a crapshoot. Some nights the feelings were acceptable. Most nights though, not so much. Kassidy just needed to know. If Lynn no longer loved her, if she was planning to leave her, Kassidy would be free to be herself . . . whatever that meant. On the other hand, if Lynn still loved her and they were just going through the proverbial rough patch, then she would still be stuck.

Wait. No, not stuck. She loved Lynn, and the relationship wasn't a burden. Right?

Maybe it wasn't a burden. Maybe it was just too routine, as was the case with most of her days. Perhaps the routine ran a little stale, even a little moldy on the bottom. This rut just did not want to go away. Though, in the rut's defense, Kassidy hadn't tried to make it go away. She seemed content to be anxious and depressed. It fueled her bad habits, and the bad habits fueled her feelings—the perfect symbiotic relationship. One that would lead her down the aisle toward a marriage with self-destruction.

That would be one hell of a reception.

Getting back to the tasks before her, Kassidy poured some coffee into her mug, added a hint of Baileys Irish Cream for flavor—it was morning, after all, and far too early for bourbon—and then walked into her home office. Over the years, the one thing, the only thing really, she appreciated was her ability to work alone. She didn't have to worry about going into a corporate office and dealing with people and their emotions. There was no dread at the prospect of seeing Reapers who'd come to collect or mark someone for the afterlife. There were no kids, no pets, no nothing. Only silence, her thoughts, and her work.

Kassidy sipped her coffee and powered on her laptop, preparing to update London. She'd check her email first, then sports scores, then the news of the day. Even with all that had happened, procrastination was still king. In the back of her mind, she was already excited about her second cup of coffee and Baileys. She was anxious. The morning events made her anxious. Her relationship made her anxious. Life felt like one giant jigsaw puzzle—but the picture was Rorschach. She was certain that something was coming, something big, and everything in her screamed that she'd be a key player in these unknown events. But with no clue as to what the big bad was, the feeling just followed her—a dark, ominous cloud over her head.

Regardless of her feelings, she followed through with her call to London.

"Hey you," said the voice on the other end.

Her voice stirred up memories and feelings from their first meeting so many years ago. She was initially drawn to London because of the stillness that surrounded the woman. Kassidy could not feel her emotions and that brought a certain sense of liberation. Sure, it was disarming at first, but then, she got to know London and that experience combined with the freedom from not having someone else's emotions mixed with her own, left Kassidy feeling like the burden that was her life had been lifted.

The mutual attraction between the two was certainly the icing on the cake.

"Hey, London."

"Please tell me you have some good news for me."

Of course, she didn't. And it pained Kassidy to tell her what happened. London was one of the few people who knew about her ability. Neither Lynn nor her best friend, David, were privy to that nugget of information. She certainly didn't tell them about Reapers. But London knew. London knew just about everything. She was special. In more ways than one.

"Jesus!" exclaimed London.

"I'm so sorry. If I'd just gotten there a little earlier, I might have . . ."

"Kass, stop that. I don't think there's anything you could have done to keep her from dying. Don't put yourself through that."

"I know," Kassidy replied. "On some level I get that. But there is some weird shit happening, like even weird for me and you."

"I'm a vampire living in Chicago, love. Weird is a walk in the park."

Kassidy shrugged in agreement. Weird took on a very different meaning in their respective worlds. She told London more about the number of strange deaths in St. John, and about the power boost she was experiencing.

"And then today, you see a Reaper ingest a soul instead of taking it to the next plane?"

"Yeah," Kassidy replied.

"Well, damn. Things sound well and truly fucked in St. John. You want me to come out and give you a hand?"

Kassidy wanted to say yes. A part of her did, at least. With London, she could just be herself. But that was precisely why she needed to stay away. Because no matter how she looked at it, Kassidy didn't truly know what it *meant* to just be herself. She had no idea who she really was, both literally and figuratively.

"No. No, don't worry. I'll get a handle on this. If I need help, I'll shout out."

"You better."

"I'm sorry again."

"I told you to stop that," said London. "I'll handle it from here. You take care of yourself over there."

They said goodbye. Kassidy reached for her coffee cup only to find it empty.

In the kitchen pouring her second cup, Kassidy peered outside at the park in the distance where a few kids enjoyed the unusually mild weather. They played, laughed, ran, doing all the things kids did. But Kassidy saw, in the distance, something moving toward them. It moved like swift fog—dark, pregnant with anticipation—and zeroed in on the kids.

"No." Kassidy startled herself. She knew what that dark figure was. She could only watch as the fog stopped at the edge of the playground, just past the unsuspecting children. Tendrils of smoke slowly swirled and formed into a person. In place of the smoke, a man stood, dressed in black, his blond hair a stark contrast. The kids behind were oblivious to his presence, but they would be, because unless he willed it, only one person could see him.

And she did.

Kassidy stood in disbelief as he stared her way from a distance. She remained still, equally afraid and angry. The man in black glanced right to left, left to right, but came back to center focus, his gaze on Kassidy's townhome. Even with the distance she could see him smiling. Still, she was certain he couldn't see her, at least not physically, so the warding was working. But that smile, so sinister, so . . . knowing. It gave her the feeling that somehow, he knew she was there.

A Wraith had found her. A *Wraith*, not a Reaper. In that moment, Kassidy no longer questioned the earlier sensation.

Someone would die soon.

And probably not well.

CHAPTER TWO

SENAYA AWOKE TO THE SOUND OF SILENCE AND THE REALIZATION that she had done it yet again—she'd had sex with a mortal. In the big scheme of things, it wasn't a big deal, except for the part where she was trying to not do that anymore, especially now that *he* was back. Until the last couple of months, she had been successful. For 103 years she'd had her lover, and for the last twenty she'd had nothing. But the recent changes in the natural order threw everything that was once normal into an unpredictable state, a frenzy of need, of emotion, of satisfying the most primal instincts in everyone—even the Reapers and Wraiths who were the root cause. Senaya had gone from twenty years of celibacy to eight weeks of debauchery. She had certain . . . interests, and it was hard to satiate them. In the wake of the dark chaos surrounding her and those like her, as if compelled, she kept trying.

Again . . . and again . . . and again.

She turned over and eyed the man next to her.

"Why is he still here?" she asked herself. "Oh . . . yeah, this is his place."

He was handsome, and not unlike a puppy in that he was young and eager to please. In fact, his leg even shook when she touched him in certain places. He damn sure was not what she needed, nor was he anything she'd ever want. He scratched an itch, just as the other guy had last night and the Cuban two nights ago. These men were simply a means to an end.

Hell, she didn't even remember their names.

Kevin? Keith?

She sat up slowly, not wanting to rouse the young pup lest he think it was time for another round. In the part of her that was still human, she recognized he was sweet. A pleaser. Also, arrogant and oblivious to the ways of the world, particularly when it came to women. He would likely die surrounded by a bunch of equally arrogant and clueless people. She would likely take pleasure in watching as he was ushered into the afterlife. She didn't do that anymore. She was a Wraith. The Reapers' leader, in fact. One of a special cadre of warriors created by the Primus himself to police the Reapers, the Nexus, and anything else he directed. She could usher souls if she chose, but now her mission was more important than escorting ungrateful human essence to the afterlife.

Her mission was him.

Everything now was for him.

For Azra-El.

For her love.

Senaya's head snapped up as she felt a familiar psychic pull. Someone was reaching out to her through the Nexus. She stood up; her naked, athletic frame illuminated faintly by the light beyond the large picture window of the studio apartment.

"Ugh, this apartment! What was I thinking?" she thought to herself. But it wasn't really the apartment that she found objectionable. It was her behavior. It was her inability to control the urges she felt. Her inability to stay true to her love, her mentor, her Primus.

She regarded the figure in the bed and smiled. Not out of satisfaction or longing. Nothing so sentimental. It had nothing to do with Kevin or Keith or whatever the hell his name was. She smiled because in a short time she would have everything she needed—in him. He was healing even more rapidly now. Before long he'd be at full strength, and she would be in his arms and his bed. He would fulfil her needs. Satisfy those growing urges.

Senaya closed her eyes, and within seconds, tendrils of black smoke swirled around her, engulfing her, and she was gone.

Senaya re-formed in a park inside the Nexus, a world just beyond the real world. As all things in the Nexus, everything took on a greenish-gray tint. Wisps of fog covered the ground, moving as if sentient. She looked around, attempting to gather her bearings, but she was unfamiliar with this area. It all appeared so suburban. Before her stood Ethan, her second, dressed in all black, his blond hair the only other color on his large frame.

"Armani?"

Ethan nodded, then inclined his head toward her.

"Casual Friday?"

Senaya glanced down and only then noticed she was still naked. It never bothered her, being naked. It was as natural to her as the sun rising in the east. This sense of freedom was a satisfying turn from the way she was raised—a middle finger to her father and the restrictive culture in which she'd grown up.

With a devilish grin, Senaya stared at Ethan, allowed her eyes to go black, the defining symbol of the Wraith's power, and willed smoke to coalesce around her. As it faded away, black leather pants, a black sleeveless silk top, and black boots covered her. The silver necklace she wore, the only thing she kept from her former life, shined bright, an elegant contrast against her clothes and mocha skin.

"I was . . . occupied earlier," she said, with no apology or embarrassment.

"We all have needs."

"Indeed." Senaya had no interest in defending her actions. Certainly not to Ethan. "So why am I here? More importantly, where is here?"

Ethan stood to the side and waved at their surroundings, like a game show host showing off prizes.

"Welcome to St. John, New York. A hidden gem only minutes from Lake Erie and a few hours from the bustling burg of Buffalo."

The sarcasm in his voice was a constant. The only person in the Reaper ranks as old as she, elevating him to Wraith had been a no-brainer. Making him her second made equal sense. He had as much knowledge, experience, and disdain for humans as she had, and he was easily managed. Manipulated was a better word. He thought he loved her, though love was an overstatement. He lusted for her, and perhaps in his mind that was love. Whatever the case, that knowledge was a weapon that Senaya wielded expertly against him when it suited her. In another time, another life, perhaps when they had been human, something might have happened between them. Even when they were only Reapers, there'd been a chance. But once they had been elevated to Wraith, once Azra-El had taken her under his wing, any such thoughts vanished as quickly as ice on Arizona asphalt in July.

"Okay. So, we have the where. Let's get to the why," Senaya said.

Ethan gave a sinister grin.

"She's here."

Senaya's eyes widened. She needed no further explanation. Since Azra-El's return, only one person had been on their collective radar.

"Where?"

"Here!" He swept his arms around toward the homes beyond the park.

"How can you be sure?"

"A Reaper I know had a run in earlier with someone who sounds a lot like our missing girl. When we exit the Nexus, you'll feel it. It's strong. The pull is breaking the barrier," Ethan said.

"Her wards are degrading."

"Or she's becoming more powerful."

"Or both," Senaya said. "In the end, that may not bode well for us."

"But for him . . ."

"Yes, for him."

Senaya stood next to Ethan. They stared at the cluster of townhomes beyond the park. In one of those homes was one of the most powerful beings in the Reaper ranks. In one of those homes lived the only being who had ever bested the Angel of Death. In one of those homes was a woman who had defeated Senaya's love, her life, her Azra-El. In one of those homes, Kassidy Simmons was alive and well.

For now.

CHAPTER THREE

KASSIDY'S MORNING HAD ESCALATED AFTER SEEING THAT WRAITH in the park, and that was saying a lot considering what she'd already seen at Karen Dodd's house. She had a pretty good idea of who it was, which made her nervous. Her anxiety, though, paled in comparison to the crushing weight of anticipation she'd felt after listening to Lynn's voicemail—a message that prompted her to go to a place that empaths avoid at all costs.

Kassidy stood across the street from St. John Memorial Hospital, pacing and shaking. Not from cold, but from the internal hurricane caused by thousands of butterflies. At this distance, she was on the edge of the myriad emotions emanating from the hospital. At least, she should have been.

But something was wrong with the natural order.

Very wrong.

She shouldn't have been able to feel much of anything, especially with the liquor and Vicodin cocktail from brunch. The combination should have been enough to dampen any emotion, just as it had countless times before. Nevertheless, pain and despair left her on edge. The agony inside the hospital was palpable.

Her stomach in knots, her teeth and fists clenched, she stopped pacing for a moment to stare at St. John Memorial. Her eyes teared up, and her long dark hair blew in the frigid winds, whipping across her cheek like a taskmaster. Reaching into her pocket, she retrieved her phone, pressed a button, and listened once again to the voicemail.

"Hey, Kass. It's me. Listen, Dad had a setback. They ran all kinds of tests on him and they found . . . something. I don't really understand it, but they've got to cut him open again. Look, I know how you feel about hospitals and being around sick people and all, but . . . I could really use you here. Mom's here, but it's not the same as having you. I just . . . I'm scared, I think. I don't know. I'm babbling now. Just . . . come. Please. I love you."

Kassidy ended the voicemail and stared at her phone. With the emotion coming from across the street, it was harder and harder to discern which feelings were hers. She loved Lynn, didn't she? Why was she so unable to put her own fear aside to be with her if she loved her? Was she a bad girlfriend? Was she a bad person? She was likely more the former than the latter. Things had been different in the beginning. Then again things were always different in the beginning of any relationship. Everything was new and exciting. There was so much wonder and antici-pation. Everything was . . . adorable. But time can be a cruel enemy. Kassidy had become more distant in the last year. She'd recognized it but was unable to stop it.

Maybe she didn't want to.

She took a deep breath, pocketed her phone, and slowly stepped toward the hospital. She stopped when she saw the first Reaper, nothing more than a gray vapor trail, enter the hospital's main entrance. Someone was near death or already gone. She remained in place, frozen, holding her breath, as if the slightest sound would alert a horde of Reapers to her presence.

She took another deep breath and continued forward. As she edged closer, emotion flowed from the hospital and dripped on her like steady rain. As she crossed the street, the rain of torment turned to a storm—heavy, wet, oppressive.

Close to the entrance, she clutched her stomach. The bombardment caused a volcanic eruption in her gut, her heart a jackhammer in her chest. She struggled to stand, then dropped to one knee when she saw *them*. Three vapors. Two, lighter in color, entered the hospital without giving her a second consideration. The darker one hovered.

There had never been a more demonic-looking creature. Ascending from Reaper to Wraith came with perks, increased power being the main prize. That power, though, took a toll on the soul, what was left of it anyway. Their power was given directly from the Primus, but he was no god. That power was not his to give. Consequently, it was tainted. They could maintain it at a cost, and that cost was the eternal deterioration of their physical form, matching the growing darkness within. This Wraith was void of anything human. Its tattered, hooded cloak covered a withered gray face. Its sunken eyes spoke of pain and agony. As it opened its mouth, Kassidy saw the jagged, spaced, and bloody teeth of a creature that died a little bit every day only to be reborn in that same instant. Wraiths were horrific, onyx-eyed creatures of darkness. Kassidy simultaneously feared and felt sorry for them.

With concentration, a Wraith could take on its former human form. Dark-gray smoke swirled about like a small tornado, and within seconds a man stood in its place. The same Wraith from the morning. His dark suit appeared expensive. His blond hair sat atop his head like a crown, perfectly sculpted. When he blinked, his black eyes became a brilliant, almost abnormal green.

Ethan!

Kassidy had met him once, a year after she'd left home. He was fit. Not overly muscular, but unquestionably well-toned. She remembered him as pretty, something she'd never said about a man before. She'd imagined he was the type who stood in front of the mirror for hours after a shower, using enough products to supply a Walmart.

At nineteen years old, her life experience had been limited, and she had never seen anyone like this Ethan—self-absorbed, absently confident, and convinced that anything and anyone was his to do with as he pleased. Back then, she likely would have let him.

What is he doing here? Why now?

Ethan walked toward her, glancing from side to side as if he could not see her. *The wards are working.* Still, if they worked as they should, this would not be happening. He stopped steps before her. Kassidy fought the pain and remained on one knee. She looked up at him, holding her breath, rigid as a corpse.

"I can't see you, but I know you're here," he said. "I can sense you, Kassidy. We all can. And you should know, we're coming for you. And so is he."

Kassidy blinked rapidly. Her lips quivered, and she felt a crinkle in the corner of her eyes as she fought tears. After what felt like an eternity, Ethan, smiling heartlessly, spun and dematerialized into dark vapor as he entered the hospital.

Kassidy stood slowly, still clutching her stomach, her head pounding. The sensations from the hospital flowed like waterfalls through the doors and windows, and she absorbed them, drowning, desperate to catch a breath for even a moment. Every emotional sting from physical pain, the shock of flat lines, both real and imminent, slammed into her, overwhelming her. She took a shaky step back from the hospital, then another and another, almost falling, until she was able to turn and run.

Kassidy made it across the street. Glancing back at the hospital, she wasn't sure what made her angrier—that she'd been found by the Wraiths after all these years, or that she was about to let down Lynn . . . again.

"I'm sorry, Lynn," she whispered. "I'm so sorry."

She knew in that moment that she did love Lynn. Not with the intensity she once had, but she loved her. Letting Lynn down made her feel guilty, unworthy. She blinked once and allowed power to flow through her, feeling the sensation of her eyes changing from blue to silver. Seconds later, light-gray tendrils of smoke wrapped around her feet and snaked their way up her body. Once engulfed, she was nothing but vapor, a vapor that rose into the air and drifted away like a leaf on a windy day.

◆　　◆　　◆

Twenty-Two Years Ago

"You can see me, can't you?" the dark figure asked.

The thing appeared, just as it always had when someone was near death. This was not the first time Kassidy watched a Reaper collect the soul of a dying person. She'd seen her first at six years old, and regularly since then. It was, however, the first time a Reaper had appeared to collect *her* soul.

Kassidy stared at him, unable to speak. Words formed in her head. They even made their way down to her throat. Her lips parted slightly to allow them to escape, but nothing emerged. Nothing but a soft exhale left her body, and with each exhale, so too a bit of her life force vanished.

"Yes. You can see me." His voice was smooth, aristocratic, and warm, despite the darkness that surrounded him. It was accented, but only a little—a southern drawl—yet the words carried an air of European sophistication. It was strange to her ears.

She lay upon the moist grass of Potter's Field in the sleepy little village of Oak Park where, as a child, she had been routinely teased and chased by her so-called friends. A part of her was happy to die. Another part knew it was sad that a sixteen-year-old girl would long for death.

"You are interesting, aren't you," the dark figure said. He knelt and peered closer at her.

Kassidy could not help but stare at the richness of his red eyes. Every Reaper she had ever seen had silver eyes. She assumed it was normal, but at times wondered if they just turned that way when they came for a soul. Perhaps it was a by-product of some strange hunger.

But this one's were red.

What does that mean?

"It takes something remarkable to call to me. Something powerful. Something . . . else."

Kassidy didn't understand. She was drowning in the lyrical sound of his voice and mesmerized by his crimson gaze.

"We need to figure out what you are, don't we?" His hand reached out and touched her forehead. His eyes glowed bright, ominous yet soothing.

A warmth radiated through her body. Her heavy eyelids closed. When she opened them, she was standing. No longer in her blue dress. She was dressed in dark jeans and her purple V-neck T-shirt. Well, not hers, but the one she'd stolen from Sarah.

Her surroundings were different somehow. She was still in the park, but a fog covered the scenery. Nothing dense though. Light, whispery, almost organic.

And it was everywhere.

She recognized Potter's Field. She looked down and identified the young girl lying on the ground in the blue homecoming dress. Kassidy took a step back, right into something. No, into someone. Whirling, she was face to face with the dark figure that had been standing above her. His features were handsome—a chiseled chin, dimples, and a movie star smile.

"Welcome to the Nexus, my dear," he said.

"The Nexus?"

"Think of it as a train station. This is the spot where souls meet Reapers and are escorted to their next . . . adventure," he said with a hint of malevolent sarcasm. "You know what a Reaper is, don't you?"

Kassidy nodded.

"How do you know? How can you see us?"

"I don't know. I've just always been able to."

The first time was when Billy Tate was hit by a car while riding his bike to school. She had not realized it then, but they'd come to collect Billy's soul. She'd screamed to anyone who would listen that a man in black was bending over Billy and helping him up. She'd pleaded for someone to step in, to stop the dark man from taking her only friend.

No one had moved.

No one else could see them.

And no one else had felt Billy's pain and fear.

"And what else have you always been able to do, Kassidy Simmons?"

The sound of her name startled her. Maybe because he knew it and she hadn't offered it first. Maybe because it seemed odd given that she was standing before him while another version of her was sprawled out on the wet grass behind her. Whatever the reason, it made her hyperaware of her surroundings. Like being awakened from a hypnotic trance.

"Who are you?" she asked.

"Fair enough." He shrugged. "I suppose we can get to the other things later. Here, we have nothing but time."

Kassidy made a mental note to ask what that meant. She didn't want to get distracted by going off on tangents.

"My name is Azra-El," he said with a slight bow.

"And you're a Reaper?"

"I'm a little bit more than that," he replied.

"Meaning?"

"Let's just say, if this whole death thing were a corporation, I'd be the president."

"So you're, like, in charge?"

"In a manner of speaking," Azra-El said. "I am responsible for maintaining the balance, and the Reapers help me do that."

"The balance of what?"

"The balance between life and death, and the afterlife. My Reapers usher the souls of the dead to the next plane of existence. I manage the Reapers."

"So, what comes after this?" Kassidy asked.

"Oh, my dear, that all depends on how good you were when you were alive."

"Like heaven or hell?"

Azra-El chuckled. Kassidy felt a flush of warmth to her cheeks. Even in this place, she still felt very human. Or as human as she had ever felt.

"The concept of a heaven or a hell is purely a human construct," Azra-El said. "But for the sake of simplicity, yes, we can call it heaven or hell."

"Well, what do you call it?"

"The place that you conceptualize as heaven, we simply call the Beyond."

"And hell?"

"The Void."

The thought of a place called a Void sent a shudder through her. She imagined a place of cold, of darkness . . . of nothingness. She thought about what she had done in life, and she felt the sting over the things she had yet to achieve.

Things she would now never accomplish.

"And they get to one of those places from here?"

Azra-El nodded.

"Based on how they lived their life?"

Azra-El nodded again.

Kassidy turned and walked over to her body. As she moved, the whispery fog cleared a path. Was it sentient? As she neared her body, the fog lifted. Kassidy regarded her prone self, then knelt. She considered the events in her life that led to this moment.

"Wondering where you'll end up?" Azra-El asked.

Kassidy said nothing.

"Life has not been kind to you, has it?"

Again, Kassidy said nothing. In some ways she was lucky. She'd been adopted by a loving family, and apart from the teasing and bullying, Oak Park had been a nice town to live in.

Until tonight.

Until Jeremy had decided that she owed him for rescuing her from the bullies after the homecoming dance.

"If nothing else, I can offer you this, Kassidy Simmons," Azra-El began.

Kassidy lifted her head and tentatively stepped forward.

"I can offer you peace of mind."

The words sounded empty. Peace of mind? What did that really mean? Would she go to the Beyond? Would there be peace there? Comfort? Warmth? Would she be happy?

"Then again . . ."

Kassidy's eyes widened. She stepped closer to him, a sense of anxiety washing over her. Not over the prospect of death. More so over the prospect of her afterlife being just as crappy as her actual life.

"What?" she asked softly.

"Well, there's this thing I can do. I shouldn't, but I can," Azra-El said.

"What is it?"

"It wouldn't be an easy life, but it would be a life." He held his hands up, palms out, as if warning her.

Kassidy couldn't feel her heart beating in this place, this Nexus. If she could have, it would've been racing. Somewhere in her mind she heard it thumping in anticipation of Azra-El's next words.

"I could make you one of us," he finally said.

"One of you? A Reaper?"

Azra-El nodded.

"And I'd have to escort souls to the Beyond or the Void?" Kassidy asked.

"Yes. And the best part, you'd be alive. Well, sort of. And powerful. Did I mention that part?"

"What kind of power?"

"The kind that makes it virtually impossible for people to mess with you. Ever."

Power. What could she do with power? Images floated through her mind. Images of people showing respect. Showing fear. People cowering as she exacted revenge. Bad things finally happening to bad people. Good people finally feeling safe.

Power.

She liked the sound of that.

CHAPTER FOUR

JUST BEYOND THE CITY LIMITS OF CHICAGO, ILLINOIS, LAY OAK PARK, a quiet, quaint village that many residents said was best city in the Midwest to raise kids. With a population of seventy-five thousand, five elementary schools, two middle schools, and two high schools—one of them private—Oak Park was a mecca for young professionals wanting to start a family without having to live within the hustle, bustle, and violence of the big city.

Bordered by four streets, Oak Park was nestled snuggly in the embrace of Chicago to the east, Elmwood Park to the north, River Forest and Forest Park to the west, and Berwyn and Cicero to the south. Crossing the border from the east, north, or south was like leaving the comfort of Kansas and entering the land of Oz. Oak Park felt colorful, brighter, and calmer. Certainly quieter than the big brother that was Chicago.

Like any suburb, it had its own unique qualities. Some of them, most of them, socioeconomic. If you were fortunate enough to live north of Lake Street, it was automatically assumed that your family had money. The homes of North Oak Park, just past the high school, were large two-story homes, with huge yards and driveways, fit for highly successful couples with multiple kids. The trees were breathtaking, especially during the fall. The leaves turned from green to yellow, and then yellow to a yellowish brown, before finally becoming that lunch-sack color associated with cooler temperatures and football season.

On the corner of Chapel and Vine stood a two-story, four-bedroom home, complete with a three-car attached garage and pool. A stereotypical white picket fence surrounded the yard, allowing a small gate in front that opened to the walkway of the home. The old-fashioned feel of the white picket fence and the tire swing hanging from the tall tree in the front yard was a peculiar juxtaposition to the home's infamous history. It had once belonged to the head of the Chicago Outfit. Organized crime leaders were notorious for running their illegal enterprise in the city while living some distance from the chaos and danger they created. These days, the house stood vacant. The current owner lived in Scottsdale, Arizona, during the fall and winter months—something about his health and bones. Mostly, it was because he hated snow and could afford to live elsewhere for part of the year.

A caretaker had come by weekly to sort the mail, rake the leaves, cut the grass, and trim the hedges. The owner, though absent, was opinionated about how a home should appear, even when he wasn't there to appreciate it. The caretaker worked hard for 250 dollars each week to make sure the home was always ready for the owner to occupy, even though it wouldn't happen for months. Inside, the windows were locked and covered. The bedrooms were empty, and the furniture was covered with white sheets.

On the oversized gray sofa with the attached chaise, opposite the nonfunctional fireplace, lay the Angel of Death.

Azra-El had been there for several days, his loyal Wraiths checking in on him from time to time as he gathered vigor. After almost two decades of slowly putting himself back together, two decades of escalating aggression and anger, he was finally able to hold his corporeal form indefinitely. He could feel himself strengthening daily.

His Reapers were out en masse, collecting souls and, by extension, feeding him, though they didn't know it. Soon his power would return, and he would lead them once again. For now, he only needed to rest, re-energize, and wait for his Wraiths to bring him the one who'd done this to him. Kassidy Simmons would stand before him and submit herself and her powers to him so he could finish what he'd begun. Her death would mean his ascension, a clear path to domination. And damnation to those who once stood in his way.

Especially the one who took his love.

Azra-El would be gone soon. The owner would return to the house in April, just in time for baseball season, to find his caretaker dead in the master bedroom. There would be no apparent cause for his death. Nothing that would make sense. He would simply be there, decomposed, in the same khaki pants, brown shoes, and white golf shirt he'd worn each Friday he'd tidied up the house.

CHAPTER FIVE

AS KASSIDY SIMMONS NEARED HER HOME, SHE RUBBED HER FACE again to wipe away the frozen tears on her cheeks and from the corners of her eyes. She hated winter, yet when given the chance to live anywhere on the map, she'd chosen another cold climate. As much as she'd complained about the frigid winters growing up in the Chicago suburbs, she stayed in St. John because she felt certain no one would think to look for her in the northern part of the country when she vanished.

As Kassidy neared the park outside the townhome she shared with Lynn, she saw the familiar snack truck operated by the Alexanders. Jean and George were a sweet retired couple who'd decided long ago that sitting at home all day watching game shows, judge shows, and talk shows was no way to spend the last years—the best years—of their lives. After forty years together, they still weren't tired of one another. Jean, a retired elementary school teacher, loved kids, just not for eight hours a day. Toward the end, summers off just weren't enough anymore. George, a retired army investigator, loved being active, but without major crimes to solve, he wasn't sure where to direct that restlessness. So, they'd decided on a snack truck. George could get out in the world and make sure things were safe for his wife, who regularly interacted with the customers—mostly children.

Jean once confided to Kassidy that she suspected George

still worked some cases, though. She'd caught him once, they'd argued, and he promised never to do it again. But that fire was always in him. He'd rush headfirst into danger just for the thrill. It bothered her on several levels. It was dangerous. He was sometimes reckless. But it mostly bothered her because she felt it was something she could never compete with. Despite their love, those moments made her feel as if she weren't enough. Thankfully those instances, those *special projects*, were few and far between.

On cold days, like today, the Alexanders sold coffee, hot cocoa, and lots of soups and sandwiches. Kassidy could smell the sweet chocolate almost two blocks away. With the way she felt, she'd stop and grab a cup, not just to warm her body but to warm her soul. Sensing the emotions of others wasn't always a good thing, but the love and warmth the Alexanders typically radiated made her heart full. Around them, Kassidy smiled more, and the weight of everyday stressors became lighter. Every step she took would be filled with hope and excitement, as if opening unexpected gifts from a lover. She'd had one of the most romantic nights in her life with Lynn after being near that loving couple for only fifteen minutes. They were the perfect drug for an empath in despair.

"Hi, Mrs. Alexander," Kassidy said, opening all of her senses, awaiting the flood of warmth and love.

"Well hello, Kassidy," Jean said. "How are you?"

"A little chilled today, but good."

"It seems a little soon for this level of cold, doesn't it?" Jean asked.

"It does," Kassidy replied. "Hopefully, it's not a prelude to a frigid winter. I don't know if I can take it."

Kassidy felt nothing. Well, she felt something. Cold. Some

— · 34 · —

goodwill from Jean, but barely enough to light a bulb. *What the hell is happening here?*

"Where's the Colonel today?" Kassidy asked.

She wasn't sure what was colder, the gust of wind that swept between her and the snack truck, or the icy daggers of angst that traveled at the speed of light from Jean right into Kassidy's heart. The little bit of goodwill circled the drain and descended into the sewers at the mention of the Colonel. Kassidy wanted to know why, but she didn't want to pry. Whatever it was angered Jean, and that wouldn't be good for Kassidy.

"He's, uh, off today," Jean said hesitantly. "He's working on some other projects."

Other projects? Oh boy!

"Oh, okay," Kassidy said. Jean was sweet, but she was angry, and her anger made Kassidy want to lash out. Somehow, she needed to keep a lid on the mini volcano inside. The quickest remedy was making fists and squeezing tight.

"You want a cocoa, hon?" Jean asked sweetly.

"Please. And thank you," Kassidy said, allowing Jean's outer calm to slip into her.

"Large?"

"Yes, please."

Jean moved deeper into the truck, and Kassidy watched the kids playing in the park. She saw a group of five kids, one girl on a swing with four standing around her. Kassidy couldn't understand why anyone would want to be on a swing in this weather. Swinging through cold air was good for no one, at any time, ever. This little girl though, she wasn't swinging. She was sitting on the swing, sure, but she wasn't moving. In fact, she was slumped over, her head down, while the other kids laughed and . . . played? No. The other kids laughed, but they weren't playing.

They were taunting her.

Kassidy trembled, not from the cold, but from the embarrassment, shame, and anger at her own ridicule at the hands of so-called friends from grade school.

Middle school.

High school.

Those same feelings flowed from that little girl on the swing. Within them, Kassidy sensed the familiar longing for comfort, for a safety net, for someone, anyone, to swoop in for a rescue. Kassidy was reminded that children were prone to create imaginary worlds in which they were invisible or strong, whether mentally strong or superpowered. Kids who could not get that sense of safety fell into the make-believe world of their choosing where they were kings, queens, princes, or princesses. They were respected and beloved and, in some cases, feared. The little girl on the swing longed for all that.

Without question, she needed a savior.

"Here you go, hon," Jean said.

Kassidy's focus snapped back. "Oh, thank you, Mrs. Alexander." Kassidy reached into her pocket for her wallet.

Opening it, she heard the faint sounds of taunting behind her, and her eyes welled up, reacting to her own distant pain as much as that little girl's. She pulled a single bill from her wallet and handed it to Jean, who took it with astonishment.

"Oh, sweetie, I'm sorry. I don't have change for this." Jean stared at the one-hundred-dollar bill.

"That's okay. I don't want change, actually," Kassidy said. Turning slightly, she pointed to the little girl on the swing. "See that little girl?"

"You mean Molly? On the swing?" Jean asked.

"Is that her name? Molly?"

"Yeah. She comes through here every couple of days. Her family doesn't have much. They're stretched check to check. It's just her, her baby brother, and her mom. Dad is off somewhere, God only knows."

Kassidy's heart sank. "Well, take this for Molly and for her family. Any time they come, please give them whatever they want. I'll come by every week and just keep adding to this."

"Oh, Kassidy, no. I can't let you—"

"No, please, Mrs.... please... Jean," Kassidy said, realizing how foreign the name sounded on her tongue, but desperate to let this woman know that doing this was important. "Please let me do this."

"Kassidy..." Jean trailed off, as if she could sense Kassidy's need.

"Please," Kassidy said one last time.

Jean took the bill and clutched it to her chest, giving Kassidy that bless-your-heart look. The sadness within Jean was mixed with pride and some determination. This wasn't the moment Kassidy had been seeking when she'd first walked to the truck, but it was a moment they both needed, nonetheless.

"You're a good woman, Kassidy," Jean said.

"I wish that were true," Kassidy said. She hated compliments. She didn't see herself as a good woman. Awful friend? Yes. Terrible girlfriend? Definitely. Killer? Monster? Without question.

Compliments on her virtues were misguided. Yet compliments were less about her and more about the people giving them. Over the years, she'd learned to just smile.

"Thank you for saying that," she added.

"You mind if I add a little twist to this gesture of yours?"

Kassidy gave a slight bow, as if to say, *the floor is yours.*

"Molly!" Jean called out loudly.

All the children turned in Jean's direction. Kassidy saw an adorable little girl with strawberry-blond curls that peeked beneath a plain black hat doing little to keep her head warm. Her freckles were beacons against red wind-blown cheeks. Her ice-blue eyes shone bright, juxtaposed against the light snow around her. She reminded Kassidy of her friend from grade school, one of her only friends—her sister, Sarah.

Molly ran to the snack truck, clearly desperate to get away from the kids around her.

"Yes, ma'am?" the little girl said with a heavy southern drawl.

"Molly, I have something for you," Jean said.

Jean reached back into the truck and produced a hot chocolate and a coin—a Susan B. Anthony silver dollar. As she handed both to Molly, the other kids raced up. Molly took the items in each hand, confused at one, ecstatic over the other.

"Molly, do you know what an investor is?" Jean asked.

Molly shook her head. The other kids snickered at her ignorance, to which Jean simply replied with a stare.

"Do any of you know what an investor is?" Jean asked with the look of a seasoned teacher asking a question about the homework that she was certain everyone had ignored.

Some glanced down. Some stared off in the distance, as if they hadn't heard the question. Molly, to her credit, just grinned shyly.

Kassidy mirrored her in solidarity.

"Well, an investor is someone who gives money to someone else to help them do something important, like start a business. A business like this snack truck. This young lady here"—Jean motioned to Kassidy—"is investing in my truck business, but she's busy and she needs someone to oversee things. She asked me if I knew anyone responsible enough to help with that, and I thought of you."

When younger, Kassidy had felt the weight of children's emotions on a more intense level. She'd assumed it was because of her inexperience with her powers. As she'd grown, the intensity, while still there, had lessened. That was, until now. Molly's elation caused Kassidy to take a step back.

"So, what do I need to do?" Molly asked eagerly.

As Jean explained Molly's duties, Kassidy quietly slipped away, though not before hearing the jealous groans of the other kids as Jean mentioned that the partnership came with free hot chocolate and snacks for Molly and her family.

Kassidy had arrived at the park seeking some salvation in the safety of the love that Jean and George shared, and instead had created salvation herself through the eyes of a nine-year-old. It did not fully erase what had happened earlier, nor would it change what would come. Right now, though, the storm within calmed.

Still, a shot of bourbon in her hot chocolate would be great.

CHAPTER SIX

KASSIDY STROLLED INTO HER TOWNHOME. TOOK OFF HER COAT. and completely missed the rack. She eyed her jacket on the floor and sighed heavily. For some reason, the thought of picking it up seemed too laborious, so she continued down the narrow hallway toward the kitchen. In her mind, all she could hear was the sound of a dozen kids making fun of her. Molly's experience at the park unsettled her more than she'd realized.

Krazy... Kassie...

Krazy... Kassie...

The voices echoed in the background of her mind like a horror-movie.

"Jesus, Kass! Get your shit together!" she said out loud, trying desperately to snap herself back to reality. She'd done a nice thing for Molly, but she was losing herself in emotion again. Forgetting the larger issues.

The deaths.

The Reapers.

The Wraiths.

The increase in her ability to sense emotion in others was making it difficult for her to control her own feelings. It was becoming easier for her to fall out of the present into an emotional abyss, especially when triggered by something painful. And her past overflowed with pain.

She made an immediate move toward the Vicodin in the kitchen cabinet above the refrigerator. In the next cupboard she grabbed the bottle of Elijah Craig, small batch. She wanted the hot chocolate but would need a cocktail to drown out the sounds of kids in her head and to assuage her guilt for not supporting Lynn.

Lynn rarely asked for anything, so for her to do it now, for something as simple as being physically present for emotional support, that was huge. Kassidy's inability to do something so very basic made her sick to her stomach. She was a bad person and an even worse girlfriend.

Fuck!

Her hands trembling, Kassidy opened and closed her fists, then shook her hands—as if that ever helped. She poured a single, took out a pill, placed it in her mouth, then took a sip to wash it down. *Do not, under any circumstances, take these pills with alcohol.* She'd heard her doctor but had not listened. No, that wasn't it. She hadn't cared. Yeah, that was more accurate.

Kassidy had never thought of herself as an addict until the last few months. Even then, she never took full ownership. Somewhere in her mind she justified it, figuring that drinking and using pain meds was simply a means to an end. The end of headaches. The end of seeing Reapers and the ever-present shadow of death everywhere. The end of feeling the emotions of everyone within arms-length of her.

The end of feeling. Period.

In the back of her mind, she knew it wasn't healthy. Kassidy had read enough studies, watched enough Dr. Phil, and experienced enough turmoil and pain to know that she would never truly escape. She knew her inability to accept and understand her own pain was the root of what ailed her. The reason she was unhappy. The reason she was such a bad friend and girlfriend.

The reason she was an addict.

She'd admitted it once, and she'd meant it. But this was largely because the only people who'd heard that admission were the participants of an AA meeting somewhere in Philadelphia. She'd gone to a meeting while working a missing persons case. In hindsight, probably not a great environment for an empath. Swept up in the honesty and vulnerability of the participants, she'd opened up about her attack at the hands of a classmate back in high school. She'd talked about how it affected her decision-making in relationships. Like the time she lied to an ex-lover to spend a weekend with Lynn, something she'd never told either of them. She'd admitted, metaphorically, that she'd made a deal with the devil. A deal that was the catalyst for everything that had happened in her life since.

A life on the run.

A life in search of . . . things.

Of feelings, of self, of understanding and acceptance . . . of unconditional love.

Kassidy had admitted it all. In a room full of strangers, people she would never see again, she'd confessed her deepest and darkest fears. They'd applauded her, supported her, uplifted her, and for thirteen minutes of a one-hour meeting, she'd felt whole.

But that might as well have been another life. She'd been working a case, essentially working undercover, so in her mind, it didn't really mean much.

She knew it as plainly as she knew the real reasons she began using in the first place. The true catalysts for her fear, her pain, and the relentless anger. She wanted to stop, desperately. But she was too afraid of what would happen if she did. Afraid of the unbearable flood of raw feelings rushing through her like a raging river. Consequently, the argument to stop was untenable.

So she drank.

She ate Vicodin like candy.

And she died a little more every day.

Kassidy stood over the kitchen sink and stared outside at the kids playing. The young girl who'd been teased was now the center of attention.

In the distance, well beyond the kids, a dark spec loomed closer, just as it had this morning. *Another Wraith.* It moved with speed; a sense of urgency as unnatural as the being itself. It flew through the park, past the kids, and directly toward Kassidy's townhome.

She stood still, almost lifeless. She tried to steady her breathing. Calming her heart was something she'd once done with regularity. She had long since lost that skill. Looking down, Kassidy watched her shirt move in rhythm with her heartbeat.

Shit!

The Wraith came to an abrupt stop in front of Kassidy's kitchen window. It hovered for a moment and then changed shape, transforming from a shapeless patch of smoke to a dark demonic figure clad in a tattered, hooded robe. It scanned left to right, moving slightly with each turn of its head. It could not see her still. Yet somehow it knew she was there. Its head phased through the double-pane glass of Kassidy's window and stared directly at her.

Kassidy stood motionless, breathless, the only sound and movement the overworked muscle in her chest. In her mind, she heard the voice of the apparition.

"You should just show yourself. We already know you're here. Your warding is degraded. Your power is growing. Surely you can sense the changes happening around you. He's coming, Kassidy. *We* are coming . . . for you. See you soon."

Senaya!

If Senaya was here, Azra-El would not be far behind. The Wraith backed away from the window, its head phasing through again. Once clear, it lingered for a moment before shooting straight up into the sky. Kassidy followed its movement until it was out of view. Her emotions rolled like a tidal wave. The pressure building inside needed a release.

She screamed.

Kassidy screamed louder than she'd ever screamed before. She pounded the countertop with both fists, lashing out like a petulant child. Her rage seemed unending, but also futile. She slid down to the ground, brought her knees to her chest, wrapped her arms around them, and wept.

He's coming for me.

CHAPTER SEVEN

KASSIDY SAT IN HER OFFICE AND STARED AT THE INFORMATION SHE needed to review. In actuality, it stared at her. To her right was her phone. It buzzed with yet another text message from her best friend, David. She hadn't read the first. She was not eager to read the fifth. His messages were mixed in with two from Lynn. Only two. She could only imagine their angry tone. To Kassidy's left was a glass with the remnants of a generous pouring of the Elijah Craig. Fortunately for the glass, the bottle was directly behind it, and Kassidy added more to bring the volume of caramel liquid to an acceptable level.

The sound of the garage door opening snapped Kassidy back to the present. She heard Lynn's car pull in followed by the garage door closing. The length of time between that and the sound of Lynn exiting her car was an eternity. The speed at which Kassidy's heart had beat when the Wraiths appeared was a slow crawl compared to now. She took a sip of her bourbon. Then another and another. Finally, she drained the rest in a single gulp.

This would not go well.

There was no way in hell this would go well.

The service door opened, and she heard Lynn walk in. Kassidy nervously cleared her throat, in part to alert Lynn as to where she was. Mostly, to be ready to explain herself without having to pause. Lynn's steps were slow and steady, stopping near the entrance to Kassidy's office. Kassidy glanced up and found her standing in the doorway, leaning against the doorjamb.

She was beautiful. Beautiful, but exhausted. Her legs were long, but she was not a tall woman. She had the body of a runner—lean and toned but not overly muscular. Her black hair was cut short, framing her face and blending well with her stunning light brown eyes. When she smiled, she radiated warmth and love.

Lynn was not smiling now.

"Hey," Kassidy said nervously.

"Hey," Lynn replied.

"How's, uh, how's Carl?"

"He's still critical, but stable," Lynn said. "They think something went wrong with the implant. They had to go back in, remove it, adjust it, then reattach. They think he'll be fine, but it's still major surgery, so it's hard to tell."

Kassidy moved back in her chair and stood up, preparing to walk over to Lynn to . . . do something. She had no idea what. But that was what one was supposed to do, right? Especially when getting ready to apologize . . . or beg for forgiveness.

"Lynn . . . babe, I . . ."

Lynn held her hand up. "I needed you there today. Needed you with me. But you weren't there. Again."

"I know. I know. I just . . . I tried. I was there, outside, and I—"

"Right. You're afraid of hospitals. You're afraid of the feelings they bring up. The memories of your past. A past, mind you, that you still keep hidden from me."

Kassidy did her best to maintain eye contact with Lynn but lost the staring contest. All she saw was pain, and standing this close to Lynn, that was all she felt as well. There was no anger, though. Only the pain of loss, of abandonment, of fear. Lynn was afraid. As sad as she was, she was afraid. Kassidy looked back up at Lynn and noticed the tears in her eyes. She should tell her. She needed to tell her. But after all this time, she just could not bring herself to do it.

"You've been running from something," Lynn began. "For as long as I've known you, you've been running. I haven't pressed you on it. Hell, I've been running with you, enabling you maybe. I don't know. Maybe I was hoping that we could outrun it together, which is crazy because I don't even know what the fuck it is we're running from. But I justified it. I justified it by telling myself that this is what love is. This is what love does. It doesn't ask questions. It just supports and strengthens and uplifts."

As Lynn spoke, Kassidy moved closer. Lynn didn't back away. She stood up straight and faced Kassidy. When within reach, Lynn stretched out and caressed Kassidy's face.

"But I'm tired, Kass," Lynn continued. "And if I'm tired, you must be exhausted. You keep trying to heal with bourbon and Vicodin, and I'm tired of competing with that too."

Kassidy felt the sting in her gut as her emotions mixed with Lynn's. She reached out and wiped the tear from Lynn's cheek, continued to caress her face, then gently pressed her forehead against Lynn's.

"I'm sorry," Kassidy said

Lynn nodded without breaking contact. "I know. I know you are, Kass."

"I love you. I do."

"I know that. I love you too. I love you with everything in me."

"And you hate me?" Kassidy asked, not really wanting to know the answer.

Lynn pulled her head back and took Kassidy's face in her

hands, staring at her. Then, in a moment of tenderness, she gently kissed her lips. That tingle, that feeling Kassidy used to get when they kissed, was missing. There was something there. There was love, there was affection and concern, but there was still something missing.

This is what the end feels like.

Lynn pulled back, kissed Kassidy on her forehead, then released her and took a full step backward. In that awkward moment, neither knew what to do with their hands. Kassidy rubbed hers together. Lynn crossed her arms over her chest.

"Whatever it is, whatever this is that's going on with you, you need to figure it out. You need to figure it out and deal with it, because what you've been doing so far"—Lynn gestured to the bourbon on the desk—"isn't working. It isn't working for you, for me, or for us."

She didn't answer my question.

"I know. I know," Kassidy said. "I really am trying to—"

She stopped. She couldn't continue with that because it was a flat-out lie. She really hadn't been trying to do much of anything. Lynn was right. She had been running for damn near twenty years. Kassidy was running and hiding from the truest part of herself. Instead of embracing all of who she was, she hid it, hid from it, and because of that Lynn had never truly known her.

No one did.

"Babe, I get it," Lynn started. "You're lost. Kind of . . . spinning. Believe me, I understand. But I can't make this better for you, and this isn't a relationship where only one person can do everything."

Kassidy nodded. She didn't know what to say, so she said nothing.

She doesn't hate me. She pities me.

They stood in silence for a few moments, occasionally regarding one another awkwardly, almost voyeuristically. Lynn rubbed her stomach. Kassidy recognized that movement and the accompanying feeling that drifted from her girlfriend.

"Why don't you let me take you to dinner. We can talk . . . maybe? If you want? Or we can just—"

"I can't. I have to get ready for the fundraiser."

"Oh my God! That's right. That's tonight. Okay. Let me grab a shower, and I'll get dressed, and we can . . ."

Kassidy let her words trail off. Lynn had cut her off with a wave of her hand, her expression a mix of pity and apology.

"I'm just gonna go on my own tonight. I think it's best."

No. Please no. Don't leave me.

Kassidy stepped back, feeling that kick to the gut again, and after several uncomfortable seconds, she nodded. She did not agree, of course. Or did she? She really didn't know. What scared her more than anything was the impression that somehow, someway, this was the end for them. But maybe it was necessary. Necessary or not, it was happening, and she had to deal with it.

"Okay. So, yeah . . . I guess that makes sense. Do you want me to drive you?"

Lynn walked up to Kassidy and kissed her again. She pressed her forehead against hers again and said softly, "I've got it."

Fuck!

Kassidy watched as Lynn backed away, turned, and walked out of the office. As Lynn's footsteps climbed the stairs to the bedroom, a wave of nausea struck Kassidy. This was all her. Elements of Lynn's emotions fluttered about, but this sensation of loss, a swarm of bees instead of butterflies, was all Kassidy.

She sat at her desk staring at the bottle of Elijah Craig. It was almost gone, and there was no excuse for that, so she emptied it into her tumbler. Picking up the glass, she just stared at the liquid inside. A part of her wanted to pour it down the drain. A larger part reminded her of everything she had experienced today. Two Wraiths, a breakup—well, at least a cooling of the relationship. No, it was a breakup.

Two Wraiths.

Ethan and Senaya.

Azra-El was coming.

Kassidy reached for her phone, scrolled through for a name, and called. She continued staring at her drink as the phone rang.

"Hello?" said the man on the other end.

"I . . . need to see you."

"I'm closing up now. I'll be home in five minutes."

"I'll see you in fifteen."

Kassidy hung up. She squeezed her glass hard, then drank it all in one gulp. She grabbed her phone, her keys, and her jacket before walking out of her office to the garage. She stopped at the service door and glanced up, listening as the shower started in her bedroom. Inside, a battle waged between anger, guilt, and sadness.

She wanted to say something. Normally, she would. But now it seemed unnecessary, maybe even unwanted. Perhaps it would only serve to make things worse.

So she simply whispered, "Goodbye."

CHAPTER EIGHT

ON ANY GIVEN NIGHT, THE BUSINESSES OF DOWNTOWN ST. JOHN thrived, even in the fall and winter months. It was as if nobody was worried about work the next day. The restaurants were reasonably priced, and most were family-owned so the food had a homemade flair. The bars were varied. Some were sports bars, some were bar and restaurant combinations, and some were where "grown folks" hung out. The alcohol was top shelf in those spots, and they usually offered live jazz or acoustic music.

There was a time when Kassidy enjoyed hanging out downtown. Back when her powers weren't as strong, she could get lost in crowds. She had greater control of her abilities then. With a cocktail or two, life had felt normal. She could work for five or six hours, head out with some friends for a few drinks or some dinner, meet a nice woman or a guy, and end the evening on a high note. The thought of it made her long for the simpler times. Now, she just felt like she was in hell.

She pulled up right outside of the bookstore owned and operated by her mentor. The store was closed, which accounted for her ability to find decent parking, but even during business hours, Keiron's store was never busy. She often wondered how he stayed operational. Other businesses nearby did well, but his survived despite itself. He lived in the loft above and owned the building outright, so that helped. Still, unless he had some special event, foot traffic was steady, but light.

After parking, Kassidy strode to the door to the far right of the bookstore entrance. She pressed a buzzer and waited. Her foot was tapping. She didn't notice it until she felt her hand tapping against her thigh. Her nerves were shot. This day had gone to shit, and her fight-or-flight instincts revved like a muscle car on the drag racing strip.

The door buzzed, jerking her out of the brain fog. She entered and headed up the stairs. She could smell something delicious. Keiron was not only a bookseller but, somehow, an excellent cook. Then again, Kassidy could burn water, so someone who could successfully microwave popcorn was a gourmet chef in her eyes.

As she rounded the corner to his loft, she saw that the door was opened. She let herself in as she always did. The fucker was making lasagna—her favorite. He had music on. Some acoustic stuff. The same stuff he played in the bookstore.

How the hell is he not tired of that after a ten-hour day?

"Hey!" she shouted as she closed the door.

"Hey, Kass," Keiron replied. "Make yourself at home."

Kassidy took her coat off and hung it on a hook on the back of the door. She sat in the oversized recliner opposite Keiron's couch. She loved that chair. She had passed out in it on more than one occasion. Usually after stumbling out of a bar alone. That was back when she had a key to Keiron's place, a luxury that was rescinded after she had lost the tenth one.

"So," Keiron began as he walked into the living room, "what have you done wrong now?"

He said it sarcastically, as he always did. She gave him the side eye, as she always did. In recent years the only reason Kassidy ever came around was because of some trouble she had caused or unwittingly found herself in. More the former than the latter. She had meant to do better. She had meant to come by more often just to say hello or hang out—to be a decent friend and human being for once. But that did not happen. It always sounded good in her head, like a sure thing. Winning the lottery or hitting on a scratch-off ticket was a surer thing.

Keiron handed her a glass, then sat on the couch opposite. He sipped his drink, keeping his eyes on her. His curiosity was just shy of anxious. Or was that her?

Kassidy took a sip of her drink and found herself pleasantly surprised.

"You've upgraded your bourbon selection. Nice."

"Yeah, well, I've got bougie friends," Keiron replied.

Kassidy laughed, nervously. There was tension, but it was self-imposed. She had never been uncomfortable with Keiron before. He was the father she had never had. No, that wasn't true. Sure, Kassidy had never known her real father, but she had a good dad in Dan Simmons. He had been amazing, patient with her, and she'd repaid that by abandoning him and the rest of the family.

She really was an awful person.

"This must have cost a small fortune."

"Costly, yes. But it's not as if I'll be drinking it every night. And since you no longer have a key, it should last me a little while."

She laughed again. These laughs were not genuine, though. They were nervous attempts to cover up her fucked-up life.

"So," Keiron began, "what's going on, Kass?"

She had no idea where to begin, so she dove in. "I saw two Wraiths today."

Keiron's eyes widened, and he moved to the edge of the couch. "What? Where?"

"The first was at the hospital, and the second—"

"Wait! Hospital? What were you doing at the hospital?"

As one of two people in the world who knew about Kassidy's abilities, Keiron was well aware of her aversion to places with overwhelming sentiment and emotion. Kassidy moved back, sitting deeper in the recliner, an effort to let the furniture carry the full weight of her burdens.

"I was there for Lynn, or at least, trying to be there for Lynn. It didn't quite work out."

"Is she okay?"

"Oh, no, she's fine. It's her father. He's having some problems. But he's stable, at least that's what she told me earlier."

"That's good," he said. "So you saw one at the hospital. Did it see you?"

"No. At least, not visually. He knew I was there."

"How?"

"I honestly don't know. He materialized in front of me but peered around me. Like a blind person does. But he knew I was there. He spoke to me."

"What did he say?"

"Essentially, that he knew I was there. And . . ."

"And?"

"And that Azra-El is back and coming for me."

"Well, shit." Keiron eased back into the couch.

"Yeah. Shit."

Kassidy took another sip of her bourbon. Followed quickly by another. She put the glass down on the end table next to her and just sat, looking everywhere but at Keiron. Her leg began to shake, and she tapped her hand against the arm of the recliner.

"And the second?" Keiron asked.

"At my house."

"What the fuck?" Keiron stood. "Do you know them?"

Kassidy nodded.

"Did the second do the same thing? Sense you more than see you?"

Kassidy nodded again.

Keiron paced around the loft. Kassidy had always liked the loft for that very reason. There was so much space. Enough to ride a bike through if you wanted. She loved her townhome, but she enjoyed space. Space to move, to breathe, to do whatever one wanted to do.

"Have you been feeling any differently recently? Any significant changes?"

"Yeah. I think my powers are growing or expanding. Something weird is happening. Usually, being across the street from the hospital is a safe distance for me. Today, I might as well have been in the lobby. And when I finally did get across the street, the emotion knocked me on my ass. I couldn't even make it to the front door."

"Does that help?" Keiron asked, pointing to her drink.

"No so much anymore. I'm drinking more, I think, and it's not doing much to dampen my abilities lately. Fucking everything else up, though, in spectacular fashion." Kassidy paused. "Actually, no, that's just me, so never mind."

Keiron just stared, seemingly uncertain how to respond. He tilted his head, silently asking for clarification.

"Forget it. It's my own shit," Kassidy said with a wave of her hand.

Keiron resumed his pacing. He was like a professor when he did this. It was as if he were calculating things in his mind. She imagined a vast array of mathematical formulas taking shape in his brain. Equations being crossed out, erased, and rewritten, all in an effort to determine an answer that was going to make every-thing okay.

"Shit, my lasagna!" he said as he sprinted to the kitchen.

"So much for genius," Kassidy whispered to herself.

She stood, grabbed her glass, and headed toward the kitchen. She didn't know why. It wasn't as if she could help. As she moved closer, a wave of cold air flowed around her. She trembled and without warning fell to her knees, sending her glass crashing to the floor.

"Kassidy? You okay?" Keiron asked from the kitchen.

She tried to respond, but the oppressive gnawing in her gut took her breath away. Her eyes fluttered, and her arms were like limp noodles attempting to hold up a stack of encyclopedias. In seconds she was sprawled out on the floor, the air flashing from light to dark, until darkness was the only thing she saw.

"Keir—"

Kassidy tried to speak, but the darkness and the cold overtook her.

CHAPTER NINE

WHEN DEREK JAMES WALKED INTO HIS SECOND-FLOOR APARTMENT, he was of one mind—throw his things to the ground, get a beer, relax in his recliner, and turn on Monday Night Football. He didn't know who was playing. He didn't particularly care. He'd just worked forty-eight straight hours, and he needed the rest of the world to be quiet for a while.

It wasn't the length of his shift that exhausted him. As a paramedic, this was nothing new. He'd pulled enough of those shifts overseas as an army medic that doing anything less seemed like a waste of a day. Despite what he'd seen in his five years here in St. John and his eight years in the army, Derek had never had days as intense as the last two. Each time he and his partner, Dani, rounded the corner into St. John Memorial, another call sent them to a new incident.

A twenty-three-year-old Caucasian female, in seemingly perfect health, had suffered an aneurism while chopping vegetables to add to her slow cooker. Forty-five-year-old Bernie Miles, the two-time St. John Rock 'N' Roll Marathon first-place finisher had a heart attack on the treadmill at the local gym. Three gunshot victims the other morning, all seemingly harmless as gunshots went. One was shot in the leg, one in the arm, and the last one in the foot—yet two of the three later died from infection. Infection!

None of the emergency calls made sense.

Healthy people were dying or getting sick. Superficial injuries and wounds endangered people as if it were the thirteenth century when the greatest medical advancements were leeches and hot pokers. Something weird was happening. But a part of Derek was aware that he too often focused on conspiracy theories, probably driven by an above average obsession with fantasy and the supernatural. The logical part of him constantly slapped his illogical side. That logical part of him lived by the mantra, "Sometimes, shit just happens."

"Except when it doesn't," he whispered to himself as he opened his beer and walked into the living room with chips and homemade salsa.

After plopping down onto his recliner, Derek turned on his television and found the game. Green Bay versus Chicago was always fun. Well, not always, but it didn't matter. Tonight, was more about unplugging from everything besides football, beer, chips, salsa, and the stuffed-crust, sausage, pepperoni, and extra-cheese pizza he'd ordered on his way home.

It was nearing halftime when his doorbell rang. Derek drank the last of his beer and moved to the door, grabbing the twenty-five dollars he'd put on the coffee table. His mouth was watering, his stomach was grumbling, and tonight's game was actually the best of the season thus far.

Opening the door, it was apparent to Derek that the weirdness of the last forty-eight hours was nowhere near its end. On the spectrum of strange, it was minimal, he supposed. But it was still on the spectrum.

Standing in front of him, holding a pizza, was a tall, blond, green-eyed man in a tailored suit. Derek was no fashion expert. He wore a uniform when he worked, and when he didn't, he wore jeans and T-shirts. But he knew this was strange, and he doubted Coleman's Pizza had changed their dress code in the week since his last order.

"Derek James?" asked the well-dressed delivery man.

"Yeah?" Derek responded with a little inflection on the end.

"Got your order ready. Sorry I'm so late," said the Armani-clad pizza man.

"Yeah, well, no problem," Derek said apprehensively. "Here you go."

Derek extended the cash to the man. The man smiled at Derek and ... just ... continued ... to ... stand ... there.

Derek wondered if he was being punked. Maybe Dani was around the corner, filming this absurd scene playing out at his front door. She was notorious for shit like that. Derek stepped forward a bit, looked to his right and left, but saw nothing, and no one. It was eerily quiet in his apartment complex.

"So I guess how this usually works is, I give you the money and you give me the pizza," Derek said with a hint of sarcasm.

Still, the stranger said nothing.

"Dude, are you new?"

That had to be the reason behind this weirdness, right? The guy was new, maybe foreign. Maybe he took the whole "dress-for-the-job-you-want" thing to a whole new level. An epic level at that. It was just pizza, for Christ's sake.

Derek's stream of consciousness stopped as a cold breeze passed between him and the delivery man. He shivered. He dropped his money as he gazed into the once green eyes of his delivery man and found them replaced with solid pools of black.

Derek froze. Words formed in his mind, but they did not escape his lips. The thud of the pizza box hitting the ground did nothing to snap him out of his daze. The delivery man's face distorted into a monstrous gray amalgam of death and decay, with a bloody grin that caused Derek to void his bladder. As the man transformed into a gray-and-black Wraith that floated effortlessly in front of him, Derek's life flashed before his eyes—a cliché he'd never put stock in until now.

The Wraith formed a sickle in one hand. It was as black as the monster's eyes. Derek watched helplessly as the monster's arm swung in an arc. The blade of the sickle passed through Derek's throat, and he instinctually reached up to stop the bleeding.

But there was no blood.

There was no blood, but something was definitely wrong. There was no blood, yet he could not breathe. There was no blood, yet he clutched at his throat and his attacker, desperate for salvation from something, from someone, from anyone.

Derek stepped forward, passed through the transparent Wraith, and toppled over the railing of his second-floor balcony, hitting the concrete ground head-first.

In his apartment, the crowd at Soldier Field roared as the Bears scored a touchdown.

CHAPTER TEN

KASSIDY STIRRED ON THE FLOOR OF KEIRON'S LOFT. SHE LIFTED HER head slightly and looked around. Everything was gray. A thin layer of mist covered the floor. Wisps of fog flowed all around her. She knew this place. She hadn't been here in ages, but she knew it.

"The fucking Nexus," she said with a groan.

She stood up slowly, glanced down, and saw her body sprawled on the floor. She was here in astral form, which was not necessarily a good thing. Fortunately, in the real world, she was with Keiron. He would protect her body until she returned. More problematic was the fact that she wasn't here by her own will. Someone else brought her here, and unless she was dead or near death, only one being could do such a thing.

"Show yourself!" she yelled, expecting to see Azra-El, the Angel of Death himself, appear.

She felt more than saw someone materialize behind her. Kassidy turned, anxious but not frightened. In the Nexus, there was no fighting, no violence. The powers of the Reaper were limited only to transporting souls to the Void or the Beyond. And of course, transporting themselves. But she'd only known of one being powerful enough to call someone to the Nexus. As the light and fog diminished around the being in front of her, Kassidy braced herself. Even here she was nervous to see Azra-El again.

Only, it wasn't him.

"Who the hell are you?" she asked.

He was a formidable, muscular man, with hazel eyes and hair cut short and faded on the sides. He smiled at her. No, more smirked. As if he were the type who had answers to every question long before they were asked. Arrogant. Cocky. Sickeningly confident.

But damn, he's handsome.

"I'm . . . a friend," he said.

"A friend? Anyone ever tell you that you resemble Denzel Washington, friend?" Kassidy asked, a hint of annoyance in her voice.

"I'm a fan of the *Equalizer* movies," he said. "Partial to the original series, of course, but I appreciate the remake and its sequel. So I'll take that as a compliment."

"You brought me here?" Kassidy asked as she walked around him.

He nodded.

"How? Who are you that you're that powerful?"

"I told you, I'm a—"

"Friend." Kassidy rolled her eyes. "Yeah, I'm full up on friends right now."

He turned to face her, and she paced in shallow steps.

"You're not a Wraith," she said as a matter of fact. "You're not even a Reaper."

The stranger stood still, betraying nothing in movement or facial expression, but the smirk remained. He casually put his hands in his pockets. The situation felt anything but casual to her.

"Then what are you? And why am I here?"

"Who and what I am is less important than why you're here.

But if it pleases you to know, let's say I represent the interests of the people who are responsible for all . . . this," he replied, waving his hand in the air.

"You represent them?"

"Most people just call me the Advocate."

When she'd first joined the Reapers, Kassidy had been told about their abilities and their function, but she'd never given much thought to their origins. She didn't care where they came from or how they came to be—she was simply happy to be living a life that seemed to mean something. Until she realized what Azra-El was making her do. Back then she'd dismissed the notion that there were other supernatural beings in the world. Had she known, had she allied herself with them, perhaps her battle with Azra-El would have ended differently.

"The Advocate?" she asked with skepticism. "Okay, I guess we can go with that. I mean, what choice do I have, really?"

"None."

Still smirking.

Son of bitch!

"I could kick your ass, snap your neck and leave you for dead," Kassidy said.

"Well," the Advocate began slowly, "we both know you can't do that. Weapons cannot be conjured here in the Nexus, and you would need every weapon at your disposal to kill someone like me."

There was no hesitation in his voice when he spoke. There was no posturing, no need to show force of any type to prove his point. He knew the rules of the Nexus. No Reaper could conjure a weapon there. There was no fighting. It was, in essence, a safe haven. If he knew that and had the power to bring her here, it was probably best for her to acquiesce.

"So, what can I do for these powers that be?"

"I'm glad you asked. It's simple really. We need you to dispatch Azra-El."

"Oh, is that all? Yeah, sure. No problem. I'll get right on that. Just, uh, send me right on back into my body, and I'll get to work."

The Advocate's smirk eased, turning softer and more inviting. And was that a chuckle she heard? She grew more than annoyed. Annoyed at the moment, at the request, and at the ridiculously handsome asshole standing in front of her. If killing Azra-El had been so easy, she would have done it twenty years ago and would not have run.

There would have been no reason to.

"We recognize that if killing Azra-El were easy, you likely would have done it twenty years ago and you wouldn't have run," the Advocate said.

What the fuck? Did he just—

"But we have a solution."

Kassidy assumed she was supposed to ask about the so-called solution, to be on the edge of her seat in anticipation for the miracle method to dispatch the Angel of Death.

"If you have a solution, then why not dispatch him yourself?"

"That is an excellent question. Unfortunately, the only answer I really have is one that you'll not be satisfied with. It's terribly cliché, and I can't quite say it with a straight face."

"Some shit about my destiny, I take it?"

The Advocate put a finger to his nose.

"Then, why now? After all this time, why now? Where the fuck were you and the people you represent when he was making me do all those things?"

"Making you?"

"Fuck you!"

"I'm just saying"—he held both hands in the air—"you seemed to be thriving. In fact, I daresay you were happy."

"So you guys knew all along?"

"Of course. But as with everything, there is a purpose. A reason to interfere, and often even greater reasons to not interfere."

Kassidy stood in front of the Advocate, angry, dumbfounded, but resigned to the fact that she could do nothing about the past. She could not undo the damage she had caused or replace the lives she had taken. Keiron had been trying to tell her that for years.

Seemed strange that it would take root in her mind now.

"It will make more sense to you later in life," the Advocate said. "For now, though, there are things in motion that could drastically change the course of existence. Azra-El has returned, and his power is growing at an exceptional rate. We don't know how or why, but it's happening, and it's creating a ripple effect."

Kassidy eyes widened as the pieces fell into place. "My powers... not only my empathic abilities, but my Reaper abilities—"

"Are growing," the Advocate finished.

"Because of him?"

"In part. Something is triggering it. Again, we don't know what. But the two of you are connected in a way that's unlike anything else he has with his Reapers. Even with his Wraiths there's no connection that strong."

"Is that why the warding is weakening? Is that why the Wraiths can sense me now?"

He nodded.

"Shit!"

"Yeah. Shit."

"It's why I can't control the emotions I'm sensing from others, too. Everything is trying to adjust," she said.

All her questions faded away. She wanted out of this. She wanted out of the Nexus, out of this madness, out of this fight. It was not hers. She had not started any of it. All she wanted, then and now, was a life that *was* hers. Free of fear, of ridicule, of judgment. She just wanted to live.

"I understand your desire to be as far away from this as possible, Kassidy. Unfortunately, that's not possible. You are the linchpin to his demise. You are the key to resetting the natural order, to stopping the untimely deaths manifesting around the world."

"Around the world? And just how am I supposed to do that?"

The Advocate's smirk returned.

"Once again, I'm glad you asked. Let's talk about the Scythe of Cronus."

◆　　◆　　◆

Twenty-Two Years Ago

"What exactly would I have to do?"

Azra-El stepped forward to stand face to face with Kassidy. "You would only need to say yes, my dear."

"And then?"

"And then the power of the Reaper would be within you."

"How would I know how to use it? How would I know what to do?"

"It's pretty instinctual. You need to let the power guide you. It won't steer you wrong. But of course, since you're a newbie and all, I'd check in on you."

Kassidy lifted an eyebrow. "Is that what most presidents of corporations do?"

Azra-El laughed. "This one does."

Kassidy paced toward her grayed body. The fog cleared again as she neared. She peered down at herself. Kneeling, she reached to touch her own lifeless form. Her hand passed right through. Kassidy's thoughts drifted off to her adoptive family. Dan, Marlene, and their daughter, Sarah, had been the only family Kassidy had ever known. Despite the occasional sisterly disagreement with Sarah, they were great friends and, in many ways, closer than some natural-born siblings. The family had given her a home, love, and unconditional support. Despite all the strange things she did as a child, the Simmons family had supported Kassidy as if she had been born to them.

"What should we do?" she asked herself.

The eyes of her body were open. Lifeless, but open. In them, Kassidy saw sadness. She saw years of unhappiness. Years of fear. Years of hiding or trying to hide. The only good thing to happen to her was her adoption by the Simmons family. As wonderful as it was, though, it was not enough. She needed the happiness that came from within. She had never had that, never known what it was like to have positive thoughts about herself. She had never learned to love herself, let alone like herself. That was why it should have been so easy to choose death.

Dying would be easy, right?

Moments ago, she'd been ready for it, welcoming it. But now, as she saw herself on the ground, it was clear that she, in fact, did not want to die. Kassidy was not ready to fade away to nothingness, seemingly forgotten by everyone. She wanted to live. She wanted a chance.

"I think we should give this a shot," she whispered. "It has to be better than what we've been doing, right?"

Kassidy arose and walked back to Azra-El. Hands clasped

behind his back, he was regal, but malevolent. Kassidy felt uneasy. There was something... dark in him. But he was the Angel of Death, after all. How could he be anything but? And now she was about to join his ranks.

"So do you, like, give me a robe and a scythe and, like, touch my head or something?"

Azra-El laughed. "No, it's nothing like that. There's no ceremony, no initiation, no party, and no monogrammed scythe."

Kassidy was embarrassed, then disappointed. She wanted to belong to something. She wanted to feel like she was a part of something greater—with a little pomp and circumstance.

But beggars can't be choosers.

"Is there a uniform? Something universal that identifies us?

Azra-El laughed again. "You can reap souls in shorts and flip flops. When you access those powers, you can literally wear anything you want. Though, you'll find that your outer appearance often reflects your mind's mood."

Kassidy pondered that for a moment. She wondered what that could mean for her. Her mood was mostly dark of late. She was often fearful ... of everything.

"Are you sure that this is what you want?" Azra-El asked.

Kassidy nodded.

"I need to hear you say it, my dear," he said with that aristocratic drawl.

"Yes," Kassidy said. "I want to be one of you."

Azra-El nodded his head. In an instant, Kassidy was in her bed, dry and warm, staring up at the ceiling of her room.

CHAPTER ELEVEN

WITH A SHARP INHALE. KASSIDY SHOT UP INTO A SEATED POSITION on the floor and found Keiron staring down at her. She clutched her chest, breathing rapidly. Returning to her body this way was always a shock to the system. With her powers strengthening, though, this return felt even more violent. She looked around, getting her bearings, then glanced up at Keiron.

"How long was I out?"

"Only a few minutes, I think. I found you on the floor."

"Yeah, sorry about the glass."

"Be sorrier about the bourbon you spilled."

Kassidy gave him the side eye, Keiron winked and grinned, then they helped each other off the floor. Keiron walked Kassidy over to the recliner and resumed his seat on the couch.

"How'd that lasagna come out?"

"Are we doing this?" Keiron asked.

Kassidy knew what he meant. She tended to ignore or laugh off anything remotely serious—a defense mechanism that sometimes helped ease the tension. Other times it just annoyed the hell out of anyone near her. It was somewhere in between the former and the latter now.

"I was pulled into the Nexus."

"Azra-El?"

"No. Denzel Washington."

By the look on his face, Keiron had officially crossed over the threshold into the land of the annoyed. She smirked, holding her head in her hands. She had a bit of head fog, but it was steadily lessening. Keiron stared at her, concern and curiosity wafting from him, along with annoyance and a desire to slap her. Kassidy was used to that.

"Some guy who resembled Denzel—loosely, mind you—pulled me in. Calls himself the Advocate. He gave me a long lecture about my duty and destiny to kill Azra-El."

"And did this so-called Advocate give you any insight as to how?"

"The Scythe of Cronus."

A jolt of fear leapt from Keiron. In all the years she'd known him, she'd never felt fear in him. In fact, for a long time, she didn't know he was capable of such an emotion. But this, now, made him seem entirely and uncomfortably human. He was always human, of course, but not to this degree.

Or was he?

"You've heard of it?"

"I have."

"You know what it can do?"

"I do."

"Then why am I just now hearing about it? From Denzel, no less."

Kassidy stood, only slightly shaken now but irritable. She walked into Keiron's kitchen and helped herself to a bottle of water from the refrigerator. When she returned to his living room, she found him standing near his bookcase. She had always loved that bookcase. She was, or course, as big a fan of books as he was. Over the years, Keiron had amassed an enviable library. Several rare pieces were in his possession. An equal number of first editions too. She was jealous. Her oldest book was a first edition of *Carrie* by Stephen King.

"The legend of the Scythe of Cronus is just that, a legend," Keiron said as he turned toward her.

"You mean, a legend like the Angel of Death and Reapers are legends?" Kassidy asked sarcastically before taking a sip of water.

"Fair enough," Keiron replied.

"If it has the power to kill Azra-El, why didn't you tell me about it? I could have used it to take him out while he was weakened. At this stage of the game, who knows if I'll be able to get close to him." Kassidy trailed off for a moment as a realization smacked her in the face. "Wait. What am I saying? Who cares? Who cares about any of this shit? I don't want to be any part of it."

Keiron walked toward Kassidy and grabbed her by the shoulders. It wasn't forceful, just a way to let her know that he needed her undivided attention. He often did that when he was ready to lecture her on something she'd screwed up. In her defense—because she wasn't always screwing up—he also did it when she needed to be comforted or reassured.

"I get it," he said. "I get it all. You've wanted nothing to do with Azra-El or anything or anyone in that world for years. But, Kassidy, we cannot always choose what we want. Destiny has a way of happening. That's why it's called destiny."

Kassidy inclined her head. Talk of fate and destiny annoyed her. She wanted to believe that life was about choice and free will. She wanted to believe there was no true endgame. More than anything she wanted to believe that all the years hiding hadn't been a waste of time. That somewhere the life she wanted was possible. A normal life, without self-medicating, without Reapers and Wraiths—without pain and trauma.

"I can't do this, Keiron. I just, I don't want any of this. I just want to live. That's all I ever wanted. Even when he … when he …"

"When he made you a Reaper?"

Kassidy nodded.

"I know. I understand. But something is happening here that's greater than your desire to run and hide."

Kassidy shook her head. She backed away from Keiron and moved toward the door. She needed to get out. She needed to leave. Not just Keiron's loft, but St. John. All of it. Even Lynn.

Especially Lynn?

"If you walk out that door, if you run, everything that happens from this moment is on you, Kassidy. Every life ruined. Every life lost. It's all on you."

Kassidy stopped as she reached for the door handle. "No, fuck that. You can't put that on me. Clearly there are people who know more than me. Fuck, you're one of them. If you all know so fucking much, you fight him."

"This is a fight you started," Keiron said.

"I started?" Kassidy asked as she turned to face Keiron. "I didn't start any of this shit. He did. I was just a kid. A screwed-up, lonely kid. He used me. He betrayed me."

"And you took out your anger on him, nearly killing him."

"Damn right I did!"

"Then you should finish the job. Just like you should have back then."

Something within snapped. Screaming, Kassidy lunged at Keiron with a speed and ferocity she hadn't known since her battle with Azra-El all those years ago. She punched, kicked, spun, and lunged, using every offensive attack she knew. Fluid and instinctual, as if she'd done it each day of her life. She felt freedom in each movement. Each punch thrown was in the face of everyone who'd ever uttered the words *fate* or *destiny*. Each kick was in the balls of everyone who'd kept her in the dark about their true agendas. Within minutes, she'd exhausted herself.

And in that moment, she realized Keiron had either blocked, ducked, or sidestepped everything she'd thrown his way.

As she bent over, hands on her knees, breathing heavy, she glared up at him. His hands were clasped behind his back, the epitome of calm and decorum.

"You been working out?" Kassidy asked.

Keiron shrugged.

Kassidy stood straight, looked at Keiron, then down and around—embarrassed. She felt better though. Like a bratty child, but better.

"I'm . . . sorry," she said, still trying to catch her breath.

"No need," Keiron replied.

Sincerity radiated from him. It made her feel even worse. He wasn't angry. He wasn't amused. He wasn't even uncomfortable in the way people get when someone does something really stupid. He was just Keiron. Good old reliable Keiron. Who'd been holding something back from her.

The Scythe of Cronus.

Her annoyance returned. But she didn't want to fight. She just wanted out.

"I have to go," she said.

"Kassidy?"

Kassidy stopped as she reached for the doorknob.

"You can't run from this. Not this time. He'll come for you. He'll come for those you love."

Pulling the door toward her, Kassidy turned her head slightly. "Not if I leave them first."

CHAPTER TWELVE

THERE WAS A TIME. NOT SO LONG AGO. WHEN PEOPLE ATTRIBUTED all the strange and unknown occurrences in the world to the gods. When crops yielded too little, the gods were angry. When there was an abundance, the gods were pleased. When battles were won, it was because the gods looked upon the winning side with favor—the losers be damned. Even in death, the gods were integral in deciding where a soul should go. Those deemed good in life went to Elysium, Valhalla, or heaven. The others, well, in any version of existence, it was hell.

There were many names given to the keeper of the various hells that existed, just as there were various names for the beings that ushered souls into the light or the dark after death. Azra-El could list all the names he'd been given over the centuries, but none suited him. He liked being called the Angel of Death, though, because there was something noble in its connotations. Angels were considered gentle, caring, and compassionate, and even though his role seemed dark, it was also necessary and beautiful.

Azra-El performed Tai Chi with graceful and elegant movements as he thought back on his life—current and former, that brief time during which he was human. That brief time during which he was happy, and in love. Azra-El wondered what life would have been like had he not died the way he had. Or had she not died the way she had.

He still remembered her face. Her long dark hair and hazel eyes, her fiery spirit. A voice like a gentle breeze on the wind—sweet, calm, and loving. When he closed his eyes and thought hard enough, he could feel her lips on his. When he closed his eyes and calmed himself, he could feel her against him as they embraced. He could smell the sweet scent of lavender on her silky skin. When those memories surfaced, he returned to a time when everything was simple, right, and . . . hopeful?

Until he'd met Kassidy Simmons, he'd all but forgotten what it was like to feel hopeful. He'd sensed something within her, something he could not name. A power unlike any he'd ever felt in a human being. Azra-El was certain that if he could tap into that power, strengthen it, absorb it, and make it his own, he could find a way to have everything he'd ever wanted in life.

Twenty years later, he was hiding out in an abandoned home, recovering from a battle with this girl who dared give him hope for a return to that happiness he'd lost so long ago. Twenty years later, he was practicing Tai Chi, loosening stiff muscles, and working through the pain inflicted on him—by a young girl.

There would be no more waiting. He'd found a way to accelerate his healing. In the process, her powers were growing. This time, there would be no long-term plan. He would take her life, her power, and he would ascend. This time, happiness would return to him by his own hand.

Azra-El stopped and bowed his head, as was his practice. He was nowhere near full strength, but that seemed to only make him more determined. The dim glow of red from his eyes pulsated like a flashlight with fading batteries. He took one step, then two, then three, before turning towards the fireplace. He stared into the flames for a short time, then closed his eyes. Concentrating, he focused on Allesandra. He saw her limp, bloody, and bruised in his arms. Even near death, she had been the most beautiful woman he'd ever known. She smiled at him, reached up, and caressed his face.

"This is not the end of us, my love," she'd said. "This life was only ever temporary. A stop on the way to an eternal life. With you."

He'd heard the words. On some level, they were sweet, romantic, and optimistic. But in that moment, all he knew was that she would be gone from him. The image burned in his mind, in his soul, and the words replayed in his brain. When Azra-El opened his eyes again, power surged within. The glow from his eyes intensified, and against the wall the color danced like small nuclear explosions.

"We were denied eternal life," he said softly to himself. "You were stolen from me in death, by Death. But soon nothing will be denied. We will be together again, my Allesandra. I'll destroy him and anyone who stands in my way."

A weak wind entered the room, and low dark clouds swirled across the floor. The clouds converged on him, encircled him, consumed him, until there was nothing left in the space he once occupied.

CHAPTER THIRTEEN

"SO YOU FUCKED IT UP?"

"Maybe. Possibly," Kassidy said.

"Probably."

Kassidy could only shrug, but David was likely right. She'd done a grade-A job of destroying her relationship with Lynn. The look in that woman's eyes this evening was burned in her mind. It wasn't anger. It wasn't love. It wasn't pity. It was all those wrapped into one tiny little atom bomb. Lynn had kissed her before she'd left. That was nice. At least she'd have that. But there was little passion in it. Love, yes, but no passion.

After everything that had occurred since the morning, especially all that weird shit with the enigmatic but ridiculously gorgeous Advocate, Kassidy needed to decompress. She'd finally responded to one of the dozen or so messages from David, and after taking a tongue lashing from him, agreed to meet him at Tully's. It was the perfect mix of a casual, friendly neighborhood pub with the madness of a chain sports bar.

"So now what?" David asked.

"I don't know."

"Oh please. You've got something in mind. Bitch, you're not thinking of leaving again, are you? Because I know that creeps into your head when shit gets real."

David didn't sugarcoat anything. He had a filter, mind you,

but it only seemed to be in place when working with his clients. He knew when to use it, and he knew when to chuck the damn thing right out the window. Usually, with her, he chucked the damn thing right out of the window. Their friendship undercut the bullshit niceties of most relationships. David was a good man, a good friend, and more often than not, just what she needed.

"I don't know." She really didn't. There was so much to do, so much to avoid, so much that she didn't want to be part of, that running seemed like the perfect course of action. *If you don't enjoy doing something anymore, you shouldn't do it, right?*

David just shook his head.

"Yeah, I know. I have a pattern," she acquiesced.

"You're seriously thinking of leaving, aren't you?"

She was about to answer when the waitress showed up with drinks and food. David had ordered wings, as usual. He had an unhealthy obsession with them. At first, he'd only ordered them as a sarcastic poke at the stereotype of a big black man eating wings like they were God's gift to the culinary arts. Over time he'd grown to love them.

Kassidy would usually just share with David. Tonight, though, she had no appetite. Except for bourbon, which the waitress set down next to her after giving David his wings and beer. Not the most nutritious meal, but it satisfied her craving.

"There's a lot going on right now. I'm trying to sort it out and deal with it. I just . . . I don't know. I guess I wonder if maybe some distance will help."

"Girl, distance is for shot put, javelin, and running marathons."

She laughed, reluctantly. David made her laugh, especially when she didn't want to. He didn't blow smoke up her ass or co-sign on her bullshit. He was not a yes man. Intuitive, he'd always had a way of helping people navigate through their crap. They'd learn how to get out of their own way, so to speak. He loved everything about life and people. He'd made it his mission in life to help others learn to love those things too, with a bit of a flourish. Not an obnoxious one, just a little flamboyance.

On her second bourbon, Kassidy was fidgety. Her leg shook, and she squeezed her glass like it was the neck of someone who'd killed her dog.

"How about we talk about you for a minute? Like why the fuck were you blowing me up all day?" Kassidy asked.

"Oh, so you just wanna stroke my ego and talk about me then? Change subjects much?"

"I'm changing it now," Kassidy said with sarcastic bite.

"For real?"

"For real, for real."

"I'll allow it," David said, before biting the meat off the tiny drumstick. With his mouth full, he pointed the naked bone at Kassidy. "We'll get back to you, though."

Kassidy nodded and laughed. Her leg stopped shaking, and she loosened her grip on her glass. For the next few minutes, she listened to David talk about how he and his partner, Matthew, had decided to move in together. She liked Matthew, mostly, though his insistence that he be called Matthew and not Matt annoyed her. Overall, he seemed to make David happy, and in the end, that's what was important.

"You sure it's not too soon?" Kassidy asked.

"YOLO!" David exclaimed, waving another naked chicken bone in the air like a bull rider.

Kassidy laughed.

"Besides, his place is bigger, and I can move my practice there. There's a separate gatehouse I can convert to an office to see clients."

As she nodded her approval, Kassidy was bowled over at the

intensity of someone's arousal. It wasn't coming from David. Someone in the bar was pretty lovestruck, though. Directed at her.

She scanned the crowd—not a difficult task on a week-night—for any sign that someone was looking her way. When Kassidy made eye contact with a woman at the bar, her pulse escalated, and she started to sweat. The woman didn't take her eyes off Kassidy.

"Um, hello?"

Kassidy snapped out of the lustful trance and refocused on David.

"I know you were not just eye fucking that heifer at the bar," David said.

"Huh?"

"Don't *huh* me. You know what, let's get back to you now," David said.

He moved his plate to the side, having demolished his wings, and grabbed his beer with both hands. Kassidy knew this move. It usually meant he was about to get serious. She put her glass to her lips and took a few sips to help brace herself for the lecture. Fortunately, no maliciousness was afoot. David was coming from a place of love and compassion. Typical.

"Look, you know I want nothing but the best for you, right?"

Kassidy nodded.

"I can't tell you what that is. Only you can. But I can tell you, just because shit feels like it's getting real, that's no reason to implode."

"All I did was look at the girl."

"Yeah, but you have a way of just looking," David said with a side eye.

Kassidy grinned. There was some truth in that. Lynn had

mentioned it on more than one occasion. It was, in fact, that look that had made Lynn take notice the night they'd met.

"See, you know you do," David continued, laughing. "Maybe it's time for you and Lynn to call it quits. Maybe it's time for you to try some new shit in general. You're not happy. You're drinking more. You're on edge. Something is going on with you."

If you only knew the half of it.

"I'm not saying you have to tell me. You know you never need to do that. What I am saying is, slow down, take a look at yourself, and address your shit before it addresses you."

He'd essentially given her the same advice Lynn had. Though with more profanity, pomp, and circumstance. They were both right, of course. She knew it. If she hadn't walked out on Keiron, he would have said the same thing. Wait. He *did* say the same thing. So did creepy, gorgeous Denzel in the Nexus. They were all right, but she wasn't ready to deal with any of it.

She wanted peace.

Quiet.

Another bourbon.

Taking a peek at the bar, she noticed that her eye candy had disappeared. Kassidy was strangely disappointed. She also saw David's brother walking toward them.

"I hear you," Kassidy said.

"Do you, bitch?"

"Yes," she said through a laugh.

"Then where are you going?" he asked.

Kassidy scooted out of the booth. She stood and held her arms out for David's brother. As they embraced, she scanned the bar for the mystery girl. Still nothing.

"How are you, Kass?" James asked.

"I'm good," she replied. "Getting a much-needed lecture from your brother about my life and my drinking."

"Damn right," David said.

"So, what are you going to do with this newfound wisdom?" James asked.

"I'm going to walk to the bar and order another. Want one?"

James laughed. David scowled slightly, then gave a sheepish smirk as he shook his head.

"I love you," Kassidy said to David.

"Shit, you better."

Kassidy strode toward the bar with her glass. She didn't have to, of course. She and David had a waitress, after all. But she needed to get away. She was close to unleashing her entire life story on David. He had no idea about her abilities. No idea about her life as a Reaper. All he'd ever known was that she had a rough childhood and was dealing with some deep-rooted issues. It served no purpose for him to know more. But tonight . . .

"What can I get you?" the bartender asked.

"Elijah Craig, small batch," Kassidy replied.

The bartender nodded.

"Good choice," said a voice behind her.

The familiar lust filled Kassidy again. Her legs almost gave out with the intensity. She shifted her gaze to the side as the mystery woman sauntered closer to the bar. Both women regarded each other, grinning. The woman was pretty. Beautiful in fact. She had brownish-red curls that fell just past her shoulders. Her eyes were a deep, dark brown, actually more chestnut. She wasn't as tall as she'd seemed from a distance. She was just a hair shorter than Kassidy. The heels on her boots helped with that.

"Yeah, I'm a fan," Kassidy said in response, with a clear double entendre.

"I'm more of a Woodford girl myself, but I definitely appreciate old Elijah."

The bartender brought Kassidy's drink to her. As he set it down, the woman asked for her bill.

"Leaving so soon?" Kassidy asked, surprised at her disappointment.

"Yeah, I have a . . . thing."

Yeah, you do.

"Ah, the proverbial, ever-mysterious thing," Kassidy said.

"Mm-hmm. Always pops up at the worst moments."

Kassidy caught a slight hint of regret in the woman. She didn't want to leave.

"That's too bad. I thought we were having an across-a-crowded-room moment," Kassidy said.

"Yeah. Yeah, we totally were. Dramatic though, right?"

"Agreed."

"I'm Traci, by the way." She extended her hand.

"Kassidy."

The women shook hands slowly, not taking their eyes off each other.

"Irish?" Traci asked.

"To be determined," Kassidy responded.

"Daddy split at birth?"

"Adopted."

"Ahhhh," Traci said, throwing her head back slightly.

"Hell, for all I know, we could be sisters."

"That would suck," Traci said.

"I don't know. There's a market for that in porn. We could make a small fortune."

They both cringed, then awkwardly laughed. Kassidy liked Traci's laugh. Or was it the bourbon in her that liked it? No, it was definitely Kassidy who liked it. Maybe a little too much.

"So, this thing—" Kassidy began.

"Birthday party," Traci said.

"Birthday party," Kassidy repeated. "Think it'll be as fun as hanging out here?"

"If you'd asked me that twenty minutes ago, I'd say yes."

"And now?"

"Now, I'm not so sure," Traci said.

As Kassidy let those words sink in, she noticed, absently, that they were still holding hands. As her eyes called attention to it, Traci took her hand back. Simultaneously, her check had arrived. She pulled a credit card from her purse and placed it on the bar. The bartender grabbed both.

"Is this a normal hangout for you?" Traci asked.

"I come through a couple times a month maybe. Used to be here a lot more, but now—"

"Life gets in the way?"

"Something like that."

"So maybe I'll see you again here some time?" Traci asked shyly.

"Maybe."

"That's not a no," Traci said as she reached for her returned credit card and receipt.

Kassidy laughed softly. Which she felt more than heard.

Traci signed her receipt. Before closing her purse, she pulled out a business card and wrote a number on the back of it. She handed it to Kassidy, who stared at it, a plethora of thoughts going through her mind.

"Maybe on a night when I don't have a thing and you don't have a thing, we could have a thing together," Traci said.

"You rehearse that?" Kassidy asked.

"Off the cuff. Too much?"

"Not too much."

"If nothing else, it'll make a great story to tell our friends," Traci said.

"Agreed."

Again, they laughed nervously. Kassidy put the card in her back pocket.

"It was nice meeting you, not-Irish Kassidy," Traci said.

"Nice meeting you too, Traci."

Kassidy stretched her hand out, and Traci took it. Such a whirlwind of desire, along with regret. Traci didn't want to go, which made Kassidy feel warm inside. She watched as Traci crossed to the door.

A rush of cold air behind her brought Kassidy's attention back. She scanned the bar to track it. Had someone come up behind her? She saw nothing out of the ordinary. No open window or door, no rush of people had passed. Seconds later, though, out of the corner of her eye, she saw something dark. A shadow? No. A cloud.

A Wraith!

Kassidy stared at it, frozen. Had it followed her? Could they finally see her now? Slowly it moved through the bar before finally picking up speed and drifting under a rear door. Kassidy clenched her fist and narrowed her eyes. Something had to give. She surveyed the bar again and found David's gaze. His face was disapproving, but that didn't matter much. Reluctantly, she slinked toward the back door, toward the Wraith, toward... death.

CHAPTER FOURTEEN

HE'D BEEN TOLD BY OTHERS THAT THE FIRST NIGHT OUT AFTER retirement would be the strangest. They told him that at some point, he'd want to call it an early night because 05:00 seemed to come faster after craft beer and multiple shots of tequila. They told him that in the back of his mind he'd still try to organize the next day because that was what good Marines did. They told him a lot of things, and he listened because they'd come before him, and good Marines respected those who'd come before them.

When he'd walked out of Tully's, he'd laughed because they were right about everything.

Ben Spada was a good man, a good friend, and a good Marine. The time had come for him to find something else to be good at. Walking along the streets of St. John at night was not the ideal time to contemplate life's meaning and purpose. But Ben was retired. What the hell else did he have to do?

Having grown up here, it was the natural first stop of his retirement tour. He had buddies coming into town in a few days, and a certain someone would be home soon from a business trip. She'd hated him when he'd enlisted. Deep down, she'd understood why he'd done it. She had told him as much. Deep down, she loved him and always would—she'd told him that too. But in the end, she did not want the life of a military wife.

Ben had spent time with her between deployments, but they'd

never spoken about his job, at least, not the specifics. Despite her feelings, she was proud of him and respected him, and it wasn't until he'd read the letter she'd left with his parents that he'd learned of that and more. That letter meant more to him than anything he'd done in life. He'd served his country with distinction. He'd saved lives, protected the innocent, gone far and above the call of duty every time he went out. Ben had earned commendations and medals for things he'd done that had never officially happened.

He was an American hero in every sense of the phrase.

So, as he walked away from the bar, when he heard a woman scream that someone had stolen her purse, it was no surprise that his first and only instinct was to help her. Ben had taken the briefest of moments to make sure she was unhurt, then set off at top speed after the perpetrator.

The chase lasted all of two minutes. Ben wasn't winded. He was focused. Relentless. He was on mission. The purse snatcher stopped to catch his breath in front of the St. John Library. Ben could see the man was breathing heavily. Assessing the situation, he felt there was minimal risk given the assailant's physical conditioning.

"Look, man, let's just make this simple," Ben said. "Take the cash, hand over the purse and everything else in it, and be on your way."

Ben hadn't been seeking a fight. He'd replace whatever money the guy would take, because at this point it didn't matter to him. He just wanted everyone to be all right tonight. Besides, judging from guy's tattered clothing, he probably needed all the money and more. The thief had a long black hoodie on, almost like a robe, with holes and stains. Ben couldn't imagine that thing keeping someone warm.

So of course, he offered the guy his coat too.

The strange man had hidden his face with the hoodie, and he was hunched over, but he stretched his left arm out and extended his hand to take Ben's coat. His emaciated, withered, skeletal hand opened, and his fingers . . . seemed to . . . lengthen. They wrapped around Ben's forearm and pulled him closer with no effort. Ben was in top physical condition with zero body fat and muscle on top of muscle, yet this . . . thing . . . handled him like a ragdoll.

When Ben had come face to face with the thing, he'd quickly realized that nothing in his training had prepared him for this. It didn't matter though. Ben Spada was a Marine. He was a hero. He would adapt and overcome because that was what he was taught. It was as natural as breathing.

Which had become difficult as a result of a skeletal hand around his throat.

Ben had looked down and found himself a couple of feet off the ground. He had tried to brace himself by grabbing the bony arm attached to the hand that held him, so he could kick himself free. Despite its appearance, the thing was a rock. Ben looked down again, as if trying to will himself to the ground. But there was no hope. If there had been, it was all gone the moment he watched the hand of the creature phase through his chest as if he were a hologram.

The creature had dropped Ben after retracting his hand. Ben watched it ingest a glowing orb, and then the creature's hands turned into weapons. Sickles.

They'd told him the first night out after retirement would be the strangest, and Ben had to laugh again at just how right they'd been.

He had not anticipated his life ending this way. In fact, after reading the letter she'd left for him, he'd imagined his life would be full of excitement with the woman who'd finally admitted that she'd loved him since they were kids. He imagined growing old with her and spending his later years with grandchildren and, medical science permitting, great-grandchildren and beyond.

But his life was ending here, on the streets of St. John, at the hands of a foul creature, all because he'd chosen to help someone.

Because that was what Marines do.

CHAPTER FIFTEEN

KASSIDY WALKED THROUGH THE BACK DOOR INTO THE ALLEYWAY behind Tully's. She saw no Wraith. Had it simply been trying to get her attention? Did it even know she was there? She continued on, stretching out her senses for any sign of the apparition, for any sign of anything. She felt nothing, which was odd. Strangely, she didn't even sense anyone inside Tully's. Considering the new range she'd experienced earlier in the day at the hospital, something seemed off again.

As she headed farther into the alley, she was startled by the rush of wind that emanated from the business next door. Within that wind gust, a dark vapor appeared, a swirl of dread and malevolence. It settled in the space in front of her, no more than ten feet away. Kassidy remained motionless as the vapor took form.

Ethan.

He stood there smiling again, as if he had no cares in the world. As a Wraith, he really didn't. As a part of Azra-El's so-called guard, he wanted for nothing. No Reaper did, but the Wraiths were the special ones, the elite, the in-crowd. It was just another reason to hate them even more.

"I know you're here, Kassidy. Why not show yourself? I'll be good if you will," he said.

Kassidy's lip curled up in a slight snarl. This whole day was fucked beyond imagination. She gave in to her anger. She wanted answers, and she wouldn't get them hiding. Maybe this asshole would give her some information. It was unlikely, but she was angry enough to step out of the darkness, if only for a moment. She closed her eyes and took a deep breath. When she opened them, they were silver. A dim light pulsed from her body.

Ethan turned his head and stared directly in her eyes.

"Well now," he said.

"What are you doing here, Ethan?" Kassidy asked.

"Nice to see you too. My goodness. Your manners have vanished over the years, I see."

Kassidy rolled her eyes.

"Why are you here?" she asked through gritted teeth.

Holding his hands up as if surrendering, Ethan replied, "I'm just here to do my job. No more, no less."

"Really? And exactly which job would that be? You're a Wraith. So are you here to escort a soul? Or are you here to police some rogue Reaper as part of Azra-El's private guard?"

"Lots of questions. Odd, considering you don't want to be a part of our family anymore. You did leave us, after all."

"Family? Is that what you call it?"

Kassidy laughed at the notion. She paced, folding her arms across her chest to keep her fists from clenching.

"If you'd bothered to stick around, you'd see that is precisely what we were. Still are, actually."

Ethan put his hands into the pockets of his tailored suit pants. He was the epitome of a gentleman. If only he weren't such a scourge.

Why are the pretty ones always clueless assholes?

"Let's pretend you didn't just say that and get back to you answering the question about why you're here."

"Touched a nerve, eh? Is it because you realize, in hindsight, that we *were* a family, and you broke some serious trust when you tried to kill the head of said family?"

Ethan's smile turned to a sinister sneer. He'd removed his hands from his pockets, and his posture was much less casual. Would he attack her?

"I left because Azra-El was not who I thought he was. Everything he'd ever told me was a lie. He was using me, using all of us. I left to be alone."

"To be alone? Oh, my dear Kassidy, in this life, this existence, you can never be—"

A door crashed open behind Ethan, cutting him off. Kassidy glanced beyond Ethan as an older man stumbled out of the building next to Tully's. He appeared to be in his late fifties, balding on top with gray on the sides, generously portioned around the midsection. There was nothing remarkable about the man.

Except for the knife sticking out of his chest.

As the man fell to the ground, Kassidy glanced from him to Ethan. Ethan's grin had returned, and he shrugged. In an instant, his eyes turned deep black. Before she knew what was happening, Kassidy threw a punch. Ethan expertly moved to the side to avoid the blow and moved again just as fast to avoid the follow-up swing Kassidy threw with her other fist. Ethan backed up and moved into a defensive stance, preparing for Kassidy's attack.

"Getting upset over this guy is really a waste of time, young pup," Ethan said. "Honestly, he's just one of many. In fact, his is the last soul we need. Though, I hear the Primus is stretching his legs tonight. Perhaps this poor bastard's soul is inconsequential after all. Nevertheless, I took a paramedic earlier, someone else just took a former Marine. Let me finish with this one, and I'll be on my way. Otherwise, we'll just take someone else—just to be certain."

Kassidy wanted to scream.

Despite their power, Reapers were trained to fight. As supernatural creatures they had some instinct to move quickly, not necessarily gracefully, but certainly with some preternatural speed. But over the centuries, turmoil in the Reaper ranks and challenges from other supernatural beings, including gods, made it necessary to adopt a more warrior-friendly mindset. With their powers, Wraiths were better fighters.

She'd beaten a Wraith once, long ago, before she even knew what they were.

But that Wraith was not Ethan.

Kassidy lunged at him again, throwing punch after punch. Ethan blocked most, but a few connected, giving her some semblance of satisfaction. She dodged and blocked his punches and kicks, mostly successfully. Ethan caught her with a kick to the gut followed by an uppercut that sent her to the ground. He stood over her, rage building, eyes dark with the emptiness of the abyss.

"You would be wise to go away, young pup."

She hated when he called her that. When she'd become a Reaper, back when Azra-El had uncharacteristically taken her under his wing, Ethan had taken to calling her that. He thought he was being cute, and back then, he was. Hell, he was still cute, but her disgust with him and the Reaper order far outweighed any schoolgirl crush she'd once had. Kassidy pushed passed her frustration, concentrated, and in an instant, she was vapor. She re-formed behind him and threw a punch, which he'd anticipated, easily blocking it.

But he was not prepared for the scythe, which had also formed in place of her hand, that entered his stomach.

Kassidy stepped back, pulled the scythe from him, spun, and slashed it across his throat. Ethan dropped to his knees, clutched his throat, and smirked.

"Welcome . . . back," he managed to get out.

He was only wounded. If she wanted to dispatch him for good, she would have to remove his life force, the way a Reaper could with a human. But she didn't have that kind of power. Sure, she once bested a Wraith, though in hindsight, she had no idea how. She even bested the Angel of Death, but that was with the aid of the black onyx daggers, which she did not currently have on her. In the end, she was only a Reaper, and that was as much a reason for his smirk as anything else. He knew she couldn't beat him, not fully. He'd heal quickly and be back to doing despicable things like whatever he'd done to the man dying in the alleyway.

The Wraiths were unchecked without Azra-El in power. They were killing people at their leisure, collecting souls for God only knew what. Perhaps for their own power. Perhaps as a source to help Azra-El heal. The thought of it, all of it, only angered Kassidy more. One sound caused her blood to boil over though.

The sound of Ethan chuckling.

Her anger turned to fury.

In his eyes, she saw joy. In his eyes, she saw the promise of further death and mayhem. In his eyes, she saw the reflection of her own, darkening. Where they had once been silver, they were now the dubious shadow of night. Her coal-black eyes startled her . . . and Ethan. A wave of power filled her. Intense. Ancient. New. Within seconds her hand phased through his chest, and when she pulled it back, the glowing purple orb that was his life force, his power, pulsated in her hand.

"Impossible," he said.

It should have been. Kassidy was only a Reaper, right?

She ingested the orb, and with his life force and power gone, sliced through Ethan's throat once more with her scythe. His eyes went wide, then sank in. His skin became dry, wrinkled, and brittle. His hair changed from blond to gray to white and receded from his scalp. Teeth fell from bleeding gums, and his skin tightened—his skeletal frame fighting for dominance and winning.

The Wraith that had been Ethan was now a hairless, dry-skinned skeleton that decayed until bones cracked and skin flaked off, before finally dispersing into a cloud of black dust.

Kassidy stared at the empty space, then down at her right hand—or what should have been a hand. The curved onyx blade dematerialized into vapor, then re-formed into five digits.

The sound of the man on the ground behind her shocked her into the present.

Kassidy ran back to him and knelt to examine the wound. There was no way to save him. The knife buried deep inside his chest had penetrated his heart. He'd be dead in minutes, less than a minute if she removed it. Through her Reaper eyes, she saw a faint red glow around him. Death was near. If she escorted his soul, her warding would be all but gone. Reapers and Wraiths would know where to find her. She could walk away and let another Reaper take him, perhaps buying herself another day or two of relative freedom. Kassidy stood, scanned the area, then walked away.

I don't want this.

I don't need this.

I just want to be left alone.

Fear stopped her in her tracks. Not her own fear, but the fear oozing from the wounded man behind her. With every breath, he was losing life, losing hope, and bathing in the fear of pain and the unknown. She wanted to leave, but she knew that pain. She'd wish that on an enemy, but not a stranger. Not an innocent. Kassidy closed her eyes and focused, and when she reopened them, she found herself in the gray-tinted world of the Nexus.

She dashed back to the body. The man was motionless, yet still had his eyes on her. Kassidy stretched out her hand, and he grabbed it. Only it wasn't him. It was his spirit, his soul. His body remained on the ground, but his soul was now beyond it. He stood and looked around, confused, scared. Kassidy placed a hand on his chest and smiled lightly at him.

"Be at peace," was all she said.

A bright blue light surrounded him, and in an instant, he was gone. Kassidy felt some relief that he'd gone to the Beyond and not the Void. She didn't know him. She'd never known any of the souls she'd reaped. But for some reason, knowing that he was truly in a better place helped ease her guilt. Somehow, this was her fault. Had she killed Azra-El all those years ago, perhaps she wouldn't be hunted now. If the Wraiths had not been after her, if her growing power hadn't been calling to them, perhaps this man would not be dead.

Did he have a wife? Children?

Question after question bombarded her. Kassidy sank down to the ground. All she wanted was to live. That was all she'd ever wanted.

No, that wasn't true. There was a time when she would have been happy to die. In many ways, she felt like that again. Like that sixteen-year-old girl who lay on the damp ground of Potter's Field, near death. Like the girl that Azra-El found and changed forever.

Wisps of fog swirled around her as it always did in this place. She sat, she wept, and then she vanished.

CHAPTER SIXTEEN

"JOHN. THANK YOU SO MUCH FOR COMING TONIGHT. YOUR PARTICI-pation and support are really going to help get this new project off the ground."

"And that sizeable donation won't hurt either, will it?"

Lynn laughed. The comment was less tongue in cheek and more passive aggressive. But she was a professional. Some would argue that she was the absolute best at what she did. Lynn got things done because she knew how to play the game.

She hated playing the game.

It was nights like this that she envied Kassidy. Kassidy didn't care about impressing anyone. She didn't care about putting her best foot forward or kissing proverbial ass to get what she wanted. Kassidy kept things simple. She was certainly capable, and she typically played nice whenever Lynn brought her to events like this, but it went against her nature to bow down, to feel like she was begging. As far as Kassidy was concerned, people shouldn't be convinced to do the right thing. If you had the means, you should help those who didn't. It was that simple.

Except when it wasn't.

"Yes, that donation definitely helps," Lynn said painfully. She'd been smiling all night. Her jaw hurt. It paled in comparison to the way her heart hurt. It didn't hurt at the prospect of losing Kassidy. It hurt because she knew Kassidy was hurting, and there was nothing Lynn could do about it. Lynn genuinely loved her. But their relationship was off course, and there was no fixing it. Maybe one day down the road when Kassidy was in a better place, maybe then they could try again. But now they each needed more than the other was able to give.

As Lynn surveyed the gala, she saw couples everywhere representing dollar signs and business arrangements under the guise of marriage. Most of them were together because it looked good—on paper, in the papers, and most definitely on banking statements. There were men and trophy wives, women who'd been born with money and married money to make more money. Lynn wondered if anyone in the room felt genuine love and affection for the person they were with. She needed to get out of there. This thing with Kassidy weighed on her, especially under the shadow of her father's hospitalization.

She sought out her boss, Sarah, to lay the groundwork for her departure. She found Sarah holding court with longtime donors and a couple of teens. The Madisons and their grandkids—future donors in Sarah's eyes, no doubt. Lynn caught her attention and watched as the executive artfully excused herself from her audience. She was ten years older than Lynn but appeared even older. Lynn had suspected that Sarah might partake of a substance or two to keep going at the speed she operated. There was just no way that someone could be that naturally energetic.

"This is a great turnout, Lynn. You and your team have outdone yourselves," Sarah said.

"You said that last time," Lynn said.

"And look at you, raising the bar. You make us look great. I need you to know how much I appreciate you."

"I do know. We all do. You do a great job of letting us know we're appreciated. I'm grateful for that."

Lynn accepted a hug. She knew that Sarah's affection for her was genuine. Lynn had suspicions and concerns about her, but when it came down to it, she was an outstanding example of an executive.

"You're trying to get out of here, aren't you?"

And she was intuitive as hell.

"Is it your dad? Is everything okay?" Sarah asked.

"Last I heard, he was unchanged. But I want to go and check on him and my mom before I head home."

"Of course," Sarah said. "Get out of here. This is going to wrap up soon anyway. We can handle it."

Lynn hugged Sarah again and made her way toward a back room to retrieve her coat and purse. When she emerged, she took one last peek at the festivities, then walked out the door.

It was cold outside. Not freezing, but cold. Lynn wrapped her coat around herself and pulled her phone from her pocket. She was shaking. Not from the temperature, but from the call she was about to make.

"Hey, Kass. It's me. Listen, I'm . . . I'm . . ." She wanted to say she was sorry. But was she? Sure. Not for what she'd said or done, but because of the way things had been. She wished she could make things better, easier. But she was tired, and frankly, she didn't know what to do.

". . . heading out of the gala. Things went pretty well tonight. People seemed happy. I'm gonna go to the hospital and see Dad and spend a little more time with my mom. So, yeah, you don't have to wait up or anything, I guess. Okay . . . I'll talk to you later."

Usually she'd end that call by saying "I love you," and she almost did, out of habit. It just didn't feel as authentic as it should have. Lynn slid into her car and sat for a long moment, staring at nothing, doing nothing.

Feeling everything.

As she drove, Lynn pressed a button on her steering wheel to change the radio station. Smooth jazz wasn't where here head was at. She needed something harder, something with an edge, something classic. "Carry On Wayward Son" blasted as she cruised down the street toward St. John Memorial Hospital.

Lynn zoned out, lost in the song, until she noticed a swirling cloud down the road. From a distance it resembled a mini tornado. No, it couldn't have been a tornado. Tornados weren't a thing in St. John. Blizzards were a thing. Besides, how ridiculous would it be to have a tornado touch down while Kansas was playing on the radio?

As she rolled closer, the cloud coalesced, almost dissipating, only . . . it took a human form. Within a few seconds, that was exactly what she saw—a man. Confusion overshadowed Lynn as she swerved at the last second to avoid him.

Are his eyes red?

The question only lingered for a moment before her SUV hit a patch of ice and spun out of control. Lynn gripped the steering wheel with both hands, turning left and right, trying hard to brake, but that only made things worse. Her SUV slammed nose first into a parked pickup. Lynn's head snapped back, then forward, her face hitting the deployed airbag.

Her neck ached. Her back was sore. Her fingers tingled. Her vision was blurry. Turning her head, she looked out her driver's-side window and saw smoke everywhere. Beyond that smoke, a dark figure strode toward her. Someone was coming to help. Thank God.

As the person drew closer, Lynn saw the two red dots in a shroud of black. Two red dots that glowed brighter and brighter as the figure approached. It was that guy in the road with . . .

those eyes. Those red eyes were now staring at her through the window. She couldn't make out the features, but even with her blurred vision, she could see the sinister grin.

Before the darkness overtook her, before she passed out, Lynn was certain she'd heard him laughing.

CHAPTER SEVENTEEN

DAVID AND JAMES STOOD OUTSIDE TULLY'S. THE POLICE ACTIVITY in the area was ridiculous. Things like this didn't happen in St. John. A dead body in an alleyway? That was like an awful movie cliché. Yet here they stood, watching an ambulance drive away with a corpse.

"Hell no," David said. "Can you believe this shit?"

James said nothing. He stared at the scene, wide-eyed and curious.

"And Kassidy just ghosted us too. I got some words for that girl when I see her next," David said.

"Seems like she's going through some things," James remarked.

"The only thing that girl is probably going through right now is that other girl's panties. I swear to God she's worse than a man sometimes."

"But no worse than you," James said.

"I beg your pardon?" David drew out the word *beg* the way their mother had when she was offended and trying to put you in your place at the same time.

"Dude, you've ghosted me, too," James said.

"I don't remember that at all."

"You don't, huh?"

"No sir."

"Do you remember that night a while back when that softball

team came in? Do you remember molesting the blond pitcher with your eyes while we ate pizza? Do you remember going up and talking to him when you got us refills on our beer?"

David stared at his brother. The questions were rapid fire, but he processed each of them. He processed, and he reminisced. He couldn't remember the blond pitcher's name. John? Jack? Hell, it could have been Nate for all he knew. But what was in a name? A pitcher by any other name would taste just . . .

"Hello?" James said, snapping his fingers at his brother.

"Huh? Okay, so I may have ghosted you. But we're not talking about me right now. And that was years ago. Why you gotta bring up old shit, man?"

James stared at his brother.

David stared back.

They both laughed out loud.

A little too loud given the current circumstances.

They glanced around to find a few people giving them the look that said, *Really? Have some respect.* They were not unaccustomed to that. David and James had been close their entire lives. David was older, but James looked out for him as if he were the older of the two. James had a bigger, athletic build. He worked out and had dabbled in martial arts. David's skills were with people, and he used that to his advantage, especially at work. His ability to tap into people's thoughts and feelings had made him popular in school. So popular, in fact, that he'd assumed that if he came out, he'd have nothing but support.

He'd been wrong.

Not everyone was keen on having a gay friend. The girls were fine, especially the ones who'd had a crush on him. Coming out seemed to restore their fragile egos, and they were his greatest allies. The guys—well, a few of the guys—they weren't so accepting. They'd bullied David. They'd scared him on occasion, blocking him into tight spaces or cornering him in a locker room. Every so often someone would come to his defense. Never often enough though. The only one who had his back ten times out of ten was his little brother, James. Their parents had been ambivalent, even going so far as to deny David's feelings. God forbid the subject come up around other family.

But James was always there.

"Dammit!" James exclaimed.

"What?"

"I left my credit card at the bar."

"Oh, so we were about to leave without paying?"

"We?"

"Well, I am with you," David said.

"There was certainly no 'we' when the check came."

"I mean, I just figured, why put them through the trouble of splitting it when I could just pay you back?"

James stared at his brother, then just shook his head. "Man, go get the car." He handed David his keys. "I'm gonna go settle up. I'm parked over there."

David followed James's finger to the metallic-blue BMW across the street. David loved that car, and he loved any moment his brother let him drive it. Even if it was only a ten-minute trip home.

As the last of the emergency vehicles left the area, David stepped into the street, careful not to slip on any of the snow-covered ice patches created by the shitty plows of the St. John Department of Streets and Sanitation. A couple of steps in, he beamed as he stared at the BMW.

A car horn snapped him back to reality.

David jumped back, turning his head so as to avoid the spray of snow in his face from the speeding Jeep.

"Asshole!" he yelled.

David brushed off the bottom of his pants, then proceeded back into the street. Steps away from his brother's car, he pressed the key fob to unlock the door. The headlights flashed, and the interior dome light popped on. Then searing heat and pain assaulted him as a car collided with his body. Bones snapped. A rush of air slammed into him as he flew back, landing on the lightly snow-covered asphalt of Main Street.

David moaned, every breath laborious, every attempt at moving an effort in futility. He heard nothing save for the ringing in his ears. He tried to open his mouth to speak, but could find no words, no breath, no energy to form any sound aside from the labored breathing.

Through his teary-eyed vision, David saw a dark figure above him. It hovered over his face like a snake. Two red orbs appeared, each gleaming bright. He wanted to wipe his eyes to get a clear view. He wanted to scream out in terror. But he couldn't. He could do nothing. He could say nothing. He could hear nothing except the ringing—a constant ringing.

That is, until the red-eyed figure laughed.

CHAPTER EIGHTEEN

KASSIDY AWOKE TO THE SOUND OF RUNNING WATER. NOT JUST running water—a shower. She lifted her head and looked around to find that absolutely nothing was familiar. She lifted the blanket covering her and . . . yep, she was naked.

Oh fuck!

She put her head back down on the pillow and worked on piecing together the events of the previous night. After Keiron and the impromptu Nexus meeting with Denzel, she'd gone to Tully's to see David and . . . oh, there it was. The Wraith, the reaping, the tears—the call.

The call!

She hadn't meant to. Then again, if she hadn't meant to, she wouldn't be naked in the woman's bed right now. Kassidy put her hand to her head and just stared at the ceiling before closing her eyes. The night replayed itself in pieces. She drank a lot, that much was certain. She'd been on a mission to wipe out the pain of recent events, and she'd almost succeeded. She wanted to forget, or at least feel numb. The bourbon helped with that. But she also wanted warmth, safety, companionship . . . love. Even the illusion of it. So, she'd called Traci, the woman she'd met at Tully's.

She traced the contours of Traci's face in her mind. Her cheekbones, her dimples, her full lips. Kassidy saw a quiet fire in

Traci's brown eyes, an energy, an excitement, a thirst for life and new experiences. In Traci, she saw the woman she'd always wanted to be. Someone who was curious, someone who felt free to explore and simply live.

The shower stopped, and the glass door opened and closed. She hurried out of bed and frantically searched for her clothes—they seemed to be everywhere. She scooped everything up, bear hugging them as if she'd fought a horde of the undead just to get them. She turned around and found Traci standing the doorway of the bathroom. Kassidy felt awkward, being naked and all, with the look on her face that surely said, *Yeah, I was totally planning to bail without saying a word.*

"You were totally planning to bail without saying a word, weren't you?" Traci asked.

How the hell did she do that?

"Uh . . ." Kassidy let the cold, empty silence speak for her. Her knees wobbled as surprise and disappointment floated through the air like a leaf on the wind, emanating from Traci and hitting her right in the heart. Strange. It wasn't that Kassidy wasn't capable of intimate feelings. It was strange that she seemed to care how someone else felt about her this soon after meeting. She was fairly certain it had nothing to do with the recent augmentation of her powers. She was feeling . . . something.

Traci giggled. She moved toward Kassidy, and like a deer in the headlights, Kassidy just stared. Traci glided more than walked. Kassidy had noticed that last night too, and it excited her.

It was exciting her now.

Traci bit her lip. Kassidy stepped back, only to find a wall that had apparently decided she shouldn't go any farther. Traci stepped closer, dropped her towel, and then took Kassidy's clothes, casually throwing them to the side.

A rush of heat flushed Kassidy, both from Traci's form, then from inside. Traci rubbed her soft body against Kassidy's, and the hardness of Traci's nipples pressed in. Kassidy touched Traci's arms, slid her hands up to Traci's shoulders, then caressed her face. Traci leaned in and kissed her—a long, slow, deep kiss that spoke volumes.

Traci pulled back, brushed a bit of hair from Kassidy's face, and said, "Good morning."

"Uh, yeah, good morning."

What the fuck is wrong with me? Why am I so flustered?

"You're too adorable," Traci said before backing up. She giggled again.

Kassidy was both turned on and confused.

"You mentioned last night that you'd probably bail on me in the morning. You also mentioned that if I caught you, I should make you feel awkward as fuck about it."

Kassidy let out a breath she hadn't realized she'd been holding. She put her hand to her chest, glanced down, then back up again to find Traci wrapping the towel around herself once more.

"Yeah, I would totally say something like that," Kassidy said.

"No one could ever accuse you of not knowing yourself."

"Ha-ha! God, how I wish that were true," Kassidy said.

Traci stopped, still smiling, but the sensations hitting Kassidy were concern and pity. No, not pity. Compassion. They'd talked about something deep last night. Glimpses came to her in bits and pieces, but she knew that they'd had, at some point in the evening or early morning, a rather in-depth conversation.

"Yeah, you kept saying that last night," Traci said. "Look, the offer still stands. I mean, if you ever need to unload, I'm happy to listen. Truly. No strings."

Nothing but sincerity in that. So much so that it almost overwhelmed Kassidy. Her eyes watered. This was neither the time nor the place for tears though. Or . . . was it?

"I know," Kassidy said. "I really appreciate you saying that too."

Kassidy gathered her clothes from the floor. She wasn't sure she wanted to leave, but something told her she should. Things needed her attention.

And there was Lynn.

When she grabbed her jeans, her phone vibrated. She pulled it out, nervous about the message. *Fuck!* She hadn't reached out to Lynn all night. She'd completely bailed on David and his brother after chasing Ethan into the alley. She still needed to wrap up her last case. This day was already going to shit, and she wasn't even dressed yet.

As Kassidy checked her messages, Traci moved back into the bathroom. She was talking, but nothing she said registered. The text messages Kassidy read were frantic and frightening.

"Oh my God," she whispered.

Kassidy checked her voicemail. The first message was from Lynn. Guilt ran through her like a freight train. In her heart, she knew they were done. Their relationship was over—at least in its current form. But still.

The second message was from James saying that David had been in an accident and was at the hospital, in critical condition. The third message, a nurse from St. John Memorial, calling her about . . . Lynn.

"Ms. Simmons? Hi, this is Carol Langford, from St. John Memorial. We have you listed as the emergency contact for Lynn Ambrose. She's here with us now. I really need you to give me a call as soon as you can . . ."

Nurse Langford rattled off a series of numbers. Between the thoughts in Kassidy's head, rereading all the text messages, and Traci talking in the background, Kassidy heard nothing.

". . . what do you think?" Traci asked as she walked back into the bedroom.

Kassidy looked up, shocked. She'd forgotten where she was that fast. Shaking, she dropped her phone, then fell to the ground, scrambling to pick up it, like it was the last communication device in existence.

Traci rushed over, grabbed the phone, and handed it to Kassidy, grabbing her shaking hands.

"Kassidy? Oh my God, Kassidy! What's wrong, hon?"

Kassidy wanted to speak. She tried to speak, but nothing would come out. She just stared at Traci's hands on top of hers. The warmth. The concern. She lifted her head and stopped trembling. She used her empathic ability to absorb Traci's strength, and she allowed it to become her own.

"I have to go," Kassidy said.

"Okay, okay. Do you need a ride somewhere? You look . . ."

Kassidy leaned forward and kissed Traci. In that kiss, she felt calm and focused. She pulled back and caressed Traci's face.

"Oh, sweetie, what is it?" Traci asked.

"I . . . I just have to go."

"Okay, okay," Traci repeated. "Here, let me help you."

Traci stood, then helped Kassidy up. She didn't push her to talk, which surprised Kassidy. It always seemed that people were forcefully trying to get her to talk, to express her feelings—but not this girl.

As Kassidy dressed, a million thoughts floated through her mind, but they all came back to one common denominator—Azra-El. He was responsible for this. He was drawing her out. He was going after people close to her. Fuck! Her family could be next.

Dan?

Sarah?

The thought of it filled her with rage. She stayed on the other side of that line, just on the other side. Traci's proximity helped.

Traci.

Traci had put on a robe and was sitting on the bed as Kassidy dressed. She looked as if she wanted to say something but knew there was nothing she could say. Kassidy put the last of her clothes on, then walked over. She put her hand out. Traci took it and stood. Kassidy hugged her, long and hard. A part of her wanted to stay in that moment. But there was work to be done. Work she could no longer run from.

"Can I ask," Traci began, "is this about Lynn?"

She knows about Lynn?

Kassidy really needed to go over what they'd discussed last night. Why the hell was it such a blur? The rest of the night certainly wasn't.

"Yes," Kassidy said, rolling with things. "And before you ask, no you didn't screw things up. She's . . . she's in the hospital. Something happened last night, and she's hurt."

"Oh my God, Kassidy. I'm sorry. I—"

"No, doll, it's not your fault. None of this is your fault."

Kassidy took Traci's face in her hands. She kissed her lightly on the lips and then on the forehead.

"I need to go and check on things."

"Yeah . . . yeah, of course," Traci said. "If I can do anything though, will you please let me know? I mean, if you need anything. I just . . ."

"I know," Kassidy said.

Traci walked Kassidy to the door. It was bittersweet, but more on the sweet side. There was something about this woman that fit. She regretted having to leave, but deep down she knew that if she didn't leave now, if she didn't step up and face her problems head on, there'd be nothing for her to come back to. Eventually, they'd come for Traci, too.

"Um, just so we're clear, you do know that nothing happened last night, right?" Traci asked.

Kassidy stopped just as she'd opened the door and glanced over her shoulder.

"I mean, it wasn't nothing. We kissed, and we were very flirty, but there was nothing else. We just talked. Well, you talked. But you were very drunk, and it just wouldn't have been right, you know?"

Kassidy wasn't sure how to respond. She turned fully to face Traci. She felt the honesty in her words.

"How did I—"

"End up naked?" Traci finished. "You just sort of stripped when we went to bed."

"I . . ."

"Yeah," Traci said with a grin. "You were hurting. It was pretty clear you needed to just escape and simply . . . be."

They both tilted their heads at the same time. There it was again. That . . . thing.

"Thank you." Kassidy kissed her again. "I um, I have to go. But I promise, I'll be back."

Kassidy left Traci standing in her doorway, bypassed the elevator and took the stairs. As she descended, she dialed Keiron. A part of her was worried that she'd have to hear some type of "I told you so" lecture. But that wasn't his style. Plus, she didn't care if he said it. It would have been right anyway. She stopped a soul from being taken last night. If Ethan was being truthful, another would be taken soon, and she'd likely be unable to stop it.

So she'd have to stop him.

She'd have to stop Azra-El.

"Hello?" Keiron said, picking up on the fifth ring.

"I need your help," Kassidy said. "I need to go home."

CHAPTER NINETEEN

LIKE MOST MORNINGS, JANE POPE AWOKE EARLY. NOT SO MUCH OUT of duty, more out of habit. She hadn't used an alarm clock in the last decade. She hadn't needed to. Five-thirty a.m. came at the same time every day, and every day she was up and ready to attack the world.

Her routine was simple. She'd brush her teeth, wash her face, and pull her hair back into a ponytail. She would change into one of her many multicolored leggings, throw on a sports bra, T-shirt, and running jacket. Typically, she'd wear white Nikes, but today she opted for the black-and-red Pumas. Jane's friends made fun of her for not having brand loyalty. She laughed it off. Such things didn't matter to her. She liked the colors and the comfort of the Pumas. Fashion only went so far when you were planning to return home in a sweaty heap of flesh and clothing.

Her prep was quick and seamless. Jane ate an apple, drank some water, and was out the door for her run by 5:45 a.m. The Midwest air was cool and crisp. Anyone unaccustomed to the weather would likely have stopped their jog after one or two blocks. Jane was not just anyone though. She'd been born and raised in the western suburbs of Chicago. She was new to Oak Park, but not the crisp temperatures of the fall.

Jane ran south to Lake Street then turned left. Once she reached East Avenue, she made another left and entered the grounds of Oak Park River Forest High School and continued to the track that surrounded the football field. Her strides were flawless. There was a rhythm to her movements, and they kept her warm—a gentle protest to the looming doom that was winter.

By 6:45 a.m. Jane was back home. Before entering, she stretched in her driveway, waving at neighbors on their way to work and the moms walking their kids to the bus stop. She was in her house by 6:55 a.m., and after starting her Keurig, she jumped into the shower by 7:00 a.m.

Jane had always been regimented. It wasn't a disorder. No obsessive-compulsive tics or rituals, and she wasn't the proverbial stick in the mud. She simply worked better with some order. It was doubly important because she worked from home. Without that discipline, she'd have been fired long ago, like so many who'd come on board with the company and utterly failed because they'd decided to fuck around all day. Jane had an appreciation for life. After two near-death experiences, she'd vowed to never take life for granted. Any part of it.

Including the opportunity to make money without leaving her home.

By 7:30 a.m., Jane was comfortably dressed, drinking her coffee, and enjoying scrambled eggs, two sausage patties, an English muffin, and a few slices of pineapple. Her eggs were perfect, light and fluffy, with just the right amount of salt and pepper. She'd added a light amount of shredded cheese—not so much, though, that it would overpower them. The sausage patties were well done, the way she liked them. A nice barbeque grill-style char covered both sides. The golden-brown English muffin glistened with melted butter in the nooks and crannies.

This was how every workday began.

At 7:50 a.m., Jane placed her dishes in the sink. She'd wash them later. There was no rush. She had enough time to brush her teeth one more time before she logged in to work and prepared for the weekly 8:00 a.m. conference call with the New York office. As she headed up the stairs of her two-story townhome, her doorbell rang.

That was not routine.

It didn't matter. At worst, she'd log in and take her weekly call without brushing her teeth. After all, who would know besides her?

Jane opened the door and greeted the lovely woman in front of her. She was athletic, with beautiful mocha skin, dark hair, and amazing eyes. They almost pulsated, like a strobe light. At one point, Jane thought she might be staring too hard at the stranger.

"I am so sorry to bother you this early," the woman said. "I was out on a run with my dog, and she got away from me."

"Oh noooo," Jane said.

"I know. I'm sick about it. She never does this, and I'm new to the area, and I have no idea where she may have gotten to."

"I'm so sorry. Yeah, this area has a lot of little places to hide. What kind a dog is she?"

"She's a yellow lab, and she's . . . she's . . ."

The woman broke off and started weeping. Such devotion to an animal was not unheard of. Jane had felt the same about her little Teddy when she'd had to put him down.

It was 7:55 a.m., and instead of sitting in front of her computer, preparing to receive her call, Jane was hugging a strange woman who'd lost her dog. After a few seconds, the woman pulled back. She was still crying, with her head down. Jane wanted to help her new neighbor, but she had a job to do.

"Listen," Jane began, "I can give you a hand searching for her in a little bit, if that would help?"

She was doing her best to be supportive, and it seemed as if her new friend was amenable to the idea. The woman raised her head, her eyes still closed, and sniffled and smiled, offering Jane some hope that they could reconnect later.

But when the woman opened her eyes, all hope of that vanished.

Her eyes were pitch black, making the once-sweet smile seem sinister. Before Jane could say a word, the strange woman thrust her fist into Jane's chest. Instead of showing blood and bone, the hand simply phased through as if Jane were a mirage. The woman retracted her fist, and Jane watched as she quickly ingested the glowing orb she held there. Jane stared in disbelief as the woman's hand turned into a curved blade.

At 7:59 a.m., Jane Pope lay dead on her floor at the entrance to her townhome.

At 8:00 a.m., her phone rang.

CHAPTER TWENTY

FOR THE SECOND DAY IN A ROW, KASSIDY AWOKE TO THE SOUND of running water. This time, there was no beautiful woman in the shower. No, this time it was the toilet in a shitty motel. She'd regretted her decision to stay there as soon as she pulled up, but she'd felt that surge of energy as soon as she crossed the city limits of her hometown. Her warding, everything that kept her hidden from the Wraiths and Reapers, the same warding that was weakening in St. John, was gone now. That was the price she paid for returning home. This rattrap of a motel wouldn't keep her hidden, but if something happened, she could at least minimize the damage and keep it contained.

Kassidy grabbed her cell phone off the nightstand to check the time. There were more messages from David's brother and a missed call from Lynn's mother, Susan. *Jesus!* That was a call she'd have to return, right? Of course it was. As far as Susan was concerned, she and Lynn weren't having any problems. Susan likely thought it was Kassidy's duty to be by Lynn's side. There was enough going on with Carl that Susan was likely pulling her hair out. But what could Kassidy say? *Sorry, I can't be there. I have to find an ancient weapon that probably doesn't even exist so I can kill the Angel of Death and save your daughter and my best friend?*

Who wouldn't buy that?

She put her phone down and stared at the ceiling. She

wondered where the numerous cracks came from, then watched as two bugs emerged from the largest of them. Kassidy tracked them as they crawled to the wall and stopped. Just stopped. As if they were napping. On another wall, a spider rested. Perhaps he was surveying the room and sizing up his new human roommate. Or maybe he was searching for a meal. The absurdity of what her life had become made Kassidy laugh.

She rose and walked into the bathroom, then pressed the button on the wall to turn on the light, which was strangely the most modern thing in the room. A push button instead of a switch? In a room that had an old box television strapped down to a rusted metal stand, that electrical work must have cost a pretty penny. Then again, considering the backlight on her cell phone was brighter than the bathroom, maybe they'd cut a few corners after all.

Turning on the faucet, she felt no shock when two spiders fell into the sink. The water took them down the drain, but not before some struggle on their part to remain in the world of the living. As she brushed her teeth, Kassidy was certain hot water would be an issue, so she turned the shower on to give it time to heat up. She needed a hot shower. She'd run out of Traci's apartment and gone back to her place to get clothes before hitting the road. At the time, a shower wasn't on her radar. Kassidy had needed to get home, to get to Oak Park to meet with Keiron's contact for that damn scythe.

She needed to save Lynn and David.

Kassidy stripped off her clothes and stepped into the shower, letting the warm spray cascade over her. If only it would wash the stress of her life away as well as the dirt and grime from travel.

"Fuck!"

The water had chilled. Kassidy screamed and scurried to the

back of the shower. The shock sent her heart into overdrive, and her frustration spiked. Did she really need to stay this far off the radar? She had shampoo in her hair, lather all over her body, and no choice but to brave the chilly stream. Kassidy stuck her head out, doing her best to get only her dark chestnut locks under the cold spray. The splash of cold on her legs and toes brought no joy, but she got the job done.

Until the water stopped completely.

At this point there was nothing to do but laugh. A hearty, maniacal, depressed laugh.

Kassidy stepped out of the shower, grabbed every towel she could find, and dried herself, still lathered in soap and with a generous amount of shampoo in her hair. She wiped the condensation from the mirror and—

"Hello, Kassidy," said the reflection of the man standing behind her.

Kassidy screamed, punched the mirror, and turned quickly, trying to press herself against the wall behind her, forgetting the sink, forgetting the shards on the floor, forgetting everything she'd ever learned about defending herself.

But there was no one.

She was alone.

Ignoring the cut on her foot, Kassidy stepped out of the bathroom, looked around, and still saw nothing. The bugs and the spider had not budged. She moved swiftly to her bag on the other side of the bed, stubbing her toe on the uneven, cigarette burned, paper-thin carpet. Kassidy dressed quickly, no longer worried about dry hair. She grabbed everything, threw it into her bag and purse, and walked into the hall, dread washing over her. There was death in the air. Someone in that motel would die today.

CHAPTER TWENTY-ONE

"SO IF ZEUS GAVE BIRTH TO ATHENA—I MEAN, SHE POPPED OUT OF the dude's head, fully grown—what happened to the mother? Where's Metis?"

"You will find that in many of the Greek myths, *the dude* is much more important than the woman."

At that, the women in the class nodded, many saying that not much had changed. The men? Some groaned. Some shrank down in their seats. A few laughed. It was the response that Octavia Lord was used to in her class. The battle of the sexes was forever in action, but at least here it was controlled and cordial—and usually over as soon as class ended.

Octavia's watch buzzed. She looked at her wrist and noted the time. Class seemed to fly by. It was the shortest of the classes she taught, so that had something to do with it. But it was also the liveliest. She enjoyed this group, perhaps more than any she'd ever taught.

But she said that every year.

"All right, class, that's it for tonight," she began. "Get caught up on your reading. We'll be discussing Perseus, yet another of Zeus's children."

Her proclamation was met with several cries of "Release the Kraken!" She laughed. It was normal, of course. It happened every year. But these days her students were generally referring to the order given by Liam Neeson. In the last few years, only once did someone recite the brief monologue by Sir Laurence Olivier. Octavia had given that student extra credit.

"I can assure you, the real story is even more entertaining than the movies," Octavia said.

As the students filed out of her classroom, Octavia rearranged chairs and picked up scraps of paper. Ever the dutiful teacher, she wiped down the dry-erase boards and made sure everything was in order before the next instructor took control of the room. That wasn't always done for her, of course, but she was of the do-unto-others method of living and working.

She assumed that some instructors didn't care one way or another because they didn't see teaching at a community college as particularly special. There were those who took the job for extra cash, those who took it because it was the only academic job they could get, and a select few who took it because they enjoyed teaching. She fell into the last camp. Some would say she was overqualified. No, not some. Everyone. Octavia Lord had a PhD in classics and classical literature, with a specialization in mythological studies, particularly Greek and Roman. Her interest in the classics was due, in large part, to her heritage and to the belief that events in human history were cyclical. She believed humanity was doomed to repeat the mistakes of the past, and so she taught in the hopes that one day, some would actually learn from those mistakes and end the cycle. Octavia knew she'd be waiting a while for that, but she had hope, and more importantly, she had time.

Octavia was surprised to find someone waiting for her by her office. Not because it wasn't a usual occurrence. Students sought her out all the time. No, she was surprised because she hadn't expected Kassidy Simmons to show up at her door. At least, not at her place of employment. She was a little taken aback but did her best not to show it.

"Miss Simmons?"

"Dr. Lord?"

"Octavia, please."

"Octavia," Kassidy acknowledged. "Nice to meet you. How do you know who I am?"

"Hmm? Oh . . . you just fit Keiron's description."

"Ah, yeah. He told you a weird, twitchy brunette was coming?"

The women stared at one another. Octavia sensed some apprehension in Kassidy's posture. Maybe because Octavia had used her name and they'd never met—at least as far as Kassidy knew. Despite the apprehension, Kassidy seemed open, almost comfortable. Octavia hoped that was the case. This was a day she had long awaited.

"Won't you come in," Octavia said, gesturing to her office, ignoring Kassidy's self-deprecating humor.

Kassidy moved aside to allow Octavia room to unlock and open her office door. She waved Kassidy in, then followed.

"Please excuse the mess," Octavia said as she placed her bag on the floor and cleared space on her desk, making room for, well, she didn't know. She'd never done that for a student. She was a professor, for crying out loud, with published works and textbooks with her name on them. It stood to reason her desk might be full. Yet she was overly concerned with making a good impression.

"This place keeps you busy, huh?" Kassidy asked.

"More so than I thought it would. But that's a good thing."

More awkward silence. Both women seemed uncomfortably comfortable. The office space helped with that. Octavia had two large bookshelves, both completely full. There were framed maps of ancient worlds and a heavy concentration of Greek and Roman decor. This atmosphere, the decoration, it was home.

"Seems like I'm in the right place," Kassidy said as she looked around. "I'm guessing you know why I'm here?"

Octavia nodded.

"Keiron seems to think you're the key to me getting some answers," Kassidy said. She leaned forward, putting her elbows on her knees and clasping her hands together, then inclined her head. "How much did he tell you? About me? About all of... this?"

Octavia sat back in her chair and crossed her legs. In her mind, though, she weighed all her options. Tell Kassidy everything and potentially freak her out? Tell her just enough to get through this meeting? Or simply keep things limited to her knowledge of the scythe and a generalized understanding of Kassidy's mission? Choosing the first put all the cards on the table and hopefully would dispel the awkwardness. The second and third, well, they had the potential to foster more distrust. There were secrets on the table. Secrets on top of secrets was nothing but a recipe for disaster.

One that neither of them might recover from.

"Keiron and I go way back," Octavia started. "We hold few secrets from another."

Kassidy sat back, crossed her legs, and raised an eyebrow. It took Octavia a minute to process the facial expression and its implication. When awareness hit, the professor laughed.

"Oh my God, no," Octavia said. "Not like that."

"Hey, no judgment," Kassidy said, holding her hands up. "You two are grown-ups."

Octavia laughed nervously. She let the thought linger for a

moment. There was no reality where she could imagine herself being anything more than friends with Keiron. These days, their relationship was more akin to that of siblings than . . . well, she couldn't even say the word with the image of his face in her head. The time for more between them had long passed.

"We are friends, period. We've collaborated on a few things over the years. Helped each other solve some crazy riddles. Our bond is not unlike brothers and sisters, forged through some very hard times."

"You make it sound like you two are warriors," Kassidy said.

"It's certainly seemed that way at times."

"Then you can appreciate the battle I'm up against?"

"Without question," Octavia said.

"And you're okay with . . . me?"

Octavia inclined her head slightly, asking a question without speaking. Kassidy did the same, as if answering the unasked question.

"You mean the fact that you're an empath and a Reaper—"

"Former Reaper," Kassidy corrected.

"Can you actually be a former Reaper?"

The question hung in the air, lingering like a kite on the delta breeze. The women stared at one another again. Kassidy seemed uncertain how to answer, and Octavia was desperately hoping she had not offended her.

Kassidy tensed and pursed her lips, as if biting back words.

"I'm . . . retired," Kassidy said.

"Fair enough." Octavia nodded, trying to move away from potential ill will.

"So, the Scythe of Cronus?" Kassidy asked.

"Yes, the scythe," Octavia began. "What do you know of it so far?"

"Not much. Just what Denzel and Keiron told me."

"Denzel..." Octavia's question trailed off in equal parts wonder and confusion.

"Long story," Kassidy said, waving it off. "I know it's both a tool and a weapon. And I know it's supposedly one of the few things that can actually kill a god."

Octavia nodded, then stood and drifted to one of her bookshelves. She removed a rather girthy text from a top shelf and brought it to her desk. As she opened it, she asked, "How's your Greek mythology?"

She was met with silence until a heavy sigh emanated from across her desk. Kassidy once again leaned forward and placed her elbows on her knees. A cynical smile spread across her face.

"Can we not do this part?" Kassidy asked.

"What part?"

"The part where we get into this long-drawn-out history of the scythe. The part where you educate me like I'm one of your students."

Octavia grinned, but a part of her was pained. Kassidy might have sensed that too, because her posture softened.

"I'm sorry," Kassidy began. "I don't mean any disrespect. It's just that I'm pressed for time. I have two friends near death, casualties of my shitty past decisions. A past that's coming back to kill me. I need to save them. I need to know if this thing is real. If it is, I need to know *where* it is so I can get it, kill Azra-El, and move on with my life."

Octavia was no empath, but she sensed the frustration and the weight Kassidy carried. She felt responsible.

"Keiron mentioned you might be a bit frustrated and impatient."

"Did he tell you about the fight?"

Octavia nodded.

"I'm just . . . tired," Kassidy said.

In that instant, the lights in the office flickered. Both women scanned the room.

"What the . . ." Octavia started; her words eclipsed by a crash through the window.

Dark vapor swished around the office and papers flew. Octavia gripped her chair, trying to hold on as the unnatural funnel cloud took control of the room. Within the sea of air and vapor, she heard a laugh—dark and menacing. Within minutes the cloud enveloped her.

She reached a hand out toward Kassidy, but to no avail. She felt herself being swept up and away through the broken window and into the dark skies above.

◆　　◆　　◆

Kassidy was flung back against the rear wall. On her feet again, she charged, only to be tossed to the side and pinned against the wall by an invisible hand. She struggled, freed herself, then dropped to her knees from the wall. Glancing out the window, she watched as the only link to her quest disappeared into nothingness.

"No!" she screamed.

Kassidy focused her power and willed herself into vapor. Her fists clenched as the cloud churned around her. In an instant, she was out the window and in pursuit.

◆　　◆　　◆

Twenty-Two Years Ago

Kassidy had lain in her bed, staring at her ceiling, wondering if the events of the night had been a terrible dream. First Jeremy.

Then the strange Reaper who'd come to her as she lay dying.

As if compelled, Kassidy now found herself back in Potter's Field. This park had always been a beautiful respite from the taunts and terrorizing of her peers. It held a myriad of memories, some good, some bad, yet she still let it envelop her like a safety blanket. Of course, that was only when the park was empty or near empty.

So being there at 4:00 a.m. was perfect. The birds weren't awake. Even the crickets were taking a cat nap. She wandered through the park and found herself in a familiar spot. Or so she thought. She'd been here before, hadn't she? Earlier in the night? Kassidy saw a familiar view of the sky between the branches of the trees. She knelt slowly, and instinctively touched the ground. Closing her eyes, she let memories invade her conscious mind.

She was running. The wetness of the grass had saturated her shoes. The water sprayed onto her ankles and lower part of her calves. Behind her, a frantic shadow moved in time with her, shouting, "Get back here, you bitch!"

Kassidy held her palm flat on the ground, but she was shaking, feeling fear. Her fear. Something had chased her through this park. No, not something. Someone.

Jeremy. Jeremy Reins.

The dark figure's features came into view. He'd gained ground. Before long, Jeremy tackled her. They tumbled and rolled on the wet grass before coming to a stop in this spot. This spot where her hand connected with the ground and its memories.

Her memories.

"I see you want to do this the hard way then," Jeremy said, just before the first slap across her face.

Kassidy winced as she felt it a second time in her memory.

She'd been looking up at the night sky between the trees. Then staring at the angry face of Jeremy Reins. He hit her again and again. "It works like this, Krazy Kassie. I help you and you help me. That's how the world works," he whispered as he bore down on her, groping her breasts, squeezing, working one hand up to her throat.

She tried screaming, but that was no good. She was overwhelmed with the complexity of emotions emanating from Jeremy. Fear, anger, lust, and exhilaration. The kind of exhilaration that came from doing something you enjoyed.

He'd done this before.

In real time, Kassidy kept her hand on the ground, her eyes closed, even as the tears escaped. Her other hand, a fist. Her teeth grinding as her jaws clenched.

Jeremy scratched and clawed at the top of her dress before finally ripping it, exposing her bra. She tried fighting him, but it was too much, so hard to focus through the emotions bombarding her. All she could see was his sinister smirk. All she could feel was his cold, wet, grimy hands on her chest.

"Get off me," she pleaded. "Stop! No! NO!"

Her screams and pleas went unheard. Jeremy kept squeezing, nuzzling her neck. "You'll like it more if you calm down. Either way, I'm good," he whispered in her ear.

Kassidy felt his erection against her. Her disgust rose. His arousal increased. She stopped moving.

Jeremy smiled. "That's better."

Kassidy spit in his face. As Jeremy reeled back in anger, Kassidy wailed against his chest and face with her fists. Jeremy covered his face with his arms. Before long, he composed himself, swept her arms aside, and punched her.

Her vision blurred. The sky above was now a haze of darkness, starlight, and blood. The haze shook as he struck her again and again. When he finally stopped, Kassidy found that she welcomed the coolness of the ground. Cool air blew across her face, soothing the aches and the fire of her bruised face.

In the distance, she heard laughter and screaming—the loud talk of teenagers. The dance was over, and the kids were nearby for the bonfire. Jeremy heard it too. She watched as his head swiveled. A wave of rage and disappointment flowed from him like an open tap.

"Fuck!" Leaning down, he whispered in her ear, "Another time, Krazy Kass. Another time." He stood, leaving her a wet, bloody mess, and ran off through the park.

Back in the present, Kassidy lifted her hand from the ground and fell back. Tears streamed down her face. It had happened. It had all been real. That part at least. Reaching up to touch her face and wipe the tears, she wondered how she'd healed so quickly. How had she returned home to her bed with her dress still intact? She let the memories flow.

"Azra-El?"

Had he been real too?

Kassidy stood, the memory of her assault fresh, her anger palpable. As if second nature, she closed her eyes and imagined herself at Jeremy's house. A swirl of light vapor enveloped her, and in an instant, she found herself traveling through the air. Before long, she was on the ground again. The vapor coalesced, and she was whole, dressed all in black, and standing in front Jeremy's house.

What the fuck?

The sensation left her disoriented, but there was no mistaking where she was. It didn't make sense though. How the hell had she arrived there? Had she teleported? Was everything else a dream? Was she just now waking up from the nightmare evening?

This is crazy!

"What the fuck is up with my clothes?" she whispered. She thought back to what Azra-El said about the outer appearance matching the mind's mood. She was feeling particularly dark and vengeful. She was feeling like a badass warrior.

Kassidy rubbed her hand against the leather of her pants and saw the boots that had replaced her shoes.

"It . . . he . . . was real?"

Jeremy's place brought back more memories. He'd been so nice. So chivalrous. He'd rescued her, for lack of a better term, from those assholes at school. They'd been up to their usual bullying and all-around shitty behavior, but at the homecoming dance, there was some extra bite in their words. Kassidy had wanted one night where she felt normal, where she felt as pretty inside as everyone said she was on the outside. But those assholes, that self-absorbed, self-righteous group of spoiled rich kids, wouldn't allow it.

How could she have thought any different?

Then out of nowhere, the new kid, Jeremy, swooped in and defended her honor. He put them in their place and then asked her to dance. He was cute, he was nice, and he was interested. She'd felt the desire in him, but she didn't think anything of it. She welcomed it at the dance. Everything felt so . . . perfect.

Until he brought her back to his house.

Until she said no.

Until she kicked him in the balls and escaped his house.

And now here she was. Back again. Only this time, something was different. Kassidy no longer felt like a victim. She looked down at herself again. Along with her black leather pants and calf-length leather boots, she wore a black top that was ... silk? Protecting her from a slight chill in the air was a three-quarter-length black leather coat.

Well, that's just overkill.

Despite the dramatic and cliché apparel, she felt good. In fact, for the first time in a long time, Kassidy felt great. Powerful.

And she looked pretty badass.

She went to the front door and grabbed the knob. The door was locked. Kassidy applied a little more pressure to the knob and turned. With a snap, the handle became a corpse in her grip, and she was inside. She listened for signs of activity. Walking through the Reins' family home intensified her anger. The loving family photos on the wall made her want to vomit. So Rockwellian. So fake. She wondered if Mr. and Mrs. Rockwell knew that their son was a sadist and rapist. Maybe that was the real reason they'd left the last town they'd lived in.

Kassidy wandered through the house to the family room, where Jeremy had taken her. Walking past a mirror she stopped, took a step back, and gazed at her reflection. Her eyes were ... silver.

"What the fu—"

A noise in the family room brought her back to the moment. She moved toward it. Crossing the threshold into the room, she saw Jeremy asleep on the couch. He wore the same clothes he'd been wearing earlier. Even had his shoes on. His knuckles were raw and red. A scratch marred his cheek, the only real wound she'd inflicted on him. Fury rose inside her. She wanted to take his head off.

She moved over to Jeremy and stood directly in front of him. He smelled of alcohol and weed, clearly taking full advantage of his parents being out of town. He'd fallen asleep sitting up. His head lolled to one side. Kassidy envisioned holding him over the edge of a cliff and letting go. She thought about hitting him with a car. She thought about punching his perfect face.

So she did.

With a start, Jeremy awakened, his hand immediately flying to this jaw. "What the fuck?" He peered around as he groaned, as if focusing on his surroundings. When he finally turned his head to face forward, he saw Kassidy standing in front him. He scrambled against the back of the couch.

"Holy shit!" he said. "What the fuck?"

Kassidy stared silently.

"Kassidy?"

Kassidy stood unmoving.

Jeremy rose from the couch and walked toward her. Rubbing his jaw, then his eyes, he stood an arm's length from her. "What are you doing in my house, you crazy..." Jeremy's question trailed off as a combination of fear and awareness fell off him like ripe apples from a tree.

"Your... your eyes. Your... face. It's..."

Kassidy could hear his heart beating in the quiet of the two-story family home. Within a few seconds, she felt a shift in him. The fear was still there, but anger was building. The same anger she'd felt in the park. His look of shock transformed to a scowl. In a flash, he pulled back his fist and punched her again.

"What the fuck are you doing in my house, you nutcase?"

Kassidy took the punch, but she didn't go down. She turned with the blow. When she faced him again, she grinned, the pain as insignificant as a pinprick into a bag of cotton balls.

Jeremy's eyes widened. He punched her two more times, with the same results. Neither blow affected her. Reaching out, Kassidy grabbed him by the throat and lifted him off the floor above her. Jeremy grabbed at her arm with both hands, struggling, silently pleading for her to release him. His feet kicked, and in one move he jabbed her in the gut. Caught off guard, Kassidy dropped him. Jeremy scrambled to his feet and ran around her, out of the family room and up the stairs.

Kassidy followed Jeremy's path. She heard a door slam and walked slowly and calmly toward the sound. Finding the only closed door on the second floor, Kassidy kicked it in. Jeremy struggled with his bedroom window. He finally turned the brass lock and slid the sash up.

"Get away from me, you crazy bitch!" Jeremy screamed.

Kassidy stalked toward him, her face expressionless but her mission clear. She had never been surer of her actions.

Jeremy turned to his window and kicked the screen out, sending it flying to the ground below. He took one last glance at Kassidy before climbing out of the window and jumping down to the ground. Kassidy looked down on Jeremy as he slowly stood after a sloppy landing. He glared back up with a sense of exasperation and accomplishment on his face.

"Fuck you, Krazy Kassie!" He held up two middle fingers.

Kassidy imagined herself down on the ground with him. In seconds, light vapor swirled around her, and she was hurled through the open window. In an instant, she re-formed behind Jeremy. As he turned to run from his home, she was there.

"Fuck you, Jeremy," Kassidy said with an icy calm. She lowered her right hand, and vapor engulfed it. In less than a second, she held a black knife. No, not a knife, not a dagger . . . a sickle. And she wasn't holding it. Her hand had *become* it.

She could see her eyes reflected in Jeremy's. Bright. Silver. Frightening. Beautiful. She swung the sickle across his throat. There was no blood, no cut, yet Jeremy clutched his throat and fell to the ground, struggling to breathe. Before long, all of the fear and desperation she'd felt from Jeremy receded to nothing.

He was dead.

"Well done, my dear. Very well done," said a voice from behind her.

Kassidy did not even turn. She recognized the voice from her memories.

"Azra-El," she said calmly. Kassidy knelt and stared into Jeremy's lifeless eyes. "Is it always like this?"

"Like what?"

"Satisfying."

Azra-El laughed. As he did, she twisted to face him. He seemed larger than the last time. Taller, broader, more... powerful. Yet she was not afraid. She felt no malice from him. In fact, she felt nothing in his presence, no emotion whatsoever. She only knew that he was her leader.

And that freedom felt good.

"Oh, just you wait. This," he gestured toward Jeremy, "is nothing."

His laugh was deep, sinister, and haunting.

CHAPTER TWENTY-TWO

KASSIDY TRACKED THE CLOUD TO POTTER'S FIELD. IT DID NOT TAKE her long to find the space it had taken form. It was the spot where everything had happened for her. The spot where her life had changed. The spot where she'd died.

Octavia sat against a tree, alive and conscious. Even from high above, Kassidy sensed that the woman was abnormally calm. As if being kidnapped by a supernatural being was as common as grabbing a grande white chocolate mocha from Starbucks. She would have to revisit that later. Now, she'd face the one who'd taken Octavia—yet another of Azra-El's Wraiths.

Kassidy reached the ground and re-formed—all but her right hand, which shaped into an onyx sickle. She walked slowly to the figure standing in front of Octavia. He faced his hostage. Octavia made eye contact with Kassidy, causing him to lift his head and slowly turn. Surprise ran through Kassidy like a wave of electrical current. Her concentration was so jarred that her hand re-formed.

"No!"

"Hey, Krazy Kass."

"You . . . you . . . can't be here. I . . ."

"Killed me? Yeah. Yeah, you did. I guess it's true what they say, huh? You never forget your first."

That sneer, that laugh, that unforgettable predatory swagger.

How could he be here? How could he be here, a Wraith, and she not know? Had he been one all along? The questions crashed, one after another, in her brain. Her eyes filled with hot, angry tears. Tears of rage, a level of rage she'd never known she was capable of. No, that wasn't true. She knew all too well that she was capable of this. She'd felt it before. She'd acted on it before. It had consumed her and turned her into something she didn't recognize. It was something she'd been running from ever since . . . the night she took his life.

"Jeremy Reins!"

"So, you still owe me a dance," Jeremy said.

"Fuck you!"

Kassidy's power flowed, her hand re-formed into the onyx sickle, and she lunged at Jeremy. He sidestepped her first swing, then her second, smiling and laughing.

"Come on, Kass. You can do better than that," he taunted.

Kassidy lunged again, swinging wildly, and following up with kicks that Jeremy effortlessly blocked or dodged. She was unhinged, a wild, almost feral supernatural animal hungry for blood and flesh. Every move was reckless. Every move flawed, bathed in anger and frustration—the uncontrolled fury of a petulant child.

With a block and counterpunch, Jeremy knocked the wind from her. He spun and returned with a roundhouse kick across her face, sending her flying. He jumped in the air like a jungle cat and landed on top of her, pinning her body to the ground, her hands above her head.

It all flooded back to her.

She struggled against him. Writhed against his body. She screamed and thrashed, just as she had that night. But just like that night, her efforts seemed futile.

"We have got to stop meeting like this," he taunted before

licking the side of her face. "Mmm, you still taste yummy. Tell me—are you finally ready to finish what we started?"

Kassidy recoiled, disgusted, angry, and afraid. Those feelings from years ago resurfaced with ease. Why? How? She'd been nothing but a girl then, desperate for acceptance and understanding, for the feeling of normalcy. But she'd never been normal. Kassidy spent so much time trying to be normal that she never took the time to actually be Kassidy. She had always been too afraid to discover who she really was. And that fear kept her from accepting her life, kept her from giving her all in every relationship, and kept her well supplied with bourbon and Vicodin.

She feared the loneliness that was her life.

And then she'd died.

She stared into Jeremy's black eyes, and just like that night long ago, she saw nothing. He was as soulless now as he was then.

"How the fuck are you even here?" she asked.

"That's the million-dollar question, isn't it? How did Jeremy Reins battle through death to get here? Truth is, it wasn't much of a battle."

"What does that mean?"

"My death, such as it was, was inevitable. Our meeting, my death, my resurrection, it was all inevitable."

Inevitable? What the hell did that mean?

"You . . . you made a deal. With Azra-El. You made a . . ."

Her words trailed off as Jeremy sneered.

"You were chosen, my dear. I got to help, and in exchange, I got this," Jeremy said, sitting up straight and raising his arms in sick and twisted triumph.

Kassidy channeled her shock and rage, brought her hands together into one large fist, and struck Jeremy in the chest, sending him flying back. She rose quickly, breathing heavily, and looked over to Octavia. The woman was standing now, as calm as a lake on a fall morning. Kassidy felt that calm strongly and let it flow through her, allowing it to guide her. She closed her eyes, took deep breaths, unclenched her fists, and stood firm.

Kassidy could hear everything. The rustle of the leaves as a gentle breeze ran through, a car alarm in the distance, and snow compacting under the weight of footsteps. She heard her own breathing, Octavia's breathing, and Jeremy rising from the ground and stalking toward her. She kept her eyes closed but tracked his every movement. She heard the ghostly whisper of his hand transforming into a sickle. He was only a few feet away when she heard his muscles tense as he raised his right arm to strike. She caught his wrist as his arm came down, opened her eyes, and struck him in the chest with her free hand, sending him flying back again.

Kassidy paced slowly toward Jeremy as he pushed off the ground, rubbing the spot where she'd struck. He scrambled to his feet and lunged at her. Kassidy blocked an overhead swing and each combination of punches and kicks. She countered, landing a punch to the side of his head and a kick to his stomach. Jeremy was doubled over when Kassidy delivered an upper cut, knocking him back.

Snow began to fall. Kassidy felt the cold flakes hit her hot cheek. She straddled Jeremy, punching him in the face once, then twice, before gripping him by the neck, just tight enough to manage his movement and let him know she was in control. His black eyes turned to their natural brown.

She'd killed those brown eyes before.

"You gonna kill me again, Krazy Kass?" Jeremy asked through a mocking, muffled laugh.

"Yeah, I was thinking about it."

"You're only a Reaper. You don't have the power to dispatch a Wraith."

Kassidy closed her eyes. When she opened them again, Jeremy grew silent. He squirmed beneath her.

"Actually, you'll be my third. But I'll enjoy this one the most," Kassidy said.

"No fucking way! Your eyes? That's impossible!"

Kassidy reached into Jeremy's chest, just as she'd done with Ethan, and removed the purple orb that was his life force. Without this, he was nothing. She ingested it, sealing his fate.

"What the . . ." His words trailed off as his gaze moved from Kassidy's now onyx eyes to the dark sickle forming in place of her raised right hand.

"Fuck you, Jeremy!"

Kassidy released his throat as her right hand swept down and through his neck, just as she'd done almost twenty years ago. This time, there would be no coming back. Not even Azra-El could resurrect a Wraith. Jeremy's body aged and crumbled into a withering bony corpse before it turned to dust and vanished into nothingness beneath her.

Powering down, she felt the sensation of her eyes changing back to blue. Her hand re-formed. Kassidy glanced back and watched as Octavia approached.

"Don't worry. I got it," Kassidy said.

"Yeah you do," Octavia said. "Any chance we can go? I'm a little cold."

That calm demeanor hadn't changed a bit.

Yeah, they would have to go somewhere and talk.

◆　◆　◆

Twenty Years Ago

The human soul was a remarkable thing. It shaped a person. Guided them. Gave them a connection to the world and those around them. In vampire lore, the fabled creatures of the night were said to have no souls, which was why they had no reflection. Hollywood had given fame to another fearsome creature—the zombie. An ambulatory, diseased, and deceased meat sack that walked around, soulless, in search of only one thing— nourishment. Of course, there were numerous accounts of the human soul searching for its other half, variations of the speech of Aristophanes in Plato's *Symposium*. And there were, of course, countless love songs, poems, and Valentine's Day cards that fed romantic musings on how souls were touched through love.

But the soul was not a thing—at least, not really.

The soul was a life force, an essence, an unknown that drove the body and mind to think, act, and react. It was the fuel for the machine that woke up every morning, showered, made coffee and breakfast, and worked at a job that eventually sucked the soul from the machine. It was the thing that lingered on after the brain and the systems within no longer found themselves compatible.

It was the very thing young Kassidy Simmons was holding in her hands.

A glowing purple orb of light that pulsated gently and evenly had resided in the body of the man now at Kassidy's feet. She didn't know much about him, only that he was a bad man. All she'd ever felt from him was anger. After following him for days, studying his movements, she'd seen the cold, empty life he'd led. When she'd sat next to him in that café earlier today, anger and guilt had poured onto her like a bursting water main. It overwhelmed her. So much so that she'd choked on her coffee, grabbing his attention and that of the dozens around them. When he'd come to her aid, she'd wretched. The proximity of his emotions almost made them one and the same. So she took the suggestion of her mentor, Azra-El, the Angel of Death. She closed

her eyes and focused on channeling his emotion into a compartment buried inside her.

A compartment that she would later open when the time was
right.

"Are you all right?" the man had asked her.

"Yeah, yeah, I will be," Kassidy said, still catching her breath.
"Just went down the wrong pipe is all."

"Here, let me help you up," he said.

Kassidy realized that at some point during her coughing fit,
she'd fallen to the ground. Strange that the emotion she'd felt
from this man had that much of an impact on her. It had
happened before, of course, but not to the extent that she'd
completely lost track of what she was physically doing.

Strange.

A barista brought Kassidy some water, and the man sat at the
table with her to make sure she was okay. He seemed concerned.
Overly concerned. But that didn't come through on an empathic
level. Despite how this man behaved, she felt nothing from him
but fear and loathing.

Mostly loathing.

"I'm really okay," Kassidy said. "You don't have to stay here
with me. I mean, thank you. But I'll be okay."

She said it with a smile, hoping that a gentle display from her
might cause him to calm down. It didn't, but she had to try.
There was something so wrong with this man. She still wasn't
clear why Azra-El had assigned him to her. Azra-El was notorious
for not giving information about those he'd personally marked
for death. He'd said she needed to understand the need for their
dispatch on her own. She needed to feel the reasons why the
person's time on earth was complete. "All for the greater good"
was what he'd said.

Since becoming a Reaper, Kassidy had dispatched dozens of people at Azra-El's request. Remarkably, each had been worse than the one before. Murderers, thieves, cheaters, rapists—monsters, one and all. This man, though, had done no such thing. At least, not in the time Kassidy had been following him.

But he felt similar to those others.

"Let me get you a cup of coffee to replace that one you spilled," he said.

"Oh, no, no, no, I couldn't let you do that. Really. It's fine. I'm fine. I think I just need to get out of here. I absolutely hate being the center of attention."

Kassidy looked around her at the faces quickly turning in another direction after making eye contact. She hated being watched. It was too reminiscent of her childhood; of the days she'd spent running from the boys and girls who'd called her Krazy Kassie. They had no idea what she could do. They only knew that at times she acted weird, and when you were a kid, that was enough to warrant incessant teasing and ridicule.

She said thank you to the man one more time and then made her retreat from the café. Once out of view, she turned around the corner, ducked into a small alcove, dematerialized into a light-gray vapor, and took to the skies. Not long after, she found herself whole again outside his home.

It didn't take much for a Reaper to enter a home. In vapor form, they needed only an opening. It didn't matter how large or small. Kassidy strolled around inside. This man was surprisingly neat for a bachelor. Everything was clean, meticulously organized. Though the small, sparsely decorated house otherwise did not seem out of the ordinary for a single man in his forties. She'd checked every room before coming to a locked door in the kitchen. Kassidy dematerialized and traveled underneath the door and down the stairs, where she materialized in the man's dark and dank basement. She flipped on a light switch. The basement was only a storage space, but given how neat and orderly it was, the moldy smell surprised her.

He had luggage and boxes stacked against a wall. Tools and various supplies against another. Straight ahead, though, was a free-standing dry-erase board on wheels, and like an old-school chalkboard, it swiveled. Nothing was written on the side facing her, so she pulled the top to flip the board around.

She stumbled back.

Taped to the whiteboard were pictures of women. One jogging, one playing with kids in a park, and another carrying groceries into her home. There were multiple pictures of a dozen women in various stages of undress. Some faces were circled in red marker. Arrows and bits of string connected one to another. As she took it all in, Kassidy noticed her own picture in the top right corner. Below it was a photo of her sister, Sarah.

Kassidy trembled. Her foot tapped the concrete floor. Her hand strummed against her thigh. Anger boiling inside came to a fever pitch when a gust of cold air filled the room along with the sense that she was not alone.

Her heart beat faster, harder, until it felt ready to burst from her chest. The dark hair cascading around her shoulders moved with a rush of air from behind. The hairs on her bare arms stood up on her goose-bumped skin.

She twirled and found the man she'd been following. His disheveled hair masked his face, making him appear darker, creepier. Black circles surrounded his sunken eyes, as if he'd been up for days and was desperately tired and malnourished.

"I see you've found my hiding spot, Kassidy," he said.

He knew her name.

How long had he been following her? Why hadn't she known?

"Why do you have a picture of me and my sister? Who the fuck are you?"

His smirk widened, showing gnarly teeth, yellow against dark-red bleeding gums.

"You don't know who I am?" he asked. "Oh, and you don't know *what* I am either, do you? He sent you after me and gave . . . you . . . nothing."

At those last three drawn-out words, he lunged. Unprepared, she bore the full weight of his body, the force of which sent them both crashing into the board and farther back into the thin false wall behind them. Coughing as the dust and debris settled, Kassidy pushed against the man on top her, a black scythe for a hand coming toward her. She dematerialized and re-formed in a standing position a few feet away, watching as the scythe swung down and impaled the concrete floor where she'd lain.

"Quick thinking, puppet," he said.

As he stood up, his sunken eyes were jet black, like pools of oil.

"What the fuck are you?" she asked again.

"You should ask your boss," the man said.

She dismissed the statement, formed a scythe of her own, and lunged forward. Each blow she threw was blocked. When he grabbed her by the arms and sent a knee to her gut, she heard whimpering. Not hers though. Doubled over in pain, she saw cages to her left . . . filled with women. Her shock was intensified by the backhand to the face that sent her flying across the room.

"I can't believe he sent a lowly Reaper after me," said the creature, stalking forward. "A young, nubile, silver-eyed Reaper. A newbie at that."

How the hell did he know that?

Kassidy pushed up to one knee and looked again at the cages of women. Many were the women from his pictures. It was difficult to tell though; their faces were dirty and gaunt. Thankfully, she didn't see Sarah among them. Her wrath took hold, and she tapped into that compartmentalized rage she'd absorbed from him earlier. It filled her, strengthened her, made her rise to her feet without even realizing it.

The man stormed toward her, swinging his right arm in a wide arc toward her neck. Kassidy ducked to her left and grabbed his arm with her right hand after he'd missed his mark. She followed with her left hand and rammed up full force against his elbow—breaking the joint. She stepped up and to his right and kicked the side of his knee—breaking that, too, and sending him to the ground.

The man stared up at Kassidy in horror. "Your . . . your eyes. They're . . . black."

Kassidy didn't understand. She didn't care. She thrust her hand into his chest, phasing through skin and bone, and retrieved a glowing purple orb. The pulsating orb that was his life force, his soul. Looking back, Kassidy wasn't sure that this man had ever had one.

She instinctively ingested it, then cut across his neck with her weapon, dispatching him permanently. As she did, she heard gasps and murmurs from the caged women. They'd witnessed everything. As Kassidy swiveled towards them, they recoiled. She turned back quickly, mostly from embarrassment, and found herself staring at her reflection in a mirror on the side wall.

Her eyes were black.

Just as his had been.

What the fuck?

Kassidy shimmered out of view of the women, entering the otherworld known as the Nexus. In there, she was safe from prying eyes. She exited the house while in that plane and made her way to a nearby payphone. Reentering the real world, she made a call to 911.

Kassidy tracked the next events through the news channels. The police descended on the home of Nathan Daniels. They processed everything they'd discovered in the basement. Days passed before the statements and psychological assessments of the freed women were completed. The repeated sentence, "Two demons fought, and the girl killed the guy," was chalked up as some type of mass psychosis brought about by physical and emotional trauma.

Kassidy would eventually understand what had happened to her to that day.

So, too, would an eighteen-year-old girl with reddish-brown hair and chestnut eyes who'd shared a cage with ten women.

CHAPTER TWENTY-THREE

SENAYA STOOD IN THE ENTRYWAY TO THE LIVING ROOM. WATCHING. waiting, admiring the Primus, *her* Primus, as he sat in meditation to heal and absorb the energy given off by his Reapers. She never fully understood how it worked. In fact, she didn't understand a lot of what had happened. Azra-El was the Primus, the Angel of Death, charged with managing the transition of souls from this world to the next, and the only one with greater power was Death himself. How had a lowly Reaper like Kassidy Simmons caused so much damage that it took nearly two decades for him to recover? Why did they have to keep her alive now?

Did he love her?
He couldn't possibly.
Could he?

Those thoughts angered her. They reminded her of the woman she'd been before—the human woman. Needy, subservient, always seeking love, adoration, validation, for simply existing. In that life, she'd been nothing more than a prize, something to be given to another and used at his discretion. She was a means to an end. For her father, she'd represented money and position through an arranged marriage with the son of a wealthy and influential family. For her husband, she'd represented a vessel into which he could pump his seed—or take out his aggression. For her mother, she'd represented envy.

Senaya was more beautiful than her mother. Everyone said so. Senaya had brushed it off out of love and adoration for the woman who'd given birth to her. But in the end, it meant nothing. So much so that on the night Senaya had taken her own life to end the abuse and use of her body and soul, her mother had sat next to her, spat in her face, and cursed her child as she'd drifted into the afterlife.

When Senaya became a Reaper, she took the lives of her husband and father first and did so with delight. But she tortured her mother. For years, she haunted her, made her feel the pain that she'd felt, until her mother had broken and apologized. When her mother had begged for forgiveness, Senaya spat in her face and sliced through her throat with the onyx sickle that was her hand.

Senaya wiped those thoughts from her mind as Azra-El stirred. Even those simple movements excited her. Everything from his walk, to his crooked smile, to his very breath set her on fire. She thought about their first night together. How different it was from their last all those years ago. Now that he was whole, would he lay with her again?

"You have a report?" Azra-El asked.

Senaya snapped back to the moment, hoping the rumors of his mind-reading abilities were false. He said he couldn't. Had he lied? Had he ever lied to her? He was certainly lying about Kassidy. There was something there he wasn't sharing. Senaya deserved to know. She above all others deserved to know. She was his and he was hers, after all. Right?

"Yes. Apologies for disturbing you, but the boy, Reins . . . he failed, Primus."

Azra-El slowly opened his eyes but remained still. The red was deep, rich, like blood. *His strength is growing.* He breathed in deep, clearly trying to remain calm. His body, still in a cross-legged position, began to rise. After floating several feet in the air, he uncrossed his legs and stood at his full height. With his hands clasped behind his back, he walked across the living room in measured strides until he reached Senaya.

Magnificent!

"What happened?"

"*She* was with the professor when the boy took her." Senaya hated saying *her* name. Kassidy. It felt bitter on her tongue. It stung her head and her heart. How could he still be protecting her? Why?

"And?"

"And she followed him. They fought, and she killed him."

"The professor is with Kassidy now?"

"Yes, Primus."

"She killed a Wraith?"

"Yes, Primus."

"Again?"

She didn't answer. An unfamiliar ripple of energy hung in the air. Senaya felt its weight emanating from Azra-El. It was so powerful she could almost taste it. The feeling was suddenly interrupted by the sting of his hand across her face, sending her flying back through the wall.

She rose from where she'd landed, her eyes now the color of deep space. She was ready for battle, for retribution, ready to inflict pain—until she realized what had just happened. He'd struck her. Her. That wasn't supposed to happen. What had she done wrong? Should she have gone after the professor herself? As he stepped toward her, she immediately took a knee before him.

"Apologies, Primus. I can . . . I will . . . fix this."

It pained her to grovel at his feet like the woman she'd once been. But this was different. This was for love.

"Rise," Azra-El said, his hand outstretched.

Senaya took it and stood. He turned her slightly and walked her backward until she reached an undamaged part of the wall. Pressed between him and the wall, heat and energy pulsed through her. The energy was different this time, more primal. She dared to look up at him and watched as his crimson eyes glowed bright red. He moved against her, closer, and she felt his hardness against her. Senaya put her hands on his waist and pulled him closer.

"Yes, you will fix this," he said. "Allow them to find the Scythe of Cronus. Be patient. Then . . . strike."

"Yes . . . Primus," she said breathlessly as he moved against her.

Senaya forgot all about Kassidy Simmons. She forgot about his lies by omission, forgot that he'd just struck her. He tore at her clothes, spun her around, and entered her.

A part of her cried out. He was using her, just as the others had done before. Senaya shut that voice down because this . . . this was different. This was something more. This was love. Right?

I am his.

He is mine.

Forever.

CHAPTER TWENTY-FOUR

KASSIDY WALKED INTO OCTAVIA'S PLACE AND GLANCED AROUND. Her home was well furnished, minimally decorated but comfortable. Most of the décor had an antique vibe. Whether authentically vintage or made to appear that way, each item was perfectly placed, creating the ideal marriage of the old world and the new.

The house was a two-bedroom brick bungalow in River Forest. The enclosed front porch allowed Octavia to sit outside even on rainy days. There were small yards in front and back.

Octavia had turned the second bedroom into a large office. The decor caught Kassidy's eye. Above the fireplace was a shield—a bit worn, but a shield, nonetheless. Kassidy recognized the symbol on the front—the symbol of the Spartan army. She had seen the movie *300* one time too many times. Behind it, hanging on the wall, were two crisscrossed spears. They seemed about as worn as the shield, yet all seemed functional.

Kassidy walked to a bookcase with several first-edition novels. She wondered if that was Keiron's influence. On top of the larger bookcase was a . . . belt, maybe? Somewhere between a bustier and WWE Championship belt.

"As I understand it, you're not really a tea kind of girl," Octavia said as she walked into the front room from her kitchen, carrying two beverages. She kept the teacup for herself and handed Kassidy the glass containing one large cube of ice and a familiar bronze liquid.

"Didn't really take you for a whiskey girl," Kassidy said as she took the glass.

"I'm not," Octavia replied. "Wine is my thing. When I'm in the mood, I'm more of a rum girl."

Kassidy let the bourbon slide down her throat. Deep down, in yet another place she hated to travel, she felt embarrassment. Embarrassment at the fact that a perfect stranger not only knew about her vice but was also watching her succumb to it.

Why did it have to taste so good?

"You've got a great place here," Kassidy said.

"Thank you," Octavia replied. "I got it pretty cheap. It felt aged. Which, as you can tell, is kind of my thing."

"You do enjoy the vintage."

"There's just something elegant about the old world," Octavia said.

"I can understand that. There's a certain sense of comfort here," Kassidy said, still fixated on the large item atop the bookcase. Pointing to it, she asked, "What's this?"

"That," Octavia began, "is the legendary girdle of Hippolyta. Once gifted to Heracles. Obtaining it was one of his twelve labors."

"Does that come with a letter of authenticity? I mean, the girdle of Hippolyta? Do you have a magic lasso in the closet too?"

Octavia gave a small giggle. "Ah yes, the modern appropriation of ancient legends. The comic book world has made good coin on those stories. I can assure you, this is indeed authentic." Octavia gazed at the artifact as if it sparked a memory.

"You seem awfully certain."

"Oh, I am."

Octavia moved over to the couch and sat down. She put her teacup down and wrung out her hands. Awkward tension filled the room, intensifying when Kassidy stopped and sat at the far side of the couch.

"So before we were interrupted—"

"Who the fuck are you?" Kassidy blurted out.

"I'm sorry?"

She could tell that Octavia was taken aback by the question and the tone. It wasn't angry. It was, if anything, a legitimate inquiry.

"You're dealing with all of this shit with just a little too much calm," Kassidy said. "You were kidnapped by a cloud that turned into a guy. You were rescued by a woman who did the same and formed weapons out of thin air. Yet you stood off to the side, as cool as an Eskimo with ice in his underwear, and just watched? That's not natural. There's nothing normal about what happened. I don't care how much you've learned and taught over the years. There's no way you should be this calm. So again, I ask, who the fuck are you?"

At that, Octavia stood and paced—a practice Kassidy knew all too well. She stretched out to tap into what Octavia was feeling, but the woman wasn't putting a lot out there. Some anxiety, which was normal under the circumstances, though Kassidy did expect more. Her anxiety was controlled. It came off in tiny bursts instead of waves. It was as if Octavia wanted to say or do something but stopped herself multiple times.

Octavia stopped pacing and faced Kassidy. She put her hands in her pockets, took a deep breath, and smiled. Still calm, cool, and collected.

"So, this isn't my first time on this particular crazy train," Octavia said.

"Meaning?"

"Meaning part of the reason I teach this stuff is because I know it, because I've seen it. When I say Keiron and I have shared adventures over the years, I mean just that. The weird world you've been living in, and avoiding, all of your life . . . is just the tip of the iceberg."

Kassidy finished her remaining bourbon in two gulps.

"I'm going to need more of this." She held her glass out.

"I'll go get the bottle."

* * *

Twenty Years Ago

"What the hell was that?" Kassidy's voice echoed in the office of the abandoned lakefront warehouse that served as Azra-El's base.

When Kassidy had first become a Reaper at sixteen, she'd been rebellious. After training, after practicing and honing her skills both as a Reaper and as an empath, she'd become even more brazen in her speech. More and more, she spoke to Azra-El as if he were a peer as opposed to someone she should engage with respect and reverence—like the other Reapers did.

Like that chick. The freaky one. Senaya.

There was something about that woman that Kassidy liked, hated, and feared. She wasn't sure what it was. Well, that's wasn't entirely true. If she were being honest, she had something of a crush on the woman. Senaya was no nonsense. Fit, hardcore, but fun and playful. She made Kassidy feel things. Things she wasn't sure she wanted to feel about another woman. At the same time, Senaya was a bitch. Arrogance and condescension were as much a part of her as her full lips, toned ass, and fearsome fighting style. The woman trained like she was an MMA fighter. Kassidy had always wondered what Senaya had been like when she was alive. Kassidy had heard rumors that Senaya had been a schoolteacher in Tombstone and may have even bedded, or been bedded by, Doc Holiday. She'd also heard rumors she'd been a nun during the inquisition. All agreed that whoever she'd been, it was a stark contrast to her role now as Azra-El's second.

"Watch your tone when speaking to the Primus," Senaya said.

Kassidy ignored her. She saw her out of the corner of her eye, of course. Senaya was, as usual, standing near Azra-El, like a parrot on the shoulder of a pirate captain. It was annoying, the way she kissed his ass. Hell, she probably did more than kiss it. Kassidy was pretty sure they were fucking. People talked about it. The Reaper grapevine was forever active. She had no proof, but rumors had to start from some grain of truth, right? Strangely, the thought of it disgusted her, excited her, and made her jealous.

But she didn't know whether she was jealous of Senaya or Azra-El.

"You sent me after a weird fucking guy who had Reaper powers," Kassidy said, ignoring Senaya and directing her question and gaze at Azra-El. "What. The actual. Fuck."

Azra-El smiled at Kassidy, as he often did. Sometimes it was soothing and comforting. Other times it was confusing as fuck. This was one of those times. Was he pleased that she'd dispatched the guy? Did he set her up? She had questions, as always. Questions whose answers were given like water rationed in the desert. She hated that. He knew it and used it to control her, just as he controlled all of his little minions. She'd be no minion though. No slave. She was more powerful and talented than any of them. Her empathic abilities sharpened and quickened her fighting instincts. Unlike other Reapers, Kassidy sensed death in humans when their end was near. She was physically stronger than the others and getting stronger each day.

She deserved to know more.

"Did you have problems with him?" Azra-El asked.

"He put me through a fucking wall! He almost killed me!"

"But you prevailed?"

Kassidy nodded.

Azra-El had a way of telling people to shut up and stop complaining without actually saying those words. She wanted to be mad. She needed to be mad. And he was taking that from her. Embarrassed, she dared to look at Senaya—who was grinning.

Which made Kassidy mad again.

"Whether I *prevailed* or not," she began, "is not the point."

"So, what is the point?" Senaya asked.

Bitch!

"The point is," she said, giving Senaya a side-eye before turning her gaze back to Azra-El, "I should be told when someone I'm sent to dispatch has abilities. Especially when they're like mine."

"And what would you have done with that information?" Azra-El asked.

"I would have been better prepared. I would have known what to anticipate. I wouldn't have been launched through a fucking wall."

"You knew nothing, yet here you stand. Alive and well. And as feisty as ever," Azra-El said.

Kassidy saw past that grin. That fucking grin. He was up to something. She couldn't sense his emotions. In fact, she could sense few of those upper-tier Reapers—like Senaya and her pretty boy, Ethan. Nevertheless, she knew Azra-El was up to something.

"Was this a test?" she asked.

"This was a mission, an assignment—a reckoning. And you negotiated things well, my dear," he said.

A nice way to dodge the question. She wasn't going to get much water rationed out to her. Seemed like today would be a day to wander the desert with other thirsty troops. No, that was nowhere near true. She wouldn't wander with the other troops. The other troops gave zero fucks about the things that concerned her. Like, what was the deal with the upper-tier Reapers? Did anyone else get the sense that some souls were taken before their time? Was she the only one who felt her power growing with each reap? At first, she'd thought it was because they were already seasoned. She thought it was because they had all they needed, knew all they needed, and were perfectly content to go about their lives—such as they were. Over the last year, Kassidy had come to realize that it wasn't so much that they were content. It was more that they were fearful. Fearful of reprisal from Azra-El, or perhaps from one of his minions—the bitch or the pretty boy, who, one could argue, was also a little bitch. Azra-El led by fear, plain and simple. He disguised it as charm and a quick wit, but that was all condescending fluff. He manipulated Reapers, and he was good at it. Even with Kassidy.

And that drove her insane.

"So, what I'm hearing is, you're not going to bother telling me what that was?" Kassidy asked with her hands on her hips. She tapped her foot absently, waiting for an answer like a petulant child.

What Kassidy liked most about being a Reaper was the speed at which they could act and react. They could will themselves into a cloud, and as that cloud, travel from place to place. When the distance wasn't too great, they did it instantaneously. They could use that speed to their advantage. Catch people off guard. Or catch another Reaper off guard.

Much like Senaya did now.

Kassidy had no idea what hit her. Until she looked up and saw Senaya standing over her, brandishing two onyx scythes with ferocity. Kassidy couldn't feel Senaya's emotion, but if she could label it, it wasn't anger—it was satisfaction.

"Your question was asked and answered, young one," Senaya said.

Senaya bent down, never taking her eyes off Kassidy. She gave a sinister smile, a knowing smile, one that said more than her mouth ever did. Then her eyes turned black. Empty. Vacant. Deadly. Just like the thing she'd dispatched earlier.

Senaya was one of them.

Kassidy scooted back against the wall, almost cowering. She felt a tingle against her skin from Senaya's weapons. "What the fuck is going on?"

"More than you realize. And more than you need to know right now," Senaya said with authority.

Kassidy peered beyond her, in search of help or rescue from Azra-El. But he'd gone. Seconds later, Senaya had gone too, leaving Kassidy curled up like a huddled mass in Azra-El's office.

For the first time, Kassidy regretted her decision to become a Reaper, and for the first time in a long time, she felt fear.

CHAPTER TWENTY-FIVE

"SO, I KNOW YOU DON'T WANT TO DO THE WHOLE 'IN THE BEGINNING' thing," Octavia said.

"Honestly, it's less about that, and more about not wanting to be involved in any of this at all. I just want it all to go away. I want my friends and family safe. I just want to be free of it."

"Understandable."

In the silence, Octavia saw fear, regret, and pain in Kassidy's eyes. She wanted to offer comfort in the moment, but she was feeling her own sense of sadness. The silence seemed never ending.

"But I suspect I'll have questions, so go back as far as you need. I've got bourbon." Kassidy tipped her glass in the air.

Octavia took a seat. She opened her laptop and pulled up a file with slides.

"Let's start with what you know about Azra-El. Tell me what you know of his past and his role," Octavia said.

"Well," Kassidy began, "it's a hierarchy. Azra-El is the Primus, the First. He's charged with helping to maintain the balance between life and death by ensuring that souls are escorted to their proper place in the afterlife."

Octavia nodded.

"He uses the Reapers to help with that. Everyone, from Reapers to Wraiths, are capable of transporting souls. Even him, but he tends to leave the reaping to the lowest level," Kassidy said. Her mouth curled up in a bit of a snarl. "And he uses the Wraiths as a personal guard or army. To police Reapers, and sometimes . . . more . . ."

Octavia observed Kassidy's face as her voice trailed off. She had to be thinking about the boy again, Jeremy. To find out that she had been betrayed by Azra-El all those years ago, in more than one way, had to be overwhelming. It was hard enough helping her calm down after she'd dispatched Reins—and apparently, she'd done that more than once to those beings.

"So, yes," Octavia said. "In the beginning, though, the very beginning, there was only one being charged with that."

"Death?"

"For our purposes, yes."

"Yeah, so with the growth in population, he created the Primus to help, then eventually to take the lead," Kassidy continued, though her curiosity was piqued.

"Azra-El is the second Primus," said Octavia. "He hasn't served as long as the first, but he is a bit more powerful."

"And more devious, no doubt."

"But even he answers to someone," Octavia said.

"So why isn't his boss checking in?"

"That . . . is a brilliant question. One that I don't have an answer for. What I do know, though, is that Thanatos, the elder god that is the embodiment of Death, is the one being Azra-El fears above all others. Except for maybe you."

"Me?"

"Think about it," Octavia said. "You are the only being in existence who's ever bested him. If you'd had the Scythe of Cronus back then, you could have killed him. You are capable of so much, and he knows that. That makes you a threat. Why else would he go after people you love first instead of just coming for you directly?"

"I don't know. Sure, I beat him, but I didn't kill him. I couldn't. I'm not strong enough. At the time, I thought maybe he'd die from his injuries. But that was terribly fucking naïve. Now I'm hearing about this scythe. What is it about this thing?"

"Yes, the scythe. So, if we look at mythology, specifically Greek, we've been told that the three most powerful weapons of the ancient gods were Zeus's thunderbolt, the trident of Poseidon, and the pitchfork of Hades. Those weapons had the power to do great things or unspeakable things, but even they could not kill a god."

"So, we're operating on the premise that the ancient gods were real?"

"You said you wanted to keep things simple, right?" Octavia asked.

Kassidy shrugged.

"Well, in that case, the gods are real. There are twelve elder gods, in fact, and a number of lesser and demi-gods. The elders held certain roles, and they held them around the world. In different cultures they were known by different names, but their function was typically the same. In some roles they became more popular. Zeus, for example, is arguably the most famous of all the gods. In other cultures, he has been known by different names, but because the name Zeus is so well known, it's the moniker he's held throughout time."

"So, he's not only real, but still alive?"

"He is."

"You say that with such certainty," Kassidy said, her gaze drifting to Hippolyta's girdle, then glancing at the spears and shield on the mantel.

"For good reason," Octavia said. "That's why I brought out the whole bottle."

Kassidy picked up the bottle of Blanton's sitting on the coffee table. She scrutinized her empty glass, then poured more.

"Okay, so the scythe . . ."

". . . is older than all those weapons," Octavia said. "It was the first weapon ever forged. Back then, though, it was less a weapon and more of a tool. Made from adamantine, the strongest metal known to man . . . then and now."

"Adamantine?" Kassidy asked.

Octavia nodded.

"That's a bit uh—"

"Again," Octavia began, "modern comics and fiction dig deep into the history and mythology of the ancient world."

Octavia scrolled through several slides on her laptop and stopped on a photo of a bearded man with wings, wearing a robe and holding a scythe. "When you see this image, what comes to mind?"

"Father Time," Kassidy replied.

"And this one?"

The image was a skeletal being, also in a robe, only this one was dark and tattered. He too held a scythe.

"The Grim Reaper," Kassidy said.

"Exactly. And you notice of course what they're holding?"

"That's the Scythe of Cronus?" Kassidy asked.

Octavia nodded. "A symbol of time, of death, and of life. This scythe was used to help create the universe. It was given to the god that embodied death because he, in essence, was uniquely tied to time and the circle of life. Over the years, as legends took on lives of their own, it became associated with other gods— primarily Cronus, the original master of time, later known as the king of the Titans, father of the Olympian gods."

"Okay, but if Azra-El is not a god, why not just find a god to kill him? Why do I have to do any of this? Let's go find his boss."

Octavia closed her laptop and faced Kassidy, whose expression held a look of exhaustion. Not so much physical exhaustion, though. Kassidy was exhausted to her very soul. Octavia again felt the pain of guilt. She tried to stifle it, but Kassidy's face told her she wasn't successful.

"You're not telling me something," Kassidy said.

"It's nothing of importance," Octavia said. "Remember, I'm trying to keep this brief and to the point. That's hard for a teacher. I feel like I'm leaving things on the table."

"Bullshit," Kassidy said.

Octavia smiled weakly. Of course there was more to say. There was so much more that Kassidy needed to know. But was this the time? Could she absorb anything else? Was it even Octavia's place to make that decision, especially considering the decisions she'd already made for Kassidy over the years?

"There's nothing more about this history that's important right now," Octavia said. "I . . . I just feel so bad that you have to deal with any of this. I told you, Keiron told me a great deal about you and your past. After hearing that, after seeing you face down someone who was complicit in making you what you are—"

"I don't need your pity," Kassidy said.

"No. Oh no, my God, please don't think I'm trying to . . . I'm sorry. I'm just so sorry for all of this," Octavia said. She wasn't trying to do anything but offer empathy for a difficult situation. The Wraiths going after her loved ones had to have Kassidy turned sideways. How could it not? She was defensive, quick to attack, and she needed calm. Could Octavia give her that? Could she give her something Kassidy had likely never had in her life?

"No, it's fine. I'm just out of sorts." Kassidy held her hands in the air to mimic an explosion.

"Yeah, I get that."

Kassidy sipped her drink and then sighed heavily.

"So, if the beings were, or are, real, then where is the scythe?"

"Ancient stories are, for the most part, real. Obviously with oral histories, some things change to help explain the unexplainable. The scythe was stolen, then recovered. It was battled over, and again recovered. To protect it, Thanatos disguised it and placed it under the protection of someone he trusted—a mortal. A very plain, very ordinary man."

"Great." Kassidy threw her hands up in the air. "That's no help. How long do you figure this guy has been dead now?"

"Who said he's dead?"

CHAPTER TWENTY-SIX

KEIRON LOCKED THE DOOR TO HIS BOOKSTORE. TURNED OFF THE main lights, then set the security code. It was the same routine every night. For him, routine was good, stability was good. The occasional surprise was acceptable, but he was happy to not have to deal with it. His closest friends knew that.

All four of them.

Of course he knew more than four people. Keiron had the great fortune and ability to touch many lives. He didn't consider them all friends though. Anyone with that title knew him well, and only four people on the planet had that privilege.

His routine led him to his back office where he finished ordering the new books for next week as well as the special requests from the day. He shut down his computer, closed his files, and made his way up the back stairs to his loft. It hadn't been a particularly difficult day. He wasn't necessarily tired, but he was looking forward to a glass of wine and some jazz.

Once inside, he grabbed a bottle of cabernet and a glass from the kitchen and walked into his living room. He wasn't fond of voice-command technology, but he made an exception when it came to music. He made his request, and as he sat down, Thelonious Monk welcomed him home and told him to relax. With much appreciation, Keiron obliged.

The first sip of wine was like ambrosia. The second sip was

much the same. The third, however, came with a companion. Unlike many, Keiron liked to keep a window cracked in the winter. He wasn't bothered by the chill. Had he remembered a secure window would offer resistance to the dark smoke swirling in his loft and slowly taking human form, he might have considered closing it when he came in.

The man before him was tall, toned, and lean. He had something of a swimmer's body. He was bald, with a goatee and inexplicable sunglasses. Perhaps he was completing a look. One that Keiron didn't understand. Human or otherwise, it was a sign of general douche-baggery. He was probably the type to use the speakerphone option in public.

"Are there no etiquette courses in Reaper school?" Keiron asked, not bothering to get up.

"There are, but I skipped class that day."

No, he was the type to FaceTime in public.

"Unfortunate," Keiron replied.

Keiron took another swallow of wine and placed his glass on the coffee table. He reluctantly stood and walked over to his guest. Keiron was forever the calm one, and it was likely that very quality that made him so approachable, respected, and liked by so many people. Those qualities, though, did not make him a pushover.

"What can I do for you, Wraith?" Keiron asked.

"Oh, you know what I am? Just like that? You're good. And it's Roderick, by the way."

"Of course it is."

Keiron had no angst against the name, but he'd never known a man named Roderick to go by anything other than Rod, unless he was in fact a douchebag. It made him wonder what the Wraith had been like when he was human.

"I want to get a message to Kassidy Simmons," Roderick said.

"Why not tell her yourself? She's back home. I'm sure you all know that by now."

"Yeah, we do. We just want to make sure she understands the importance of our message. You know, sometimes you have to leave a few in multiple locations."

"And what would you like me to tell her?"

Roderick paced. He had that Cheshire Cat grin. Keiron suspected that, in life, that grin had made him the center of attention with women. That likely hadn't changed either. There were no rules against copulating with humans, after all, at least according to Kassidy. Keiron, with his hands in his pockets, watched and waited, not knowing what was coming next, but not concerned about it either.

"See, that's the thing." Roderick stopped and faced Keiron, "I don't want the message to get lost in translation. Like . . . like . . . you know how stories change as they go through a grapevine?" he asked, matter of fact, as if talking to a buddy at the bar. "By the time the message gets where it's supposed to go, in no way, shape, or form does it resemble the original."

"So, what do you propose?" Keiron asked.

"Well, I was thinking it would be best for me"—Roderick paused for dramatic effect—"to carve it into your chest."

Roderick stared at Keiron with demonic intensity.

"Oh."

Roderick's eyes went black. His left hand misted to smoke and transformed into a scythe. A southpaw. Perhaps he'd been an artist in life. It was a strange thought, but Keiron had noticed that most of the great artists he'd known were left-handed. They were also all mild mannered, even tempered. He couldn't think of one who suggested something like carving into his chest. There was that woman in Brazil though. She'd scratched his back. They weren't exactly working on anything artistic at the time, though there was a great deal of nudity involved. The memory brought a smile to his face. The woman was . . . spirited.

"The fuck are you smiling at, dude?" Roderick asked.

"Just thinking of the spanking I gave to the last person who scratched my skin."

"Oh, this won't be anything like that, my friend."

"You got that right," Keiron said. "This will be much more pleasurable."

Roderick moved forward with speed and intensity. He spun with a downward arc to strike Keiron in the head with his scythe. But his target was no longer there. Roderick, stunned, stood still, and took off his sunglasses. He turned around and was met with a kick to the face that sent him back flying across the couch and smashing onto the coffee table.

Keiron watched his wine spill on the floor.

"Alexa, play 'Public Enemy,'" he said.

As the unit acknowledged his request, Keiron walked over to his bookcase, opened a center console, and retrieved two onyx daggers. He turned to face the Wraith staggering to his feet and followed the Wraith's eyes as they wandered to Keiron's hands.

The Cheshire Cat grin faded into shock.

"What the fuck are you?" Roderick asked.

With a smirk of his own, Keiron said, "Probably someone you should have studied up on in Reaper school."

Keiron leapt forward with his daggers in hand while, in the background, Chuck D welcomed everyone to the Terrordome.

◆　◆　◆

Twenty Years Ago

"You're going to need to let them go," Azra-El said.

Deep down, Kassidy knew that. What she didn't know was how.

"And do what?" she asked.

"Move on. With me. With your new family."

"And then what? Just spend the rest of my life ushering souls to heaven or hell?"

"Does that sound so bad?" Azra-El asked.

This ... man had a way of speaking that made everything seem elementary. Everything he uttered sounded like the best idea ever. Kassidy surveyed the house again, focused on the interior through the large living room window. The house where she'd grown up. The only home she had ever known. Inside, Dan was stretching, and as he did, Marlene, Kassidy's sweet adoptive mother, walked behind him from the kitchen. She kissed him on the cheek and kept going until Kassidy could no longer see her.

"Actually, it sounds kind of lonely," Kassidy said, taking in the loving scene in the house.

"When I found you, you were ready for death. Now you want to live? Among people who've done nothing but torment you? Your entire life has been hell. You've been living in the Void, Love, and you didn't even know it. Now ... now you have a chance to take control. Now *you* can give *them* hell."

"What are you talking about?"

"We can do much more than usher souls, my dear. You got a taste of that already."

"You mean revenge? Killing?"

"I mean reckoning," Azra-El replied.

As he spoke, his eyes turned dark crimson, and Kassidy flinched backward. She moved, not from fear but from the weight and intensity of his words. She peered through the window again, and Dan had his hands on Marlene's shoulders. He kissed her on the forehead. He always did that, and every time Kassidy beamed. To her, that was the most loving gesture anyone could offer. He said something to Marlene, causing her to chuckle, and then he walked away. Seconds later, Kassidy watched as he emerged from the house and set off on his regular morning run.

For every memory of the kindness of her family there was with another memory of cruelty from the kids of the neighborhood. The kids, the school, and the not-so-subtle stares from neighborhood parents. Everyone in town either feared her or hated her, everyone except for this family.

But at what cost to them?

Dan's business barely stayed afloat because people didn't want to do business with the guy with the weird kid. All the moms in town laughed and gossiped behind Marlene's back. And Sarah? She fought her way through the days defending her crazy kid sister. She barely had friends because the other kids were either scared or just assholes.

Surely they would be better off without her. Right? Surely the best way to thank them, to show her love, would be for her to leave.

Surely.

"I'm listening," she said.

CHAPTER TWENTY-SEVEN

ONE WAS HARD PRESSED TO FIND ANYONE WHO DISLIKED DAN Simmons. He was a hard-working family man. The kind of man fathers would trust with their daughters. The type of man mothers wanted their sons to emulate. He was among the best examples of humanity. He, of course, didn't see himself that way, but that was also what made him so well loved.

Dan knelt and cleared the loose paper that blew around the cemetery from the base of his wife's headstone. While others thought of him as a good man, Dan rarely saw himself as anything of substance without his Marlene. She had been everything to him. He'd slipped once. So caught up in grief he'd forgotten the promise he'd made to live a good life, a long life. He lost his way and thought his only salvation was to be with her again. Miraculously, he survived his attempt to die by suicide. He believes it was because of Marlene, and that has carried him each day since. Even in death she gave him strength, purpose, and unconditional love.

He placed the tulips against the granite headstone, just as he did every other week. He placed his right hand against the stone, traced her name, and bowed his head in prayer, just as he did every other week. He opened his eyes. A single tear fell down his cheek and took a slight detour around the loving smile on his face.

Just as it had every other week.

With his salt-and-pepper hair blowing in the cool breeze, he told her about their daughter Sarah and her little girl. He joked about Sarah getting a taste of her own medicine now that she had a daughter of her own. Dan mentioned that Sarah and Mark were going to try for another child now that little Kassidy was older.

Of course, whenever he talked about the cute, rambunctious little Kassidy, it always led to him talking about her namesake. Dan longed for the day when he could tell Marlene that Kassidy had returned. That she'd showed up at the house, happy and healthy, full of love. He longed for the day when he could tell Marlene that she could truly rest in peace because their youngest daughter was home.

But he couldn't do that this week, just as he couldn't do it two weeks ago or two weeks before that. So instead he talked about their daughter. The times Kassidy had made them all laugh or cry with joy. Birthdays, family trips, and the impromptu food fight they had while making Thanksgiving dinner one year. The first and only year they'd ended up celebrating Thanksgiving at Steve Lee's Chinese Kitchen.

When Dan stood to leave, he lowered his head, kissed two fingers, and lightly touched the top of Marlene's headstone. He told her he loved her. He told her he'd see her again in a couple of weeks and have lunch with her. Dan Simmons blew a final kiss, just as he did every other week. He trudged back toward his car, just as he did every other week. Unlike those other times, though, two women stood next to his car. Two women who, from a distance, almost appeared to be sisters. As he moved closer, he realized they weren't sisters, but ghosts. One of them, the blue-eyed brunette, he'd not seen in almost two decades. The other, he'd not seen in almost three. He was, of course, more focused on the former. His pace quickened and then slowed as he edged closer, fearful it was a dream. Fearful she truly *was* a ghost. Her image blurred as the tears welled in his eyes.

Finally, he'd have news to tell Marlene.

"K-K-Kassidy," he managed to get out.

"Hey, Dad," Kassidy said.

The embrace they shared was one of love, of safety, and even some remorse. It was heavy, even for a nonempath like Dan.

"I'm sorry," he began, "this must be overwhelming for your—"

"No!" Kassidy exclaimed when he tried to pull away. "It's okay. Most of this is me."

They laughed, they cried, and for a brief moment in time, all was right in Dan's world. Until he remembered that Dr. Octavia Lord was standing off to the side. He stood back and studied Kassidy with all the love and pride a father could give. Then he turned his head slightly to acknowledge Octavia.

"It's been a long time."

"It has indeed. You look good, Dan."

"Meh, I'm older, a little slower, but I guess I'm good." He swung his gaze back toward Kassidy. "Especially now."

Kassidy grinned. Though it seemed to be out of love and adoration, Dan sensed some guilt too. But it pleased him, nonetheless.

"So I guess if you two are here, together no less, some shit is about to hit the fan?"

"You could say that," Octavia said.

"Maybe we should go home then," Dan said.

"Yeah," Kassidy replied. "Let's go home."

CHAPTER TWENTY-EIGHT

KASSIDY STARED AT THE PICTURE OF HER SISTER, SARAH, ON THE mantel. Sarah looked as she always had—practically perfect in every way, just like Mary Poppins. Sarah's hair was always pristine. The perfect color, the perfect highlights, the perfect length, and the perfect style. Her makeup was so light and flawless, you could barely tell she had any on. Her smile was one of confidence and purpose, even when she didn't feel like she had either. And the little girl sitting on her lap was a miniature version of all that.

"She named her Kassidy?"

"Yep. She said she wanted to make damn sure that there was always a Kassidy running through this house," Dan replied with a slight laugh.

Kassidy looked back at the photo, tracing the images with her finger. How could she have left all this? Why had she so easily been led away by Azra-El? Had her life truly been that bad that she'd had to run away, that she'd had to die in some ridiculous effort to live?

Octavia walked in from the kitchen and ended a call. She appeared confused, and Kassidy sensed concern.

"Everything okay?" Dan asked. Despite not having empathic abilities like Kassidy, Dan was, in his own right, intuitive, particularly with his children.

"I think so," Octavia said. "Having some trouble reaching a friend though. Hopefully, he's getting my messages."

Kassidy knew Octavia had been calling Keiron, but she forced her attention back to Dan. He was equal parts excited and nervous, much like she was. She did her best to manage the emotions jockeying for lead position. He'd made coffee, and she added bourbon to it from her flask. He asked no questions, but she knew they were there. Moving over to the couch, she sat and sipped at her coffee as Octavia settled in to the recliner on her right.

"I'm sorry," Kassidy said to Dan. "I'm sorry I wasn't here for you when mom died. I should have been, I know. I should have been here with all of you. I was just . . . just so. . ."

She didn't know what to say. Kassidy had dreaded this for years. Coming face to face with her selfishness was something she'd honestly hoped to avoid for another decade or two. She sensed sadness from Dan. She'd expected anger, so in many ways this was so much more pleasant. Uncomfortable, but the alternative was too much to bear.

"We looked for you," Dan began. "We tried to find you so that we could tell you. I mean, we didn't know if you were alive or dead, but if you were alive, we didn't want you to find out in the papers or from someone that wasn't family."

Kassidy could do nothing but nod.

"I wish you had been here," Dan continued. "But I know you, and selfish is not a word I'd use to describe you. Whatever it was—anger, fear . . . whatever, it's in the past."

"But I should have been here to help you or at least support you. It couldn't have been easy."

"No. It definitely was not easy . . ."

As Dan's voice trailed off, Kassidy felt a sensation of shame.

It surrounded him like a cocoon.

"What is it?" Kassidy asked.

Dan lowered his head for a moment. When he raised it, a tear fell, leaving a moist trail along his cheek. Kassidy reached out, and he grabbed her hand and held it.

"I wasn't as strong as I should have been," he said. "I tried to . . ."

Kassidy gasped. She knew what he was going to say. She could feel the struggle within him. The pain was still there, mixed with embarrassment. She realized then that they'd both felt the sense of failure to the family. She moved to hug him, as much for her peace as his. The embrace didn't wash away everything, but it served its purpose—they were no longer alone in their shame.

"She must have been watching over you then," Kassidy said.

"I wholeheartedly believe that. Otherwise, I wouldn't be here now."

Kassidy kissed her father on the cheek, then pressed her forehead against his. She wanted to go back in time and wipe away the distance and the dumb decisions. She wanted so much to just make everything okay. Dan kissed her cheek, then pulled back and wiped tears away.

"So," Dan began nervously, "how did you two connect?"

His eyes shifted from Kassidy to Octavia, but they lingered in Octavia's direction.

Kassidy sensed that his real question was more along the lines of, "How much does Kassidy know?" Which of course only fueled her suspicions that the good professor had not told her everything. She'd leave that alone for the time being. But somebody was going to tell her everything once this shit was settled.

"I guess the best way to answer that is with a long story," Kassidy said.

"I hope part of that story includes some info on where you've been," Dan said.

There was no bite to his statement. Nevertheless, in those thirteen words Dan expressed interest, excitement, anger, disappointment, concern, and love.

Always love.

Kassidy nodded and closed her eyes. She took a deep breath and then, for the first time in ages, told someone the story of homecoming night. She felt the anger roll off Dan like an out-of-control locomotive as she talked about Jeremy Reins and what he'd done to her. She moved closer to Dan, placed a hand on his, and did her best to help him regain some calm. It mostly worked—until she got to Azra-El.

When she finished catching Dan up, she wasn't sure what to make of his expression. She reached out with her abilities to gauge any emotion, and strangely, there was nothing. Well, not entirely nothing. In actuality there was everything. Everything all at once, but none stronger than the other. It was as if he were emotionally numb. He didn't know what to feel. He didn't know how to feel. He was just simply there, staring blankly.

"Dad?" she asked.

No response.

"DAD?!" she asked louder.

Still nothing.

Had she broken him? Did she overload him with too much information? He'd always known about her abilities. The empathic stuff was just a drop in the bucket. When she was younger and talked about sensing death, he'd assumed it was tied into her empathic power. When she said she could see beings hovering around bodies when they were sick or dead, he'd dismissed that as the ramblings of a child burdened with abilities and an overactive imagination. She'd accepted all that, which was why she'd stopped talking about seeing Reapers in her preteens. But now she was telling him all that was real, very real. And a published college professor was corroborating everything. She must have broken him. It had to be too much.

"Dad?" she asked softly, touching his shoulder.

Dan's eyes shifted. He blinked.

"It's . . . all real?" he asked.

"Yeah, dad. It's all real."

"And you think he's coming for you now?"

"I know he is," Kassidy said. "He's already attacked two people close to me. One of his people tried to take Octavia. He's after me, and I don't think he'll stop until he kills me."

Kassidy watched as Dan stood up. He went nowhere, though. He put his hands on his hips, then moved them to his sides, then moved toward the kitchen, only to come right back.

"Dan, I know it's a lot to take in," Octavia said.

Dan gave her a look that made Kassidy shiver. There was definitely more going on between these two. Octavia had said she'd met Dan about fifteen years ago as a favor to Keiron who'd simply wanted to check in on the man and his family to ensure none of Kassidy's enemies were after them. That had to be bullshit. The anger Dan directed at Octavia was reserved for people he knew well.

"Sorry," Octavia said as Dan's frustration registered with her.

Dan sat next to Kassidy again. His deep sigh was an attempt to radiate some calm through his body, but Kassidy didn't feel its impact.

"So, you've been dealing with this alone for all this time?" he asked.

"Yes . . . and no," Kassidy said.

Dan inclined his head. As he did, Kassidy blushed. They were headed for a subject change that could be just as shocking as the first. But if she were going to die soon, did it really matter?

"You have someone? Someone in your life?" Dan asked.

Kassidy nodded.

"Are you married? Kids?"

"No to both. Definitely no kids. I mean, can you imagine?"

"So, a boyfriend?"

Kassidy took a deep breath and tried to prepare herself for any backlash. It wasn't that she was afraid Dan would disapprove. He would never openly show any disappointment, but she could always feel it if it was there.

That was worse than any physical pain she could imagine.

"A girlfriend actually," Kassidy said.

"And?"

"And we live together. A nice little townhome in St. John, New York."

"And?"

He was searching for something, but she didn't know what. She wasn't feeling anything negative from him. Just curiosity and concern.

"And what, dad?"

"And are you happy?"

Kassidy was both relieved and distressed. She had needed someone to ask that question. She needed her dad to ask her that question.

"I was, I think. But I've really fucked it up."

Dan opened his arms wide, and Kassidy, as she'd done hundreds of times as a child, moved into them. She felt comforted immediately. The stress of being hunted, of not being able to help Lynn and David, bore down on her like a wet wool blanket. She didn't cry. She simply lived in the moment.

"So this Azra-El character," Dan began, "we need to kill him."

Kassidy nodded against his chest.

"How can I help?" he asked.

She stepped back, then turned to Octavia, who was smiling as she leaned forward in the recliner.

"I'm glad you asked, Dan. You're about to help Kassidy save the world."

◆　　◆　　◆

Twenty Years Ago

Kassidy was apprehensive about her next assignment from Azra-El. After the last guy, after almost losing that battle with . . . whatever that thing was, after seeing Senaya's eyes and learning she was the same kind of creature, Kassidy wasn't sure about much of anything anymore. Amazing how one act could completely unravel everything.

And why did my eyes change too?

She found herself in the sleepy little town of St. John, New York. Downtown seemed quaint, not unlike downtown Oak Park. There were sections, small streets actually, that were still cobblestone. The main thoroughfare was called Main Street because, why not? On that street were bars and restaurants, privately owned businesses, and one nondescript bookstore.

Sitting in a coffee shop across the street from the bookstore, Kassidy watched people come and go while the owner sat at the checkout counter and read. Occasionally, he'd get up, walk out of sight, and return with a snack or something to drink. But he otherwise seemed harmless.

Why does Azra-El want this guy dispatched?

When Kassidy had first become a Reaper, it was very clear

that they were drawn to those who were near death or already dead. Tasks weren't divided up. She'd feel the pull, she'd go to the source, and she'd carry out her duty and move on. But these rogue reapings she'd been sent on just felt weird. Azra-El said that these people had escaped their fate through some sort of supernatural intervention, and that it was her duty as a Reaper to maintain the balance of life and death. It made sense to her, to some degree. Plus, he was her leader, her Primus, she was bound to him in that way, and despite her occasionally rebellious behavior, she obeyed. Those orders certainly made sense with that creature she'd dispatched in that basement. But this guy? This guy seemed too normal, too good, too innocent.

Kassidy took her final sip of coffee and walked across the street to get a better feel for the bookseller.

Entering the store, she was bombarded with scents. Sweet and soothing aromas that somehow meshed well with the underlying smell of leather covers and paper. Kassidy felt safe in this environment. She could not explain why. She only knew that she was completely and utterly safe—from everything.

"Can I help you, young lady?" the bookseller asked.

He seemed to be a nice man. She sensed nothing from him but peace and calm. No malicious intent. No rogue thoughts or inappropriate urges. The guy wasn't flat, or dull, or without emotion. He was . . . chill, to borrow the vernacular.

"I don't know. I'm just kind of browsing, I guess. Not even really sure what I'm looking for."

"Not much of a reader then?" he asked.

"Meh." Kassidy shrugged. "I read a lot in school. I like to read. It just takes a lot to get me interested, I guess."

Kassidy walked to the checkout counter toward the seller. He was handsome in a classic way. The black goatee suited his

Mediterranean complexion. His dark hair was cut short, buzzed on the sides, but faded toward the ears—almost military. He didn't have the intensity of most military men she'd come across though. Whatever he was, he was calm, cool, and didn't seem worried about a thing. Was that what it was like to be confident?

"That's not so uncommon these days. People need to be invested in a story within the first few paragraphs, and the chapters need to be short and sweet. Our attention span isn't what it used to be," he said.

"Yeah. Like with movies and television shows too. There's got to be a quick—"

"Hook," they said together.

Why the hell does Azra-El want this guy dispatched?

"What was the last book you read that you really liked?" he asked.

"Honestly?"

He nodded.

"*Carrie*," Kassidy replied.

The bookseller's eyebrows went up, and he inclined his head, as if approving but surprised. Or was he?

"The story of a young girl with extraordinary gifts who finds herself ridiculed for being different, only to exact revenge in the end. Interesting choice," he said.

"Why interesting?"

"Well, most people think of it as horror. They like the revenge factor. Others like it for what I consider the right reason."

"And what's that?" Kassidy asked.

"Because they connect with the girl and her struggle."

Oddly enough, that was the very reason she liked the novel. She was uniquely qualified to understand exactly what Carrie was experiencing. Every part of it sang to her. Every emotion was an echo. Every urge Carrie experienced served as a reminder of what Kassidy had suffered. Yeah, Carrie was less a favorite and more a kindred spirit. A sister even. Someone who, like her, needed protection from abuse and exploitation.

"Been a teenage girl long, have you?" Kassidy asked with a little bite.

"No. Never actually. But I've been confused, lied to, abused, and overprotective of those like me," the bookseller said.

Who the fuck is this guy?

"Fair enough, I suppose," Kassidy said, embarrassed, yet feeling unjudged.

"Are you new in town?" the bookseller asked.

"Keying in on my Midwest accent?"

"A little. Mostly, this is a small area, and I've been here awhile. I've never seen you around."

From anyone else, this would seem like a really bad pickup line. But Kassidy felt no ulterior motives from him. He was a straight-up good guy. Maybe this was a test. Maybe Azra-El was testing her to see if she was blindly loyal or capable of making sound decisions, even if they were contrary to his mandates. Maybe Azra-El respected critical thinking. All those blind mice he was leading probably irked the hell out of him. He needed smart people on his team. She'd been thinking that for months. Was he grooming her?

"I'm actually just passing through town. I'll probably head out tomorrow. Maybe the day after."

"No real plan, eh?" he asked.

"I guess not. I mean, I was here to see someone, but I'm starting to think that wasn't such a good idea."

"Hmm, that's curious."

"Isn't it though?" Kassidy replied. "I think I ran into an

unexpected speedbump, is all. Just not sure my original plan is the best plan."

"It takes a smart individual with an open mind and an ability to think critically to change plans abruptly like that. You may go far in this world," the bookseller said.

"Maybe," Kassidy said. "Then again, I could be dead tomorrow."

The bookseller chuckled. It wasn't condescending or judgmental. He was simply in tune with her humor, even with its dark undertones. It was weird how quickly she was warming up to this man. This man she was supposed to kill.

"Well, before you leave, either this town or this existence, you should check out a couple of books. You might find them interesting. Follow me."

Kassidy followed him to a back room. Normally, she'd be on guard. In any movie she'd ever seen, a young woman following an older man into a back room never worked out well. Kassidy was naïve in some ways, but she was an empath, and she trusted her senses and the emotions of others. In this store, with this man, she was safe.

The back room was less a storage space or office and more a separate store. On two of the four walls were books, most of them first editions. The smell of old paper and worn leather permeated every part of the room. On a third wall were antiques and . . . trinkets? Keepsakes? Maybe they had some sort of sentimental or collectors' value. There were swords, axes, and daggers, but they appeared strange juxtaposed against something that looked like an ancient brass Rubik's Cube and a silver handcrafted thunder-bolt.

"You bring a lot of first dates here?" Kassidy asked.

"Great way to weed out who's worthy of my time and who's not," the bookseller replied.

"You've got a high opinion of yourself."

"We all should," he replied.

That statement shot Kassidy right in the heart. It seemed aimed at her. If it wasn't, it certainly fit.

"Ah, here we are," he said, walking over to a wall of books. "I think you'll find this particularly interesting."

The man grabbed a book from the wall. It was bound in black leather. Less like a book and more like . . . a journal, maybe? He held it out to her, unbound the leather strap, and opened it.

"This is the journal of a young woman named Allesandra. A warrior of sorts."

"Of sorts?" Kassidy asked.

"Well, the notion of gods, men, and warriors is complicated. This young girl was the daughter of mortals, but she battled gods and monsters in ancient Greece. I won't spoil it for you. But I will tell you this. In her lifetime, she had to overcome ridicule. With no special powers at all, she defeated deadly supernatural creatures and found her path in life. So, if you liked *Carrie*, you'll likely enjoy these journal entries."

"Journal entries? Seems a bit voyeuristic."

The bookseller shrugged.

"And she battled supernatural creatures?"

He nodded again.

"With good looks and charm?"

The bookseller chuckled. "With patience, intelligence, a great mentor, and those daggers over there." He pointed to a wall.

Kassidy walked over to the weapons wall and studied the onyx blades. She touched the metal, and her fingertips tingled. They felt similar to the metal of the Reaper scythes and seemed even more similar to the metal in the scythe of that black-eyed creature she had fought. Like the scythe Senaya constructed.

When she'd held it close to Kassidy's face, it made her skin tingle.

Why does he have these blades?

"Where did you find these?" Kassidy asked.

"I'm a collector of books and rare antiquities. I came across these a long time ago and kept them. Somewhat of an homage to ancient times. I'm sentimental like that."

"An old soul?

"Very much so."

Kassidy turned back to the daggers.

"The metal was known as celestial onyx. Makes it sound as if it is magical or otherworldly," the bookseller said.

"And it's not?"

"The ancient world is full of stories of magic and sorcery, gods and goddesses—things to explain what was unexplainable. In those days, people didn't know enough to know what they didn't know."

"I don't think that's really changed much," Kassidy said.

The bookseller chuckled at that. "I can't argue with you on that. Very astute for someone so young."

"Usually people call me cynical, but I'll take astute. Makes me sound less like a bitch."

The bookseller laughed again. Warmth radiated through Kassidy, and she was overwhelmed with a sense of comfort she'd not felt since her time at home with Dan and Marlene. Despite all the mystery, she knew, to the depths of her soul, that she could trust this man with her life.

"Anyhow, the metal is actually a substance known as adamantine. The hardest substance known to exist."

"Harder than diamonds?"

"Harder than anything. Legend has it, it's the only substance that can kill an immortal."

"You mean, like . . . gods?" Kassidy asked.

"Depends on the god. Lesser gods, maybe. But most certainly other types of immortal beings and such."

Like Reapers.

Like the Angel of Death.

"Even the famed thunderbolt of Zeus can only kill certain gods. I suspect if there were such a weapon, the gods would have confiscated it long ago."

"There's really nothing?" Kassidy asked.

"Nothing outside the deepest and darkest of legend. There was talk of a blade that was made of pure adamantine, but it was lost shortly after the great war between the Titans and Olympians," the bookseller said.

"These aren't pure?"

"No. No adamantine weapon is pure. These daggers are a mix of metals. Predominantly adamantine, hence the effect it has on immortals. But definitely not pure."

What about my sickle?

Kassidy walked away from the daggers. Standing near them stirred up feelings of excitement—a hunger, a thirst for aggression and violence. She wanted to attack.

The feel of the leather in her hands caused her to refocus on the journal she'd been handed. She opened it, sifting through the pages, giving it a cursory glance.

"And you'd just part with this journal for li'l ol' me?" Kassidy asked, feigning playfulness.

"I'd let you borrow it. I'll want that back at some point," the bookseller said.

"You trust me to bring this back?"

"I do."

"Just like that?"

"Just like that."

This guy was weird. But her curiosity was on high alert. Especially about those daggers. Those daggers, that metal, and the thing that she'd dispatched a couple of weeks ago—and most certainly, Senaya.

"You're awfully trusting of strangers," Kassidy said.

The bookseller extended his hand. "My name is Keiron. Pleased to meet you, Miss . . ."

"Simmons." Kassidy accepted his handshake. "Kassidy Simmons."

"Well, see, now we're no longer strangers."

CHAPTER TWENTY-NINE

THE FOOT TRAFFIC IN THE HALLS OF ST. JOHN MEMORIAL HOSPITAL moved at a slow yet steady pace. The town was small, though, so compared to the big city it stood to reason there wouldn't be a constant rush of people. The mood in the hospital was somber. People were getting sick, and an abnormal number of patients lingered near death. Doctors found themselves at a loss to understand what seemed to be a freak phenomenon. It raised flags, but not enough to warrant requests for help from other hospitals or researchers.

That suited Azra-El just fine.

Every illness led to death, and every death led to a reaping, which only served to strengthen him. The by-product, of course, was strengthening Kassidy too. But that mattered less and less to him. The more power she had, the more he could eventually absorb, and that would all but guarantee his ascension.

He walked the halls inconspicuously, checking in on the chaos he'd set in motion. He was determined to make Kassidy recognize the importance of joining his side. He would make her see how imperative it was that she acquiesce to his will. If it wasn't enough that her best friend and lover were near death, he'd up the ante and hold the souls of an entire town hostage.

He stopped at the door of Lynn Ambrose and walked in. Stepping up to her bed, he peered down at her with a crooked grin. Azra-El reached out and brushed an errant strand of hair from her face. It was a loving gesture, gentle. He examined his hand after, as if dismayed he was capable of such compassion. But of course he was capable of compassion, of love. Of course he was capable of caring for someone more than he cared for himself.

He was doing this for his beloved, after all.

"So, you're the one that helped her hold things together all these years?" Azra-El asked rhetorically. "It's a shame, really. I think you would have had a long and wonderful life otherwise. Strange how fate gives us everything we want only to snatch it away at a moment's notice."

Azra-El pulled up a chair and sat down. Lynn's chestnut hair reminded him of Allesandra's long curls. Unlike his love, Lynn's skin was tanned. Allesandra's hair always provided the perfect contrast to her fair, smooth skin. He missed her. He missed her more and more each day. That longing only made him more determined to make his plan work. He'd be with her again. He would make this happen.

"She'll come for you and the guy downstairs. She'll come for all of you," Azra-El said. "She'll come for you, and she'll try to save you, because that's what love does."

Azra-El edged closer to the bed and adjusted the blanket covering Lynn's sleeping form. Satisfied, he sat back and crossed one leg over the other.

"I honestly don't care if she saves you or not," he said.

As if proving a point, Azra-El raised his hand, extended his thumb and forefinger, then slowly brought them together. A red glow engulfed Lynn. Within seconds her monitors changed from a steady beep to a flat line. Azra-El sat there quietly, full of righteousness and power.

"All I care about is taking her life and adding her power to my own. With her power and the Scythe of Cronus in my hands, I will have my beloved Allesandra at my side again."

Azra-El closed his eyes, nodded his head, and the flat line ceased. First one beep, then two, then three. Her heartbeat steadied, and Azra-El rose and stood over Lynn Ambrose once more.

"I am sorry for you. You have no idea what you've gotten yourself into. That's a fate thing, though, and I have nothing to do with that. Death is my workplace, and soon it will be my domain to control as I see fit."

Azra-El strode out of the room. His power was nearing its peak. He could feel it strengthening with every step he took. His senses were sharp, and he felt the essences of almost all his Reapers and Wraiths again. He couldn't feel Kassidy though. He could sense her power growing, but he couldn't feel her. This was the time to escalate. Stretching out with his senses, he connected his mind to Senaya's. He needed his second. He had a mission for her.

CHAPTER THIRTY

"THIS IS THE PART WHERE YOU'LL WANT TO SIT DOWN AND STRAP in," Kassidy said.

Dan nodded at his daughter. He didn't have a clue about what he was getting himself into, though he was certain it wouldn't be good. He turned his attention toward Octavia.

She still looks the same. How can she not have aged?

"How are you so calm in all of this?" he asked Kassidy.

"Oh, I'm not. Just lots of years of hiding shit," she said.

"And you"—his eyes pointed toward Octavia—"how long have you been involved or known about all of this?"

Dan caught a side glance of Kassidy. She gave him a curious look. He recognized it as her "I'm processing things" look. She was analyzing something, putting pieces together. She'd have questions soon. What did she know? What could he answer?

"I'm something of an expert in classical literature and mythology. I suppose you could say, I've known about this for a long time."

"Known that it was real?" Dan asked.

"Every legend is rooted in fact. Even rumors start somewhere."

"So where do I come in?" Dan asked.

"The Scythe of Cronus is among the most powerful weapons ever created. It was fashioned shortly after the creation of the Universe and as a result has some unique properties. In the right hands, in the right conditions, it's a tool. In the wrong hands, you have death, destruction, chaos . . . end-of-the-world shit."

"Oh, that old story," Dan said.

"You've heard it?" Octavia asked.

"I've seen the movie."

They smiled tensely at each another. Dan caught another glimpse of Kassidy. She was doing that thing again.

"Anyhow," Octavia began, "after some struggle among the elder gods, the scythe eventually found itself under the control of the god of Death. Death, or Thanatos, the name he preferred, had no interest in petty squabbles and gathering power. He was content with his role. He gained control of the scythe and decided that it may be in the best interest of humanity to have it hidden."

"Very magnanimous of him," Dan said.

"It was necessary. Had he not done that, there's really no telling where we'd be today."

Dan had accepted a long time ago that his adopted daughter was different from other kids. He'd thought—no, he'd hoped that would be the worst thing he'd have to deal with. In the big scheme of things, raising an empath was nothing. That was something they could easily manage with time, patience, and practice. Reapers and Wraiths were entirely different animals. The Angel of Death was real? Thanatos? Elder gods and weapons? And Kassidy was in the center of it, along with Octavia Lord—the woman who'd given Kassidy to him and Marlene almost thirty-eight years ago.

"So, what did he do with it?" Dan asked. His fear of the answer must have hit Kassidy. He felt her hand on his. He covered it with his other hand. Dan attempted to smile, attempted to let her know he was okay. But he knew better than to try.

"Most of the elder gods had mortals they trusted. Usually, these mortals were priests of their temples. As you can imagine, having a temple to honor and worship Death was a bit . . . it just wasn't something you'd do. Nevertheless, Thanatos had a man he trusted. A man named Antolychus."

"Should I assume he gave this Antolychus guy the scythe?" Dan asked.

Octavia nodded.

"Should I also assume that this Antolychus guy is somehow connected with me?"

Octavia nodded again.

"Dad," Kassidy said, "the scythe is not only an instrument of death but also a tool that controls space, time, hell . . . even life."

Dan stared at Kassidy. He'd heard her words, but what he was really stuck on was hearing her call him *Dad*. Mostly she called him Dan. Not out of spite, but more so in an attempt to protect herself and her feelings. She'd been too young to remember her birth parents, too young to know even that she'd been passed from one family to another. When she'd found out, though, she'd been angry. The anger quickly downgraded to fear—fear that Dan and Marlene would abandon her too. Especially given that she was the weird kid in town. So, when she called him *Dad*, it was a sign that she was slipping into a comfort zone, a safe zone. He was happy that she slipped into that now.

"What are you getting at?" Dan asked.

"Thanatos chose to hide the weapon with someone he trusted," Octavia said.

"Yeah, I got that part," Dan said.

"But he was concerned about the protection of the scythe over time. So, to protect it throughout history, he imbued its, well, guardian—for lack of a better word—with extended life."

"Immortality?" Dan asked.

"Not quite. Immortals, as legends go, cannot die except under very specific circumstances or by specific weaponry," Octavia said.

"Like this Scythe of . . . Cronus?"

Octavia nodded.

Instinct told Dan that shit was about to get weirder. He wasn't sure if he could handle it, but he had to try. Kassidy was back, and she needed his help. She'd run from him, from the family, had been gone so long because she felt she couldn't be herself. He wouldn't put her in that position again.

"Okay, so the guy isn't immortal then. So, what, he just has a long life?" Dan asked.

"Essentially, yes. He is mortal in every sense of the word. He ages, gets sick, all the things that people go through. But when he's near death, he is called to the Scythe of Cronus. It's part of the spell, the magical link, that connects him to it. Once he has it, he uses the scythe to regenerate. After he completes this ritual, he uses a spell to create a new life narrative for himself. He then hides the scythe in a different location and that same spell causes him to consciously forget who and what he truly is. He lives the new life he's crafted until the cycle needs to repeat. But—"

"Assuming that I buy into all of this magic and mythology, how does this tie in to me exactly?"

Dan looked back and forth between Octavia and Kassidy. Kassidy was wringing her hands. He wondered how much of her discomfort was this discussion and how much was the need for more bourbon. It had not gone unnoticed that she'd poured the last of it into her coffee. The coffee mug was now empty. What had happened to his little girl? He put a hand on her shoulder, silently willing her to relax.

"Go on," Dan said. "I know the good part is coming."

"Antolychus accepted the challenge and went on to live a long life. He traveled, he learned, he loved, all the while protecting the most powerful weapon in existence, with no elder god ever knowing what he was doing. He assimilated with the times with each regeneration. During one of his lives, he used the name Anthony. He found a nice trade and worked as a silversmith. He worked by day and studied by night, as he did with every trade he undertook. Instead of taking the last name of Smith, as many people did who took up that trade, he opted for—"

"Simmons," Dan said.

Octavia nodded.

"Anthony Simmons was my great-great-grandfather," Dan said.

Octavia shook her head.

Dan raised an eyebrow and inclined his head.

"Anthony Simmons . . . is you."

If this was all bullshit, it was incredibly elaborate. Dan's head was truly spinning. Of course the logical side of him was concerned. Concerned for his safety in the presence of people who seemed to truly believe what they were saying. He was concerned for Kassidy, because she'd clearly had a psychotic break and he had no idea how to deal with that. If this is what she truly believed, it was no wonder she drank bourbon by the gallon. He needed to get focused. He needed to ask questions. More than anything, he just wanted to hug her, to comfort her, but he couldn't. Not because he was speechless—but because she was vanishing before his eyes.

"Kassidy!"

Dan Simmons grabbed at empty air attempting to keep his daughter at his side.

He failed.

CHAPTER THIRTY-ONE

KASSIDY WAS IN THE NEXUS. IN A HOUSE. BUT NO LONGER HER family home. The house seemed a little older but fairly well maintained. Much of the furniture was covered except for one recliner and one couch. She saw a giant hole in the wall that led from the foyer to the dining room. From what she could tell, it had been made recently.

Why the fuck am I here?

"Denzel?" Kassidy called out. No answer. Kassidy stepped toward the couch looking for any clue about who'd been here. She found nothing but the recently burned logs in the fireplace.

"My favorite Reaper has returned," Azra-El said.

She shuddered when she heard his voice, then froze. She wanted to run. She wanted to attack. But none of that would do any good in the moment. He was strong enough now to summon her. Without the scythe, she'd likely have no chance against him. She hated admitting it but besting him twenty years ago was likely due to him being caught off guard by her audacity.

"I'm not a Reaper anymore," she said.

"Well now, if that were true, I wouldn't have two dead Wraiths and you wouldn't be here."

At that, Kassidy turned to face her one-time mentor, her one-time savior. The fury of the last several days filled her. The sight of him, though, the softness of his face, those eyes. He'd been good to her once. How could such a good man be so—

"You son of a bitch! I'm not here willingly. As for those Wraiths . . ." Kassidy's voice trailed off as her hand shifted into a sickle. She rushed at Azra-El, pressing the weapon to his throat. "Fucking Jeremy Reins! You brought him back? You fucking used him to lure me into your world? I'm going to end you once and for all!"

Kassidy saw concern in Azra-El's eyes. That concern softened, and then he sneered. That sinister sneer that spoke more than his words ever did.

"You shouldn't be able to do that here, Reaper," he said, pointing to the sickle at his throat with his eyes.

"What?" Kassidy asked absently.

Holy shit!

Kassidy gasped at the weapon pressed to his throat. He was right. She shouldn't be able to do that. No Reaper, no Wraith could manifest weapons in the Nexus. The only one with that power was the Primus or Death himself.

She backed away, staring at the sickle, then willed it to transform back into a hand.

"Perhaps now you see why I found you so interesting," Azra-El said.

"Found?"

"Okay, found and still find. Happy?"

There was that fucking smile again.

"What do you want?"

"Come on. Can't we catch up? How've you been, love?"

"Fuck you! That's how I've been. Now what do you want?"

"Okay, fine. I want to kill you, of course. That goes without saying." He shrugged his shoulders. Nonchalant. Playfulness intertwined with menace.

Kassidy inched back from him, each step slow and deliberate. She tried to drift out of the Nexus but couldn't. *He's fucking blocking me! Shit!*

"We didn't finish our last conversation, my dear. It was like we were talking, and then all of a sudden, you stabbed me with those blades. I don't even know where you found those fucking things. But I never got a chance to argue my point."

"Which was?"

"That you and I need to work together to establish some new rules to the natural order."

"Oh, that line of horseshit," Kassidy said.

"You wound me." Azra-El, held his hand to his chest, feigning offense.

"Yeah, I did wound you. Sadly, not enough."

Azra-El's hands dropped to his side.

"Touché."

His eyes radiated a dim red. She did her best to remain calm, but every Reaper knew that when his eyes glowed that way, he was angry.

"You're after my power, aren't you? You wanted to fatten me up, make me stronger, then kill me and absorb my abilities. That was your plan."

"I mean, can you blame me?" he asked with a sly grin. "Look, in any corporation, the idea is to get promoted, right? Not to stay in the same position doing the same thing millennia after millennia."

Kassidy's fists clenched tighter. She shifted from side to side, doing her best to keep her rage in check. "So that night you found me, that was set up?"

Azra-El nodded.

"In exchange for power and immortality, you instructed a boy to terrorize me? To beat me? To . . . rape me?"

Azra-El held up a hand.

"Whoa. I told him I needed you to be down and out. I needed you in a state near death."

"But you didn't care how he did it?"

Azra-El shrugged.

"And all so you could have power? You ruined my life for power?" Kassidy asked.

"Ruined your life? Ruined your life! I saved you, you ungrateful little bitch! I gave you a chance to take vengeance. Vengeance on him, on all the Jeremy Reins of the world. On everyone who'd ever treated you wrong. I gave you a chance to be powerful for once in your miserable fucking life! And for that gift, you spat in my face and tried to kill me."

"You orchestrated all of it. You took away any chance for me to be normal, to find my own way. You turned me into a monster, a killer, all in an effort to make you more powerful. You didn't save me. It was all for you. I was happy to die. I was happy to fade away."

Kassidy advanced toward Azra-El again. Her power building. Fists clenched.

"Then why did you say yes?"

Those six words stopped her in her tracks. She relaxed her fists.

"Cat got your tongue? Or are you afraid of the truth?"

"What truth?"

"That deep within there's a darkness, a hunger, a thirst for power, for reckoning. You needed what I gave you, and when it was offered, you willingly accepted."

"You tricked me. With what I went through, what human being wouldn't want that?"

Azra-El laughed again. His eyes dimmed, transitioning from

red to their natural state. "Sweetheart, you're not human. Do you think most humans walk around feeling the emotions of others? Sensing when death is near? Do you think they see Reapers and Wraiths as easily as they see stop signs and clouds in the sky? Even now you have abilities beyond the norm. You bested two Wraiths in the last few days. You bested me twenty years ago. No, my dear, whatever you are, it isn't human. Far from it. Why do you think I chose you?"

Kassidy shivered. In anger. In fear. In curiosity. What the hell did he mean? What did he think she was? She wanted to be at his throat again, weapon in hand, demanding answers. But she stayed still. She could not let him—

What the . . .

"Looks like you're not quite at full strength yet," Kassidy said with a grin.

Like an old television with a dying tube, Azra-El began to fade from view. She let her anger go as she watched his frustration. His hands shimmered as he was pulled into the real world. Kassidy waved at him. She felt the bind tying her to the Nexus break.

"I wouldn't get too happy, my dear," Azra-El sneered. "I still have your girlfriend . . . what's her name, Lauren? Lucy?"

"Lynn!"

"Ah yes, that's it—Lynn. I have her, and I have your other friend David. They seem awful, by the way. I can't believe you haven't visited them yet."

"You son of a—"

"Tsk-tsk. If you want to save them, find the scythe, bring it to me, and surrender yourself. You wanted to die, right? I'm here to make that wish come true."

Kassidy leapt forward and flew through empty space as Azra-El vanished from the Nexus. She whirled, somehow expecting him to be behind her or to her side, only in the real world. He'd been staying in this abandoned house. She was certain of that. Now that she knew, he'd vacate this hiding space. He couldn't stay in the Nexus for some reason, but he had enough power to reappear elsewhere.

He knew about the scythe, that they were searching for it. That was why they'd kidnapped Octavia. If they knew about her, what else had they figured out? Did they know about Dan? Did they know the family connection to Thanatos? Kassidy's mind swirled.

So she screamed.

Windows and mirrors shattered as she screamed herself out of the Nexus. After a few moments, she dematerialized into vapor. She had to get back to Octavia and Dan. Those two were the key to everything.

CHAPTER THIRTY-TWO

OCTAVIA WAS ACCUSTOMED TO THINGS NOT GOING TO PLAN. Though, had she ever really had a plan? Keiron had contacted her, and she'd jumped at the chance to assist him. That was the way they were with each other. Of course, it didn't hurt that this request had come with the opportunity to connect with Kassidy. In hindsight, that prospect was the true drive. An opportunity to establish a relationship.

An opportunity to make amends.

When Octavia was younger, she'd been born to a wealthy family of status and privilege. As the younger of two girls, she'd lived in the shadow of her sister. She loved her sister dearly. Idolized her, even. In many ways she wanted to be just like her. At times, she wanted to *be* her. This led to resentment, and by the time they were of age, that resentment grew into something sinister.

Back then, marriages were arranged, particularly among well-to-do families. Their father, Zyantony, announced that Octavia's sister was to be married to a wealthy heir from the next city over. For six months, everything revolved around that wedding, around everything but Octavia.

The benefit of maturity was recognizing your challenges, your opportunities for improvement, and moving on. Knowing, though, did not lessen the embarrassment and shame she felt about her youthful jealousy.

Octavia had been entitled, as most children of privilege were. She wanted to be acknowledged in any way—at the very least, as much as her sister. Going virtually unnoticed, especially as everyone prepared for an upcoming union, no one paid attention to her when she'd overheard her father talk about the financial hardship the family was experiencing. No one paid attention when she'd spied her mother taking food from the market without paying.

No one paid attention when she caught her sister spending time with a man who was not her betrothed.

Octavia used that knowledge. The young man her sister truly loved, Tyran, was a commoner. He came from poor parents who had long since died. Octavia admitted to him her knowledge of their love. Her sister would never confirm it, but he did. Happily. He seemed so desperate to talk to someone, anyone, about their relationship. Octavia led him to believe that she could influence her father's feelings about him.

He realized the folly of that when the affair came to light and he was forbidden to come anywhere near the family home. Nevertheless, Octavia was there with her support and continued encouragement. She even suggested Tyran marry her sister in secret—that way, no one could ever tear them apart.

When she found out her sister's betrothed was coming to visit, she gathered as much information as she could about the travel route and passed it on to Tyran. She knew he'd likely do something violent. He was a man of purpose. It seemed when he set his mind to it, he would do anything to achieve his goal. In this, his goal was love and happiness. In this, Octavia could use him for her own needs. The need to see her sister removed as the favorite. The need to see Allesandra disowned for loving and marrying a commoner. The need to finally be seen herself as worthy of a wealthy husband and all the power that went with it.

When word came that there would be no wedding, that the suitor and his party had been slaughtered en route to visit the family, Octavia's world crashed. The family rallied around Allesandra. When it was discovered that Tyran had been the instrument of that slaughter, her world burned. Allesandra left to search for a missing Tyran. The family became obsessed with finding her. Octavia was all but forgotten.

◆　　◆　　◆

Octavia walked into the living room of the Simmons family home and stared at the pictures of their loving family. Guilt shadowed her. She'd stolen that chance for happiness from her sister. She had not anticipated her sister's response in the wake of Tyran's punishment. She had not anticipated her sister losing her life and soul in her efforts to save her true love. She had not anticipated her sister being impregnated by the man—the being, rather—that had exacted revenge on Tyran. She certainly had not anticipated saving her sister and helping her hide inside the fabled Nexus, where she would live and give birth to a daughter.

For all of that, Octavia had been punished.

Cursed by a god and destined to live a life of loneliness.

Octavia Lord spent her life trying to repay the sins of her selfishness and betrayal. She learned to fight and defend. She learned the best ways to reach others through compassion and shared knowledge. It was what made her an ally against injustice and a champion of education. Helping Kassidy, she hoped, would finally settle unspoken debts to her family, to her sister.

Through Kassidy—her niece—Octavia could finally restore her personal honor.

CHAPTER THIRTY-THREE

DAN DID HIS BEST NOT TO OVERREACT. BUT WHEN IT CAME TO HIS family, he really didn't have a strong governor. Common sense often flew out the window.

He argued briefly with Octavia about finding Kassidy after she'd vanished. Octavia told him to stay and wait. She suggested that staying together might be safer than being separated. He blew up at her before he got in his car and bolted from the house. He had no idea where, or if, he was going to find his daughter. If he were being honest, his leaving had nothing to do with finding her. He needed to be away from Octavia, away from all the shit he'd just learned. He didn't know if he was freaked out more about the concepts of Reapers, Wraiths, ancient gods, or the fact that he was . . . immortal. Or at least something close to it.

There was so much more to adjust to. Like the fact that he'd gone from being a priest of Thanatos to a suburban father. He'd heard the explanation, but it just didn't make sense. How could he not know he'd lived this long? How could he not remember being an ancient priest?

Dan's thoughts twisted. In his brain, every question that had ever gone unanswered demanded an answer now. He wanted to know why his mother never let him visit the Johnsons' house down the street. For some reason, they could come over. Jimmy and Mark were always welcome, but he could never go over there.

The whole family moved after their dad had dropped off the face of the earth. Everything about that was weird. Nevertheless, he wanted answers now. He wanted to know what had happened to his dog. Had he really just accidentally gotten out of the yard? Things seemed fishy, even when he was eight years old.

But that had never happened, had it? None of it was real. It was all a part of some spell that he had essentially put on himself. That's what he was supposed to believe now.

"I've got to find Kassidy," he said to himself, trying to knock himself back into the present. He couldn't get her back just to lose her again. This time, potentially, for good.

Marlene would never forgive me.

He drove a little longer, wandered, really. His mind was flooded with information, with questions, with . . . doubt. *What if this is some mass psychosis? What if Kassidy is not in her right mind, or is being brainwashed by Octavia?*

"Damn! Damnit! God. Damn. It!" Dan screamed, as he banged his hand on the steering wheel.

The buzz of his phone snapped his mental break. Pulling over to the side of the road, he read the text message. *She's back.* Two simple words that somehow lifted the weight of the heavens from his shoulders.

He stepped out of his car. Years ago, Marlene had urged him to take in deep breaths of fresh air whenever he felt overwhelmed. She knew he'd never meditate or try yoga. He got plenty of exercise with his morning runs. He was happier when the weather was cool and crisp. In those moments, Dan was focused, relaxed, and ready for anything. So she encouraged him to take deep breaths to calm himself, especially on those cool mornings and evenings, and it worked—every time.

This time was no exception.

As he exhaled, Dan opened his eyes and felt ready for anything. He walked back to his car. As he lifted the door handle, a chill brushed the back of his neck, colder than the brisk wind that drifted through the evening.

"Nice night isn't it?" said a voice from behind.

Startled, Dan dropped his keys on the snow-dusted asphalt. "Jesus Christ!"

"Can't say I've ever been mistaken for him," said the stranger. "But I'll take that as a compliment, I suppose."

Dan let the shock flow away and allowed himself a chuckle, more at ease when the stranger laughed along with him. Dan bent to pick up his keys. When he stood, the stranger was gone. Dan twisted side to side, seeing nothing.

There weren't even any tracks in the light snow.

"Fuck . . ."

Dan quickly slid into his car. It didn't start. He tried again, nothing. The third time was a charm. As he put it in gear, he caught a hint of movement in his peripheral vision.

"Hey, pal, I don't suppose you can give me a ride?" asked a muffled voice.

Dan jumped again, turning to the passenger-side window. The stranger had returned, his face staring at Dan from the outside.

"I mean, the winter feels mild, thankfully, but it's still a bit chilly. I'm not going too far."

Dan placed his head on his steering wheel, doing his best to catch his breath. In this moment, Dan was reminded just why he hated surprise parties, scary movies, roller coasters, and almost all things Halloween.

"Look, pal, I'm sorry. I don't mean to be rude. Any other time, I'd be happy to help, but—"

"You should just drive, Dan," said the stranger in a much clearer and closer voice.

With his head still resting against the steering wheel, Dan turned it slightly. The stranger now sat in the passenger seat. What the fuck? Had the door even opened? His head shot back when he realized that the stranger's eyes glowed dimly.

"Jesus Christ! What the fuck is this?"

"This? This is nothing, Dan. Just needed a lift. I was feeling dead on my feet."

The man gestured with a hand for Dan to drive. With shaky hands, Dan complied, the light crunch of snow compacting beneath his tires seeming to echo like a symphony playing in an empty amphitheater.

"You're him, aren't you?" Dan asked.

"Jesus Christ?" asked the stranger. "No, but I knew him. Nice guy. Owes me seventy thousand dollars. You know, when you adjust for inflation."

"You're the Azra guy, the Angel of Death."

"Ah, that guy. You got me, Dan. I am he," Azra-El said. "I'm going to guess you haven't really heard a lot of good things about me?"

"You'd guess right," Dan replied.

"In my defense, I'm often misunderstood. Much like Lucifer, who's also a very nice guy, I might add. I get a lot of bad press simply for doing my job."

"Your job is killing innocent people before their time?" Dan asked with a bite.

"My job, Dan, is to balance the scales," Azra-El said with some annoyance.

Dan said nothing. He kept driving, though he didn't know where to go. He couldn't go home. Kassidy was back at the house, and he'd be damned if he'd bring her enemy to their doorstep. He drove aimlessly—scared for himself, for Kassidy, for everyone.

"She's going to stop you, you know."

Dan's statement was met with laughter. Psychotic, maniacal, loud laughter.

"You have a lot of faith in her. A lot of faith in a child who just abandoned you and your entire family . . . for another family."

"You were never her family!" Dan shouted as he slammed on the brakes. "You—"

His words were cut off by the realization he was in his car alone. His head swiveled, but Dan saw nothing inside or outside the vehicle. He let out the breath he didn't know he was holding and sat forward, both hands now on the steering wheel as if they were keeping his entire life balanced. After a few seconds, he continued driving, slowly, deliberately, frightfully—wondering if his unwanted passenger would return.

He needed to let Kassidy and Octavia know about Azra-El's appearance, but he didn't want to bring more danger to the house. Dan reached for his phone to call Octavia. All the while, his mind a torrent of thought. He hadn't been prepared for this. He hadn't been prepared for the madness of Kassidy's world.

He hadn't been prepared for the hooded winged skeletal figure standing in the middle of the road as he rounded the corner.

Dan swerved left then right to avoid the creature. His phone fell to the floor. Despite the snow being light, there was enough to cause havoc on the road when vehicles were speeding or out of control— or both. Dan could do nothing to regain control. He'd driven for decades with nothing more than a parking ticket. Even that ticket had been discharged because of extenuating circumstances.

After all this time, Dan Simmons was about to have his first and last car accident.

In fact, Dan Simmons would soon have his last everything.

CHAPTER THIRTY-FOUR

THE GLASS IN KASSIDY'S HAND SHATTERED AS SHE SWALLOWED THE last of her father's Woodford Reserve. Remarkably, she had no cuts or scratches. She brushed her hand free of fragments and dust before walking to the kitchen sink to wash.

"I'll just grab something to clean that up," Octavia said with some apprehension.

Kassidy heard cabinet doors opening as Octavia searched for something to clean the mess, but Kassidy was in her own world. She was still fixated on the words Azra-El had said to her. She wasn't human. She felt human. Perhaps that was a part of the problem. She felt human—or rather, felt humans, all humans. She felt their every emotion. She tried to recall the first time she experienced her empathic abilities. But she couldn't. She couldn't recall one specific time. They had just always been there.

Right now they were focused on the anxiety that surrounded Octavia Lord. Until minutes ago, this woman had been iceberg cool. Now she was the proverbial squirrel in the middle of the busy street.

"What's going on with you?" Kassidy asked as she dried her hands.

The brushing of glass onto the dustpan stopped. She watched Octavia empty the shards into the trash can.

"Well, you literally vanished only to reappear in a cloud of smoke, and then you beelined it to the kitchen, downed bourbon, and broke the glass in your hand. I guess I'm just taking it all in."

Kassidy stared at Octavia. She was lying.

"So, you're telling me, out of everything you've seen, with everything you know, this is what gets to you? A shattered glass?"

"That's what I'm saying," Octavia replied as she returned the broom and dustpan to the pantry.

Kassidy kept her eyes on her. There was some truth in what she was saying. Sincerity and concern were apparent. It was the reason behind those feelings that bothered Kassidy. Octavia was invested in this, originally, because she was a friend of Keiron. Something had shifted though. Ever since they'd come face to face with Dan, Olivia had changed. Her emotional investment felt even more personal.

"You're hiding something from me," Kassidy said.

Octavia paused for the briefest of moments, then inexplicably walked into the living room without saying a word. Kassidy felt her cheeks flush with heat as she followed the professor.

"Hey," Kassidy shouted, "I'm talking to you, dammit."

Kassidy found Octavia staring at family photographs on the mantel above the fireplace. It wasn't the visual of Octavia that stopped Kassidy. It was the invisible wall of guilt she slammed into. It surrounded Octavia like a shield. Kassidy moved slowly and deliberately to break through.

"You seem happy here," Octavia said, pointing to a picture of Kassidy and her sister in a hammock.

"I was. I think," Kassidy said. "I was six when that was taken. At our grandparents' cabin in Wisconsin. We'd gone there for a few weeks one summer. I mean, we went a lot, but that particular time, we stayed longer."

"Why?"

Kassidy hesitated.

"That was the year I first saw Reapers, the first time I actually sensed someone's death before they died."

"That boy from your class?" Octavia asked, still staring at the photograph.

"Yeah, Billy Tate."

Kassidy looked from the photo to Octavia, who finally shifted her gaze. Her emotions were palpable now. Kassidy could taste the sweetness of love, the bitterness of anger, and the guilt that left the aftertaste of chalky aspirin. What was going on with this woman?

"After it happened, the kids at school made fun of me. The whole town really freaked out at my reaction. So as soon as class was over for the summer, Dan and Marlene packed me and Sarah up and took us on a road trip to let things cool down. And, probably, to give us all time to figure out what the fuck was going on with me." Kassidy shrugged.

"You know where I come from, don't you?" Kassidy asked, her eyes still on Octavia.

Apprehensively, Octavia nodded.

"How? And don't tell me because of your research. This all goes far beyond that."

Kassidy was suddenly disappointed that she'd drunk the last of the bourbon. Her hands fidgeted. Her foot tapped inside her shoe.

Octavia was antsy as well.

"It does," she said. "And I suppose now is as good a time as any to talk about that. Maybe we should wait for Dan to—"

"No!" Kassidy shouted. "No more waiting. Tell me what you know. Now!"

Kassidy was as startled as Octavia by the outburst. So much

for calm. There were truths out there. Maybe those truths could save lives, and maybe they couldn't. Maybe they'd have no effect at all. Whatever the case, she deserved . . . something.

"All right," Octavia said with a shaky voice. "It is not a coincidence that you were adopted by the priest of Thanatos."

Kassidy took a step back, fearful of where this conversation was heading.

"Your abilities, your empathic power, your power to sense death and see Reapers . . . are a product of biology, of your heritage," Octavia said. "That heritage is what Azra-El sensed in you. He doesn't understand its origins, but he recognizes the power. That's why he wants you, why he needs you. You're the key to getting to the scythe so he can kill Thanatos and ascend to godhood."

"Why me?"

Kassidy stepped back farther, but Octavia matched her steps and reached out, grabbing Kassidy by the hands. Her knees went limp, and she allowed Octavia to guide her backward until she felt Dan's recliner against the back of her legs. Kassidy lowered herself to sit as Octavia knelt in front of her.

"Because, Kassidy . . . you are a daughter of Death. Thanatos is your father."

CHAPTER THIRTY-FIVE

SENAYA INHALED DEEPLY AS AZRA-EL THRUST INTO HER ONE LAST time. She felt him pour inside of her, and with each pulse she wished that they were still human. She wished that each wave of his seed brought with it the hope of a child, his child, that she could carry and share with him for the rest of their days.

But that life was not to be.

Instead of that life, she lived one in which the man she loved snuck around in the dark and fucked her until he came, only to leave as soon as he was done with her. There were no tender kisses, no soft caresses, and certainly no concerns about her pleasure. She didn't even protest when he called her Allesandra—which happened often.

Thankfully, tonight it didn't.

No, tonight he'd called to her after finding a new abandoned residence to take root in. A condo with a view of the city. She'd come to him, and without a word he'd grabbed her, bent her over the dining room table, lifted her skirt, and entered her—hard and urgent. Senaya said nothing. She cried out when he entered her, but then moaned, because she knew he liked it. As his desire for her rose, so did her desire to please. So did her own pleasure.

Pleasure that meant nothing to him.

When he finished, he removed himself and walked away. Still bent over the table, Senaya pulled her skirt back down, then stood and turned. He didn't wipe himself off, and he made no eye contact. He never did right after. He simply put his cock back into his pants, pulled his zipper up, and went about his business as if nothing had happened.

"Where are we with the old man?" Azra-El asked.

"His soul is secure with the others." Senaya clenched her legs tightly, crossing them at the ankles while standing in front of him as she felt his essence sliding slowly down her inner thigh. It excited her. It didn't matter that he didn't acknowledge she was his lover. She didn't care how he treated her or that he only used her when he needed release. She was chosen. Chosen as his right hand to lead in his absence. Chosen as his confidante and refuge for pleasure.

"Chosen as his whore!" screamed an inner voice that she pushed down.

"Good. Do we know where she is?" he asked.

"We believe she's at his home now, Primus."

She saw it coming this time, but knew that if she made any defensive move, there would be hell to pay. There would be no flying through a wall though. This time she'd brace herself for the strike, giving him satisfaction while mitigating her humiliation.

The strike came hard against her cheek. She rolled with the momentum and turned her body.

It didn't hurt.

Physically.

"You believe? You *believe*? Why don't you go and check!" he demanded.

Senaya stood at attention, feeling more of his seed escape down her inner thigh. When she turned to vapor, that sensation would be gone. And when she re-formed again, all evidence would be gone. Senaya wanted to linger, to feel it a little longer.

But duty called.

And there would be another time.

"Yes, Primus," she said with a slight bow.

"Once you've confirmed that, have the old man dispatched. She needs to know that I'm done playing games," Azra-El said.

"Yes, Primus," she said with hidden delight.

The last image she saw was of her leader, her love, her abuser, sneering as she vanished.

CHAPTER THIRTY-SIX

KASSIDY DIDN'T OFTEN HAVE DIFFICULTY WITH WORDS. THERE WERE some monumental moments in her life where she'd been rendered speechless. Her first kiss. Her first kiss with a woman. Her first sexual encounter. Her first sexual encounter with a woman. Not that she was speechless only during sexual situations, but those stood out because she'd felt vulnerable.

Much like now.

"Kassidy?" Octavia said.

Kassidy heard her name, but it sounded distant, almost as if she were in the Nexus and Octavia were in the real world.

"Kassidy?" Octavia gently shook Kassidy's shoulders.

Kassidy made her way back to reality. She blinked several times, as if somehow that would help her make sense of things, or if she blinked hard and fast enough, she could blow the revelation away. But there was only the truth. The truth of her.

"That's. Not. Possible."

"I know it's a lot to take in," Octavia said, "but it's the truth. Thanatos is your father."

Kassidy shook her head, as if trying to awaken from the strangest of dreams.

"Kassidy, look at me," Octavia said.

The woman's hand on Kassidy's chin stopped her shaking. She allowed the gentle touch to guide her. Opening her eyes, she saw Octavia staring back at her with tears and felt a steady flow of compassion.

"You are his daughter. That is why you have abilities. That is why you are so connected to death and why, unlike other Reapers, you did not have to die to join their ranks."

Kassidy's eyes widened. "Wait. What?"

"Kassidy, you never died."

"That's impossible. You can't become a Reaper unless you die."

"You can if you're the child of a death god," Octavia said. "As you are."

Everything Azra-El ever told her had been a lie. He hadn't saved her from anything. He'd *caused* everything. He altered the course of her history to suit his needs.

"He . . . ruined everything," Kassidy whispered.

"What?" Octavia asked, leaning in slightly.

"Azra-El. He ruined everything. He . . . ruined my life. And for what?"

"For power," Octavia said. "For your power."

"He knows, then?"

"No, I can't imagine how. He only knows that you're different. But he doesn't know how or why."

"And my mother?"

Octavia glanced down. She said nothing, her emotions betraying her once again.

"She's . . . gone, isn't she?"

Octavia said nothing, choosing instead to wipe away a tear on Kassidy's cheek.

"Your mother's name was Allesandra. My sister."

"Your . . . sister?" Kassidy said. "Oh my God! Keiron gave me her journal when I first met him. He knew her, didn't he? He knows about all of this, doesn't he? He's known about me my whole life!"

Octavia's silence spoke volumes.

"Fuck!"

Kassidy sank back into the recliner, confused and relieved, as the day she'd hoped for had finally come—the day she found out who she really was. She felt light-headed, overwhelmed, but she allowed herself to absorb all of it. She looked at Octavia, this woman who was a stranger to her, and felt—

Something is coming!

Kassidy stood abruptly and stepped forward to cover Octavia seconds before the crash through the front door. Large wooden splinters and shards of glass exploded into the living room. The sound of a storm came with it, followed by the appearance of three large, dark funnel clouds. Each cloud entered the house and moved about with speed and urgency, destroying everything they came into contact with. Mirrors shattered, papers scattered, and furniture flew against one wall or another. Kassidy and Octavia huddled together under the weight of the winds, covering each other's heads.

After what seemed like an eternity, the winds died down and coalesced into human forms. Kassidy and Octavia uncovered their heads and found Senaya standing between two male Wraiths of formidable size.

"Hey, ladies," Senaya said. "Sorry about the mess."

Kassidy and Octavia helped each other up and stood in front of their unwanted guests. They separated slightly, giving them both room to move in case they needed to flee. Or fight.

"What do you want, Senaya?" Kassidy asked.

"We were in the neighborhood and thought we'd stop by." Senaya said with sinister sarcasm.

"I'm going to kill you," Kassidy said.

"Tsk-tsk. Is that any way to talk to guests? I would have thought your father raised you better than that."

An image of Dan flashed into Kassidy's mind. He was supposed to be on his way back to the house. She'd forgotten completely. He should be here now.

"What have you done with him?" Kassidy asked through gritted teeth.

She took a step closer to Senaya. In her peripheral vision she noticed Octavia had done the same. Was she stepping up to fight?

"Now, now, young Kassidy. You needn't worry. He's safe for the time being. And by *time being*, I mean, for about another three minutes. Could be the same for that lovely girlfriend of yours and that cute bestie. Francis over here has his eye on him, by the way." Senaya gestured to the Wraith on her left who grinned.

Kassidy's power surged, and her right hand materialized into an onyx sickle. Her new guests' eyes went black as their weapons manifested.

"You really don't want to do this, little girl. You got lucky with the others. But let's face it—it was one-on-one, and they really weren't that good. Do you really think you have a chance against us? Three against one is not the way you want to end your life."

"Three against three," Octavia said, stepping forward and catching a black onyx dagger in midair.

Kassidy glanced past her uninvited guests to see Keiron standing in the doorway, holding a dagger of his own.

"What did I miss?" he asked.

CHAPTER THIRTY-SEVEN

WHEN ALLESANDRA WAS FIFTEEN, SHE WAS PROMISED TO ANOTHER. Such were the traditions of the times. Even then, Azra-El was not one to follow tradition in order to get what he desired. He was eighteen when he first laid eyes on her, when he decided that she was the most beautiful woman he had ever seen, when he decided that she would be his wife.

Their courtship was unorthodox, mostly because no one knew it was happening, least of all Allesandra. Azra-El, then known as Tyran, made every effort to put himself in her path on a regular basis. He befriended her father and soon found himself on hunting trips with him. He was cordial to her mother when he saw her shopping in the town square. He made every effort to make Allesandra laugh when in her presence, because in that laugh was the promise of affection. In that laugh was comfort, beauty, and safety.

In that laugh was love.

Allesandra had never met the man she was promised to, but young Tyran was certain the man paled in comparison to him. There were rumors that the man was, in fact, the son of an elder god. In Tyran's mind, only fools believed in such things. Over the course of one year, Tyran managed to win Allesandra's heart, much to the dismay of her father, who was counting on her marriage to help change their financial circumstance. Her mother believed in love, and quietly supported her daughter and Tyran. Allesandra's father, however, was a traditionalist. Arranged marriages strengthened both families, and he would not jeopardize his legacy by allowing a commoner to wed his oldest child, no matter how much he liked him.

Tyran's love knew no limits, nor did his affection for Allesandra's parents. He knew he was putting them in an awful position, just as he knew he should walk away from it all, especially with the knowledge that her intended was to arrive to meet her on her sixteenth birthday. He knew all this, but he didn't care. This was true love, and it could not be stopped.

Days before Allesandra's birthday, Tyran set out on horseback to intercept her husband-to-be. He wanted to see what type of man would get to spend the rest of his life with a woman who did not belong to him. On his second night out, he came upon a group of four men who'd made camp. Just as he always did, he charmed them enough to be invited to join.

Among them was Lyric, a young lord from the neighboring city on his way to meet his betrothed. Tyran sized the man up. Tall, brown haired, with blue eyes and handsome features, the man had the build of a warrior, the swagger of royalty, and the humility of an old soul. Tyran could not help but like him, even though this was clearly the man who stood in his path.

The group eventually settled down for the night so that they could continue their journey at first light. With the amount of wine they'd consumed, it would likely be a hard sleep and a difficult awakening.

Tyran's thoughts raced, but he focused on one thing—his love for Allesandra. He wanted nothing but the best for her, and it was hard to argue that this suitor was unworthy. Lyric had wealth and charm, and he could no doubt provide her with a comfortable life and many children. She would want for nothing. Her family would be happy and content.

But she wouldn't be with Tyran.

In that moment, he knew what he would do.

As his dagger blade sliced across the neck of the suitor, Tyran covered the man's mouth. It brought Tyran no joy to kill him. As the crimson line across the man's neck flowed to either side of his head, his eyes popped open. Tyran stared absently at the look of horror. He moved his hand to cover the man's nose as well and hoped that the other men were too drunk to be roused by the grunting and flailing. One of them stirred, causing Tyran's heart to beat faster, but it settled when the guard merely turned over in his sleep.

As the life left the suitor's body, Tyran said a silent prayer. He actually meant it. He even mouthed an apology, a whisper carried across a windless night upon dead ears. If this man were the son of an elder god, perhaps he'd be welcomed to the afterlife with favor.

Tyran quickly dispatched the remaining three men. He slashed each of their throats, then returned to each in turn to stab them in the heart. When he sat back to see what he'd done, he smiled. Allesandra would be his forever. Tyran had told her that love would find a way, and it had.

That was the night Death himself appeared before him.

The night that his fate was sealed.

The night he lost his life in exchange for those he'd taken.

He'd become a Reaper, Death's attempt to show him the value and beauty of humanity. Those lessons were lost on him though. He was bitter and angry, fueled by fear and loathing of a being he'd rarely see but would always kneel to. As a Reaper, he attempted to indulge in his former life. He went so far as to tell

Allesandra about what he'd done, about the consequences of his actions, and somehow she had not shunned him. She'd grown to love him even more, so much so that she'd sought ways to fight Death himself to release her love.

She was fierce, but in the end, it had not been enough.

Death took her from Tyran. Not just her life, not just her soul—all of her. Thanatos made Allesandra his and his alone, further torturing Azra-El for the choices he'd made in life. Torturing Azra-El for killing his son.

•   •   •

Azra-El stared out onto the city of Chicago, feeling the cold air blow across his face. It had been another lifetime ago, to be sure, but it had defined him in that life and the next. It defined him as a man who would do anything for the one he loved. Even kill the god of Death. He'd wanted this for so long that it was hard to think of a time when he'd thought of anything else.

Except when Senaya was around.

She'd been with him as he'd healed over the last two decades. She'd dedicated herself to his recovery and led the Wraiths in his stead while keeping the Reapers in line. She made him long for more.

But he could not betray his mission.

He could not betray his Allesandra.

This was all for her. Everything he'd done to this point had been for her. He would bring her back. She would be his immortal queen as he ruled as a god. She was his first and true love.

But what of Senaya?

What was she?

She was a distraction. A beautiful, sensual distraction. She made him feel things that only one person had ever made him feel. She was tempting him, making him betray Allesandra's memory, making him second-guess his mission to bring her back. Senaya was leading him astray, trying to steal his heart.

A heart could not serve two masters, could it?

He tried to push her away, to escape the confusion. He used her, abused her, belittled her, and yet she always came back to him. Why did she always come back? Didn't she know what she was doing? Did she know what *he* was doing?

Azra-El took a deep breath. The frigid air swam through him like a living being, filling his lungs and numbing his mind. With his eyes closed, he thought about his first love. As he settled on the image of Allesandra's face, a warmth inside overpowered the cold that surrounded him.

He felt warmer still as Allesandra's brown eyes turned green. He burned with fire as her long, curly, flowing brown locks turned to a jet-black pixie cut. When Allesandra's pink lips turned into full red lips, the same lips he'd felt on his only hours ago ... when Allesandra's face changed to that of Senaya, causing his heart to beat faster and faster, Azra-El let out the breath he'd been holding.

And he screamed.

◆   ◆   ◆

Twenty Years Ago

When the first celestial onyx dagger drew blood along Azra-El's cheek, Kassidy's confidence swelled. Up to this moment, she wasn't sure if attacking the Angel of Death, her Primus, was the right thing to do. She'd contemplated running. Vanishing. Hiding in the Nexus for the rest of her days. But his power over the Reapers was absolute. When he wanted to find them, he need only think it. The link was unbreakable. She didn't want to spend her life looking over her shoulder. One of two things would happen if she fought him: She'd win, or she'd lose.

Either way, Kassidy would be free.

The red glow in his eyes intensified as he wiped the blood from his cheek. He grinned and licked the crimson smear from his fingers. He seemed elated, almost proud. That was not the reaction she expected.

"I take it you have something on your mind, Reaper?"

Kassidy said nothing. She simply gripped the onyx daggers tighter and moved forward for another strike. She faked a move to the right, ducked, and spun to come at him on the left, but he blocked it expertly. She kicked at him, and he sidestepped. She moved faster and faster, and every move was matched. Frustrated and angry, she backed up to reorient herself.

"Liar!" she screamed, her voice echoing in the empty warehouse Azra-El and his cohorts had been using for years.

"You wound me," Azra-El said. "Literally and figuratively. As much as I'm enjoying this little tango, I do not take this sort of insubordination lightly. Explain yourself before I get angry. And most importantly, tell me where you found those blades."

His face changed when he referenced the blades. Kassidy caught that. He was trying to be calm and cool, but the blades worried him. Just as it said in Allesandra's journal, the blades could hurt the Primus.

"You . . . you lied to me. All those people I . . . I dispatched . . . I . . . I *killed*. It wasn't their time. You son of a bitch! You turned me into a monster! Why? Why would you do this to me?"

Kassidy spoke through tears. Angry, hot tears. She felt the sting of every life she'd snuffed out.

"Do what? Save you from death? Offer you a life beyond the wretched one you were living? Give you power?"

"You made me a killer!" Kassidy spat back.

"You wanted this life!" Azra-El shouted. "You wanted it. You begged for it. You took to it as if born to it. This is what you are."

At those words, Kassidy exploded. She moved in a blur, a furious rage. Her opponent moved and blocked, but he was no match for her ferocity. Kassidy wanted revenge. Eighteen months of training, of taking souls Azra-El had arbitrarily marked for death, culminated in this moment of white-hot rage.

The onyx daggers, stolen from the shop of that bookseller, were the only weapons to stop Azra-El. He'd manifested his scythes and blocked her swings, but Kassidy's bloodlust overwhelmed him. The blade in her left hand pierced his right side, between his ribs. He stumbled, the blade still inside. She spun and delivered a roundhouse directly to his chest, sending him flying back against the concrete wall of the building. Then she threw the second dagger toward Azra-El's limp body, and it found a home in his chest.

His scream brought her pleasure.

Just like the night she'd dispatched Jeremy Reins.

Kassidy walked slowly to him, straddled him, and punched him in the face. Once, twice, three times. She ripped the dagger from his chest and wiped the blood on her thigh. With her left hand, she grabbed the dagger embedded in his side and pushed further—twisting.

Azra-El's power subsided, and his eyes reflected hers. They'd changed from silver to black.

"You are more like me than you know, little one." Azra-El laughed.

"I'm nothing like you!"

"Oh, but you are. You think this is a victory? Taking me out? Someone has to take my place. In the end, there still has to be balance."

"You lied to me. You used me. You made me a killer. The only balance that's needed is the end of your miserable existence."

Kassidy ripped the other blade from Azra-El's side. She crisscrossed both against his throat and pressed hard.

"Once you walk down this path, you'll never find peace. They'll come for you," Azra-El said.

"They?" Kassidy asked. "You mean your precious Wraiths?"

Azra-El gave a small snarl.

"Yeah, I know all about them. I know what they are, and I know you used those unsanctioned deaths, all those kills I made, to create them. You gave them a portion of your power and then used those deaths to fuel them. Don't you worry though. I took one out. I can take the rest out too."

With that, Kassidy spread her arms apart, cutting across Azra-El's throat. But he did not turn to dust and drift off into the ether. His wounds bled more, but his throat did not. His eyes stared forward, in surprise, but he did not move.

It was done.

He was no more.

In the background, Kassidy heard a rush of wind, loud, furious, and swift. They were coming to his aid, his precious Wraiths. A part of her wanted to stay and fight. Take them on and destroy them all. But she was spent. With her daggers in hand, she dematerialized, and floated off to a new life.

To a life of freedom and redemption.

CHAPTER THIRTY-EIGHT

"WELL, IT'S JUST ONE BIG HAPPY REUNION HERE, ISN'T IT?" SENAYA SAID.

Keiron walked around the trio of Wraiths to stand with Octavia and Kassidy. Senaya kept her gaze on him as he took his place.

"You look good, old man. What's it been, two, three hundred years since our last rodeo?"

Kassidy's face contorted. She hadn't known. This added some joy to Senaya's day.

"What is it that you want, Senaya?" Keiron asked, clearly trying to change the subject.

Senaya rolled with it, though she desperately wanted to be a fly on the wall in the conversations to come.

"As I was telling the ladies before you arrived, we were in the neighborhood and thought we'd stop by. You know, catch up with our favorite Reaper."

"I'm not a fucking Reaper anymore!" Kassidy exclaimed.

"Well, honey," Senaya began with a chuckle, "that sickle you formed tells a different story. Once a Reaper, always a Reaper."

"I'm so tired of hearing that," Kassidy said.

Senaya took satisfaction in the tension growing in her foe. Kassidy's jaws clenched, her eyes narrowed, and her brow furrowed as a second sickle manifested in her free hand. Senaya widened her grin. She waited with practiced restraint and bathed in the psychological torture.

"Double fisting, eh? You know, I heard you had a problem. I thought it was booze though. Tell me, is that why your girl left you?"

Kassidy stepped forward, but Senaya stood firm as Keiron held back the lost Reaper.

"Are you here to fight or talk?" Kassidy asked.

"Actually, neither. Just wanted to deliver a message really. But then you came all hard, brandishing weapons and whatnot, and then this one"—Senaya pointed to Keiron—"shows up all dramatic and shit, throwing daggers in the air. I tell you, if this is modern hospitality, send me back to the Middle Ages."

"Give your message and move on," Octavia said.

"Ah, yes, the professor. We almost had you, didn't we? If not for this 'non-Reaper,' as she wants to be known, you'd be under lock and key, telling us everything."

"Don't be so sure," Octavia said.

"In any event, we just wanted to remind you to deliver the Scythe of Cronus and yourself, of course, to Azra-El. It's like . . . a courtesy call. Isn't that what they do in this century?" Senaya swiveled her head to each of her companions for confirmation. They just grinned, which was fine. These two were merely muscle. Guards to keep her Primus safe. "Oh, and one more thing," Senaya said, pretending to look at a watch on her wrist, "your daddy is off to the Beyond. That's a good thing, right? He can see your mommy again. Maybe both of them."

Senaya hadn't expected Kassidy to lunge at her, but she certainly wasn't caught off guard. As if scripted, a battle ensued. Senaya blocked, ducked, and dodged everything Kassidy threw at her. Her companions fought the professor and Keiron respectively, and strangely, the battles appeared to be evenly matched. She expected that from Keiron. But the professor held her own remarkably well, for a teacher.

Senaya feigned retreat, bent slightly, and held up her right forearm to block Kassidy's sickle from coming down on her head. She manifested her own weapons and charged Kassidy, oddly pleased at the skill with which Kassidy defended herself.

"I see you haven't forgotten what I taught you," Senaya said.

"Fuck you, bitch!"

Kassidy moved faster, pushing Senaya back toward the door. Senaya blocked each blow, but the intensity had increased, causing her concentration to waver enough for her hands to re-form.

"Maybe after we're done here, I can go visit your sis and send her up for a reunion too."

It was enough of a taunt to cause Kassidy to lower her guard. Senaya grinned and struck the girl twice with a closed fist, which she followed with a kick to the stomach.

Kassidy doubled over.

"Losing your focus, love bug?" Senaya asked before delivering an uppercut that sent Kassidy sailing back against the wall. Kassidy landed hard and slid to the floor. Senaya laughed. "I see those baby blues have returned. Power running near empty, is it?"

Keiron and the professor paused to glance towards Kassidy, opening them up to brutal attacks. The Wraiths stabbed their respective opponents in the belly. Keiron and the professor fell to their knees. The professor dropped her dagger, grabbed at her stomach, and toppled over.

"That's two down," Senaya said.

She glanced at Keiron, who scowled at her. With a surprising surge of energy, he rose to one knee, unsheathed a hidden dagger held at his ankle, and drove it into the Wraith before him.

"Son of a bitch!" Senaya exclaimed.

She could do nothing to stop what was coming next. The

blade, just like the sickles the Wraiths manifested, was made of celestial onyx, the only metal that could damage an immortal, the only weapon that could kill a Reaper or Wraith. Keiron's opponent cried out, then slowly dissipated into black vapor before vanishing forever.

With one final breath, Keiron turned to her and said, "You won't win this."

Senaya sauntered over to Keiron and bent slightly.

"My dear, we are well on our way."

Keiron slumped over, face first. Kassidy yelled out, and Senaya whirled, facing her. At the height of her scream, Kassidy's eyes turned black, and she dematerialized into black vapor, reforming in front of Senaya with two sickles.

"What the fuck?" Senaya said. "That's not possible."

Senaya ducked a swing from Kassidy, narrowly missing a slice across the throat. She wasn't quick enough to avoid Kassidy's follow through, which sliced her forearm.

"Get her, damn you!" Senaya screamed to the remaining Wraith.

He surged toward Kassidy, but his movements were sloppy, ragged, and uncoordinated. Within seconds he took multiple hits to the face and a kick to the gut followed by a fatal blow across his stomach. Still stunned by Kassidy's transformation, the sound of Kassidy striding toward her snapped Senaya back to attention, as her guard vanished into ash. She blocked blow after blow before finally catching Kassidy off guard with a fake lunge. Senaya's final blow was a roundhouse kick to the face that dropped Kassidy to the ground. Senaya stood over her, surprised as Kassidy tried to rise again. Her eyes changed from black to silver.

"Damn you! All you had to do was die!" Senaya yelled in disbelief.

She punched Kassidy again, driving the girl back to the ground.

"Bring the scythe. Surrender your life. Your friends live. It's that fucking simple."

With a final kick to the head to knock Kassidy unconscious, Senaya dematerialized to vapor and left the Simmons home.

CHAPTER THIRTY-NINE

THE NEXUS EXISTED BETWEEN WORLDS. IN MANY WAYS, IT WAS A world of its own. It came complete with its own rules, its own feeling, its own sense of self. Time was different there. Legend had it that a woman, hiding from a god, had once found her way into the Nexus and given birth to her first and only child. When she finally decided to leave with her child, generations had passed. Horses had been replaced with machines that traveled at high speeds, and man took to the skies in metal tubes with wings. Buildings touched the heavens, and voices could be heard in devices with pictures. What seemed like a year, maybe only a few months in the Nexus, had been an eternity outside of it.

Kassidy knew exactly where she was. There was no questioning that. She thought about that old Nexus legend, and for the first time in all her travels in and out of that place, she wondered whether she should even bother returning to the real world. She'd always felt so at home in the Nexus anyway.

What was left for her?

Who was left for her?

Would anyone even know she was gone?

Kassidy rose to her feet. The Nexus was typically an ethereal manifestation of the real world you'd just left. The grayish-green tint of the Nexus gave no comfort. The rolling tendrils of fog and cloud always seemed sentient. She saw bodies and furniture. She was still in her family home, but here, everything was so lifeless.

Where is Octavia's spirit?

Where's Keiron's?

As familiar as this was, something was different. The Nexus felt colder. Kassidy could actually see her breath as she exhaled. She couldn't even remember breathing in this place in the past. The grayish green was darker, more ominous. Fear was unusual for a Reaper, especially in this place. Yet that was all she felt.

"Fancy seeing you here."

Kassidy whirled, following the voice toward the open door of the home, and found a familiar face.

"Denzel!"

"Beg your pardon?"

"What the fuck is going on?"

Kassidy marched toward the being in front of her. He'd changed his suit. It was a dark-gray three-piece ensemble, complete with handkerchief and timepiece. This man was a throwback. Was he old, or did he just appreciate old styles?

Kassidy glared into his dark eyes. That familiar smirk radiated across his face. She hated that damned smirk. It was cute, actually. Downright sexy, and that, more than anything, was why she hated it.

"Why did you pull me back in here?" Kassidy asked.

"I didn't."

"Then how did I get here?"

"Well, let's examine that, shall we? There are only three reasons a Reaper enters the Nexus. To escort a soul to the next plane, because they are pulled in by a more powerful force, or—"

"Because they want to," Kassidy said.

"So, since I didn't bring you here, and since I see no souls, the real question is, why do you want to be here?"

Kassidy kicked at the fog rolling along the ground. She'd always been fascinated by how the fog responded to movements. There was absolutely no reason to be fascinated by such a thing, and yet it provided a distraction every time.

Kassidy stared at the devastation in her family home, no less horrific through the veil of the Nexus. All she'd ever wanted in life was to be normal. When she couldn't have that, she'd embraced everything she was. At least, she thought she had. But even that was twisted and perverted, and so she ran, as fast and as far as she could—only to find that her life, such as it was, was not something she could ever escape. She wanted out, but something wouldn't allow that.

Or . . . someone.

"Who are you?" she turned her attention back toward the mystery man.

"Denzel?"

Kassidy rolled her eyes, then closed them tightly. She wanted to scream, but she held back.

"Who . . . the fuck . . . are you?"

There was a palpable pause, and in that moment, she opened her eyes. A part of her expected fake Denzel to be gone. To her surprise and satisfaction, he wasn't. His smirk was gone though. He still carried an air of superiority, of confidence, of power, but that smirk was finally gone.

"My name is Jacen Lucas," he said. "I'm an associate, shall we say, of your father's."

That was not an answer Kassidy expected. An associate? What did that even mean? And exactly how many people knew she was the daughter of Thanatos?

Why are people lying to me?

"Are you a god?"

"A god? No. I'm something different. God-adjacent, if you will," Jacen said.

"I don't understand what that means," Kassidy said. "Fuck! I don't understand any of this! Why am I here?"

"I thought we—"

"Don't you say a fucking word," Kassidy said through clenched teeth.

She walked over to Octavia and knelt, waving away the fog from her aunt's body. She felt Jacen's presence. He was closer, but not too close. A wise move.

"Are you able to give me answers? Or are you just here to be a cryptic fucking cliché and speak in riddles and shit?"

"I am here to give as much information and direction as I can, without actually doing for you what you must do for yourself," he answered.

"So, cryptic fucking riddles then?"

He laughed faintly. For some reason, it didn't annoy her. It didn't endear him to her, but at the very least it didn't annoy her. That was some kind of progress.

"Can I assume you're here to give me a message?"

"You can assume anything you want," Jacen replied.

Kassidy was startled by his sarcasm. Generally only Keiron talked to her that way. She inclined her head toward Jacen, a sign of respect, and turned back to Octavia. Everything felt unfair.

Then again, most of the events of her life felt unfair.

"I understand that none of this is easy, Kassidy. But we are all pawns in the greater scheme of things. We must all play our part," Jacen said with a grandiose Shakespearean gesture.

Jacen stepped closer and knelt beside Kassidy. She felt his gaze on her but felt no discomfort. If anything, she felt calm and strangely supported.

"I didn't ask for this. Any of this," she said.

"I know."

"I don't want any of this. Can you just take me away? Can you send me to the Void?"

"No."

"Why not?"

"Several reasons," Jacen said. "Principle among them, that is not your destiny."

"Then what is?"

"Balance, my dear. Your destiny is to restore the balance. Azra-El has done terrible things over the years, and it has upset that balance."

"Then why can't my father restore it?"

She searched his face for an answer. His stare was blank, clinical, yet educational. Without saying a word, he challenged her to put the pieces together and answer the question herself. She didn't know what the hell he was trying to get at, though. Nothing made sense, and her mind felt like a building in an uncontrolled explosion. Pieces of data flew everywhere, a debris field of unorganized chaos, and at its core, the detonator—her emotions.

"Think, Kassidy," Jacen said softly.

Kassidy closed her eyes. She tried to let the emotion drain away. She focused on recent events, on her father, David and Lynn. Each thought led to a wince of pain. She tensed and ground her teeth, smothering a scream.

"Get your shit together, Kassidy!" she said to herself. She needed to focus. She needed to find some semblance of balance. Her emotions were all over the place and that would not help her back in the real world. Taking a deep breath, she let her thoughts wander, searching for one thing that had brought her joy amid the recent destruction.

"Traci," she whispered.

Allowing thoughts of meeting Traci to fill her mind, Kassidy's tension drifted away as she pictured their night together. She didn't remember the details, though she had a sense she'd been happy—at the very least, she'd felt safe. Even the next morning, with the madness unfolding, Traci had simply been present. Traci hadn't judged her, hadn't second-guessed her, and offered nothing but unconditional understanding—all without really even knowing her. That gave her hope. Hope that despite all around her, there were still good people in the world. People who would let her simply be Kassidy—whatever that meant. That hope eased her tension.

With calm overtaking her, the pieces of her complex puzzle connected. Azra-El's return, the augmentation of her powers, the emergence of the Reapers and Wraiths—more people dying. People were dying, and Azra-El was feeding from that. That was how he upset the balance. The natural order would demand a response to his rise in power though. It would demand balance to the overreaching power Azra-El was demonstrating.

"My power is growing as his does," Kassidy said softly.

"Yes," Jacen said, drawing out the word, acknowledging her growing understanding.

"It's growing to counteract his, but it's not enough. That's why I need the Scythe of Cronus."

Kassidy opened her eyes and turned her head slightly to regard Jacen. His smirk had returned, but she paid little attention to it. Understanding washed over her.

She knew why she was here.

She knew why she had to stop him.

Only one question remained.

"If you're here, and I'm left to clean up this clusterfuck, where is my father?"

"Your father," Jacen said, "is missing."

CHAPTER FORTY

"IS IT DONE?"

"Yes, Primus," Senaya said.

"Casualties?"

"Two," Senaya said. "The Wraiths that accompanied me were destroyed, Primus."

"By whom?"

"By . . . her."

Senaya braced herself for a blow to the gut, or the head, or anywhere he saw fit to inflict pain. Those Wraiths meant nothing to Azra-El. If she'd told him their names, he'd have no fucking clue who they were or what they'd done for him in his absence. Of course, she'd deliberately not informed her leader how she and those Wraiths orchestrated the imprisonment of Thanatos. She wanted to save that as a surprise. She wanted Azra-El to know that it was she who planned the capture of the god. She wanted him to know that it was she who was instrumental in Azra-El's ascension—all but assured once he had the Scythe of Cronus.

Once that bitch was dead.

Her thoughts had wandered, returning to the present when she realized he had not struck her. This brought some relief, and much confusion.

"Good."

That's all? That's all he has to say. Good?

"Primus?" Senaya spoke hesitantly. "About the girl . . ."

"Kassidy," he corrected.

"Yes, Kassidy." She held back her rage at his correction and the bile gathering in the back of her throat at the mention of her name. "I wonder if . . . I wonder if her power isn't growing beyond our expectation?"

She braced herself again. Senaya was a trusted lieutenant and advisor, but only advised when asked, and Azra-El had not asked in decades. She'd never be his equal, but she at least wanted to feel as if her thoughts and opinions mattered. Senaya wanted the respect she once had. Respect that had been hers before that bitch Kassidy Simmons appeared on their radar. Senaya wanted to be more than just a punching bag and an occasional plaything.

She wanted to stand at the side of a god.

"Explain," Azra-El said, his eyes glowing red.

"When we fought, for several moments, her eyes, they . . . they turned black."

Azra-El expression was unexpected. There was no sign of concern. He asked no follow-up question. He simply allowed his glowing eyes to dim to their natural brown, and he chuckled.

CHAPTER FORTY-ONE

KASSIDY'S MOTHER WAS GONE. HER FATHER WAS MISSING. *How can a god be missing? How was any of this even . . .*

Her thoughts trailed as she focused on Octavia's body. Kassidy shifted her vision, an ability that allowed her to see death at its various stages. When death was near, when someone was marked, as she called it, a reddish glow surrounded them. When she was younger, she didn't have the strength to control that ability. At any given moment she'd simply see a red glow surround a person, and before long, they were gone. With a child's curiosity, she'd linger and watch as the red glow dimmed from a bright red to a pale pink, and then, inexplicably, to a flat gray, which was, for her, the absence of life and the beacon that called them—the Reapers. But no Reapers came for Octavia, and her soul was nowhere to be found.

When Kassidy peered closer, she understood why.

"She's immortal," she said in a low voice.

"She is indeed," Jacen said. "The blow of a Reaper blade is not fatal to her, but it will take a little longer to heal from."

With a sense of relief, Kassidy let her body fall limp. She was exhausted, more so mentally than physically. She was about to ask Jacen another question about her father, when movement caught her eye.

"Keiron?"

His body stirred before settling to a position on all fours. Kassidy again shifted her vision. The normal blue hue that surrounded humans was nonexistent. In its stead was the brightness of gold. It enveloped him like sunshine.

Keiron frowned at the destruction surrounding him. Scanning the room, he found Octavia and Kassidy's bodies. Rushing to Kassidy, he knelt and checked her pulse. He seemed relieved when he found it. Kassidy watched as he took the hand of her slumbering form and held it, gently stroking it.

"Come on, Kass," he said, "I need you to wake up. There's work to be done."

Kassidy stood and stared blankly.

"You never told me why you were here, in the Nexus," she said.

"I'm here to help," Jacen replied.

"And yet you've done nothing."

"And still, you've asked nothing of me," he countered.

Without averting her gaze from Keiron, Kassidy asked, "Where is the Scythe of Cronus?"

"In all honesty, I do not know."

"Then again, what good are you to me?"

The voice in the back of her mind screamed at her to hurt him, to make him tell her everything he knew. But she suspected it would accomplish nothing. She had no clue about the limits of his power. For all she knew, he could blink and wipe her from existence. Unlikely, of course, but anything was possible.

"I can tell you this much, Kassidy Simmons. You're thinking too much. Overthinking in fact. Your father hid the scythe, leaving it for you to find."

"And how do I find it, dammit? Where do I start?"

That fucking smirk returned to his face, and Kassidy was

seconds away from letting the voice in the back of her mind take control.

"Consider whom he entrusted it to," Jacen said.

"How does that help?"

"Stop being so stubborn and think, dammit!"

Kassidy began to respond, then thought better of it. Not out of fear, but because she realized she was being a bitch. A petulant child who wanted her way. An easy way.

"He gave it to the person he trusted most," Kassidy said.

"What would you do if tasked to protect something so important? Where would you hide it?"

"Someplace that's important to me. With ... someone who means ..."

Oh shit!

"Dan's suicide attempt! He would have subconsciously gone to it, then he would have moved it after he was done. It's—"

Before her words could escape, Jacen Lucas shimmered out of view. Frustrated and confused, Kassidy glanced back down at Keiron. He was stroking her head, comforting her, still begging her to open her eyes. When she'd first awakened in the Nexus, Kassidy had been fully prepared to stay forever. Ready to run from anything and everything in the real world. She knew now that she couldn't.

She had to go back.

CHAPTER FORTY-TWO

KEIRON HELPED KASSIDY TO HER FEET. SHE WAS UNSTEADY. MORE so psychologically than physically. Moving away from Keiron, she edged toward Octavia again, knelt, then lifted her aunt with a strength she'd never known. Octavia was as light as air. Kassidy walked effortlessly to the couch, lowered Octavia to it, then lovingly brushed hair from her face.

"She'll be okay," Keiron said.

"I know."

"You—"

"What are you?"

"Pardon?"

Kassidy turned to face Keiron, wonder, sadness, and disappointment on her face. He heard the question. He was stalling. She could sense conflict within him, but it was soon overshadowed with relief. That shift was accompanied by a slight grin.

"You both had the same wound," Kassidy said, nodding her head toward Octavia. "I get why she's not dead, though I don't understand how she's immortal. What I don't get is why *you're* still here."

"She told you?"

Kassidy nodded.

"Everything?"

"Obviously not." She held her arms out toward him in the universal what-the-fuck gesture.

Keiron wandered toward the fireplace and stared at the one photo that remained undamaged from the battle. A picture of Dan Simmons sitting on the front porch of their lake house, with Kassidy and Sarah sitting on either side of him. Dan and Sarah seemed happy. Kassidy was smiling, but that smile was a mask. Even in the photo, anyone who knew her well could see that.

"I've known your father since he was born," Keiron said. "Even as a child it was easy to see that he would grow to be a good man. He's one of the best I've known in all my years on this earth."

Kassidy eyes teared up, which made her mad, for many reasons. Chief among them was that she felt as if she was tearing up far too often. She was hard pressed to recall a time when she'd been so emotional. Even when she felt the emotions of others, she was able to control their physical manifestation, but lately her life overwhelmed her.

Of course, being lied to by another so-called friend also sparked her anger.

"Exactly how long have you been alive?"

"Honestly, I'm not even sure anymore. A couple thousand years, give or take." He shrugged.

"Then what? What the fuck are you? A god? Are you . . . are you my . . . are you Tha—"

"No. No, Kassidy. I am definitely not Thanatos."

Kassidy felt relief and sadness simultaneously. Not from Keiron, but from herself. As angry as she was, given all he'd done for her throughout her life, the brief thought of Keiron being her father had given her a sense of joy and peace. Of course, it also made her cringe, as she recalled the crush she'd had on him when she was younger.

Younger. Dammit!

"Jesus Christ, you haven't fucking aged a day since I've known you. Why the hell didn't I see it?"

"Honestly, I don't think you wanted to. You didn't want to, you weren't ready to, and now . . . now it's being thrust upon you. All of this is being shoved in your faced, and you're forced to deal with and accept things that you never wanted and weren't prepared for."

"Why didn't anyone tell me?"

"I think we hoped to spare you from it all. We were hoping you'd be able to drift through life unscathed. Live without the sins of your father following you through the ether."

"Good plan."

Keiron shrugged again, and Kassidy moved into the kitchen. In the back of her mind was a sense of urgency, a fire doused by the waters of ambivalence. There was much to be done, but she was frozen with indecision. Or was it fear? Kassidy did the same thing she did each time she was faced with these sensations.

She searched the kitchen for something to drown her sorrows. She remembered she'd finished the bourbon earlier, so she settled for vodka.

"Drinking is not going to solve this," Keiron said in the background.

"I'm sorry—what are you again?" she asked, completely ignoring his statement as she drank.

"My father, like yours, was a god."

Kassidy laughed uncomfortably as she poured more vodka. She gulped it, all in one fluid motion. It burned her throat. There was nothing smooth about the colorless spirit sliding down her esophagus.

"Which one? Maybe we're related," she said, wincing as the liquid continued to burn.

"I'm pretty sure we are. They're all related in some way."

Another pour.

Another drink.

Another anxious, uncomfortable laugh.

"So, Keiron, who's your daddy?"

As her one-time crush, mentor, and best friend leaned back against the kitchen wall, Kassidy pushed the bottle and glass away from her, then braced herself against the kitchen sink. Something in his hesitation made her uncomfortable.

"Cronus, or the elder god most commonly associated with him. That was the name he used when I was born, though," he said flatly.

Kassidy threw her hands in the air.

"Sure. Why the fuck not. Of course your dad was the owner of the very weapon I'm supposed to find. The one you said was just a legend. I don't suppose you've known all along where the fucking thing is? I mean, maybe your dad and my dad collaborated. Blood is thicker than water, right?"

"Kassidy—"

"Nope. Nope. Just don't. You've had a couple thousand years, give or take, to live with all of this shit. I've had a couple days. A drop in the bucket comparatively, wouldn't you say?"

It was rhetorical, of course, and she was thankful Keiron recognized that too. Fortunately, he wasn't a horse's ass like . . .

Horse's ass? No. Way!

"You changed your name, didn't you? You're . . . you're . . . Chiron. You're a fucking centaur!"

"Clearly not." He gestured toward his legs.

"In all those myths, though . . ."

"I was extremely skilled at horseback riding." He held up his hands up. "I was trick riding before it was a thing. They used to say it was as if I were one with the horse. I think something was lost in translation."

"I'd say so." Kassidy wanted to insert an inappropriate joke about horse genitalia, but then she remembered she was mad. "Why didn't you tell me this? Any of this!"

As he moved toward her, she shrank into herself, making herself small, feeling like a little girl again. All this adulting—adulting with gods and monsters no less—was draining.

"I mean, people keep telling me I wasn't ready to accept it, but nobody seems willing to entertain the notion that if I'd known this at an early age, everything would feel normal—the one fucking thing I always wanted to feel."

A wave of guilt hit Kassidy like an uppercut. She'd never felt anything so strong. It caused her to lose balance for a moment. It wasn't just coming from Keiron though. His guilt was strong, but this was on another level. There was enough emotion for multiple people. Shaking it off, she watched Octavia stagger into the kitchen, holding her stomach and moving to stand next to Keiron. *Well there you have it.* Their faces wore a collective look of apology and acknowledgment that they'd seriously fucked up.

Kassidy could only shake her head and laugh.

Then she dematerialized into vapor and escaped.

CHAPTER FORTY-THREE

IT NEVER FAILED. WHENEVER KASSIDY FELT LOST OR SAD, WHENEVER she needed to get away to gain perspective or to simply escape until she felt strong enough to cope, she came to this spot in the city. With the Adler Planetarium on her right and the Shedd Aquarium to her left, there was nothing but a majestic view of downtown Chicago before her. The headlights of the cars traveling down Lake Shore Drive shone amongst the bright lights of the buildings and skyscrapers. In the distance, Navy Pier was illuminated.

During the day, downtown Chicago was beautiful. Amid the gray and sterile concrete resided a city rich with culture, sophistication, and just enough arrogance to know that it was something special. To the residents, it was home. Even when it was ugly, it was home. The tourists looked beyond the concrete, steel, and asphalt and saw the architecture and historic buildings that stood the test of time. They saw a river that ran through the heart of downtown lined with businesses, walkways, and passersby. There was a sense of urgency, but also a respect . . . for time. Times past . . . and times yet to come.

So much life.

So much joy.

So many people oblivious to the danger that awaited them because she was unable to act.

But she wasn't unable. She wasn't even unwilling. Her girlfriend—her ex-girlfriend—lay near death in a faraway hospital because of her. Her friend David was the same, and for the same reason. Dan Simmons, the man who'd raised her, was dead. Again, because of her. She was the daughter of Death, and it seemed, in light of all the pending doom around her, she was living up to that legacy.

But here with this view, this space was her safe place, her sanctuary, her personal Nexus. Here, no one could harm her. Here, there were answers to all the questions of life—and death.

Kassidy closed her eyes and breathed deeply. The cold air filled her lungs, and when she let out that breath, she felt lighter, as if she could fly.

"What's a nice girl like you doing in a place like this?"

Startled, Kassidy shot to her feet and turned around, her right hand in the form of a sickle, ready for battle.

"Well, that's new."

"Oh my God! Lynn?"

Kassidy stared in disbelief as Lynn's eyes traveled from Kassidy's hand to her face and back again. After a short time, awareness set in, and Kassidy's hand re-formed.

"Neat trick," Lynn said.

Kassidy said nothing. She was speechless for what seemed like the hundredth time this week. Lynn walked down the small hill to the concrete walkway where Kassidy stood. Her movements seemed effortless. There was something . . . off. Kassidy wanted to step toward her and embrace her, but she couldn't.

She'd never be able to again.

"You're . . . you're gone," Kassidy said softly.

Lynn nodded once.

"I'm too late? I can't save you now?"

"Before you start beating yourself up, babe," Lynn began, holding her hand up, "you need to know that even if you had killed the big bad wolf, I still would have died. My injuries were far too extensive. Nothing you would have done was going to prevent that."

Kassidy's legs weakened. She fell against the concrete rise and slid down, landing hard on her ass. Lynn ran to her, knelt, and placed her hand on Kassidy's leg.

Kassidy felt her touch.

She shouldn't be able to do that.

"How?" Kassidy asked, looking from her leg to Lynn's face.

"I don't know how these things work. I died. Some hot dude showed up and asked a favor, asked me to talk to you. I agreed, but only if I could touch you, because without that sensation one last time, even heaven would feel like hell."

Kassidy put one hand on top of Lynn's, then caressed her face with the other. She was so soft. Softer than she'd been in life, and that was saying something. Kassidy traced Lynn's lips with her thumb, then leaned in for a kiss. It was slow, deliberate, and despite everything, so warm.

"I'm so sorry, Lynn. This is all my fault. Everything . . . it's . . . it's because of me. Because of my past, my father, my—"

"Shhh. It's all right, sweetheart. It's all going to be all right."

"How is this all right?" Kassidy asked. "Nothing about this is all right. You're dead. My dad is dead. David is—"

"David is going to be okay. He woke up about an hour ago."

"Seriously?"

"Yeah."

"Are you sure?"

"Positive. Saw it with my own eyes," Lynn said.

"How? His soul . . ."

"Was liberated like mine was."

Kassidy sat confused. None of this made sense. *Why would Azra-El hold David's and Lynn's souls hostage only to let them be taken? Was it a trap? Was this even the real Lynn?*

"The hot guy that I made the deal with. He did it," Lynn said.

"The hot guy?"

A pang of jealousy jabbed Kassidy at the thought of Lynn referring to a man as hot. There was an air of reverence in Lynn's voice that made Kassidy's gut churn. She recognized the hypocrisy of those feelings given her recent night with Traci, so she pushed them aside.

"Wait," Kassidy said. "Did this guy look like Denzel Washington in a three-piece suit?"

"I got more of a Chadwick Boseman vibe. But spot on with the suit. You've met him?"

Kassidy nodded.

"Jacen. Jacen Lucas," Kassidy said.

"Yeah, that's what he said."

"Boseman, huh? Black Panther?"

"You know it," Lynn replied.

Both women laughed, and Kassidy realized that she had genuinely laughed so infrequently lately, that when she did, it sounded like a stranger. It felt good. In that same moment, she wondered if she'd ever laugh that way again. Without Lynn, could she?

"You've got a lot on your mind, babe, and a lot to do. Jacen told me everything, or rather, showed me. He's got some weird kind of ability. It's like my head is full of knowledge about Reapers and Wraiths . . . and you."

"You know everything?"

Lynn nodded.

Shame filled every cell in Kassidy's body. She wondered if it was strong enough for Lynn to feel. Hell, she felt so much shame, Lynn could probably taste it on her tongue if she stuck it out.

"How can you not see that none of this is your fault?" Lynn asked.

"How is it not?"

"You're just as much a pawn in all of this as I am."

"And if you'd never met me, you wouldn't have had to make a deal with a brooding vampire look-alike to see me one last time," Kassidy said.

"But I did meet you. And I did have to make that deal. And you know what? Fuck it!"

Kassidy stood with Lynn, her eyes locked on hers.

"Kass, it is what it fucking is. You can either cry about it and give up, or you can get off your ass and accept that this is your life. Yours! You can do with it what you will, but what you can't deny is who you are."

"I don't know who I am!" Kassidy screamed.

"Yes. You. Do."

Kassidy shook from the anxiety. Was her last talk with Lynn going to be a fight? She didn't have it in her to argue. The last time they'd spoken, things were cold and painful. She couldn't do that now.

When she felt Lynn's hand on her cheek, she knew it wouldn't be that way again.

"You know exactly who you are, Kass. Now more than ever, you know exactly who you are. That is how you will survive. That is how you will save everyone else and defeat this asshole."

Kassidy heard the words, but all she saw was the face of the woman she'd loved in life and disappointed to death, literally.

"Does it even matter now?" Kassidy asked.

As she said the words, she felt Lynn move to stand behind her, then felt the softness and warmth of her body against hers. Lynn's arms wrapped around her, and Lynn rested her head on Kassidy's shoulder. Kassidy had never felt so safe. A part of her wanted to stay in this moment forever.

"That is why it matters," Lynn said, gesturing toward the city. "Everything you see there, everything you love, will be gone if you don't step up and do what you need to do."

"But I love you," Kassidy said.

With a squeeze, Lynn replied, "I know you do. I love you, too. That will never change for either of us. But for those people, those millions in this city and so many others, you are the only hope they have to enjoy the same thing we felt and will always feel for one another."

Once again a wave of guilt crashed upon her. "Lynn . . . I . . . I . . ."

Lynn spun her around and kissed her on the lips and forehead. Caressing Kassidy's face again, she said, "I know, love. I know what happened . . . and it's okay."

She knows about Traci? Oh my God!

"How can you possibly forgive me?" Kassidy asked.

"There's nothing to forgive. Our love is forever, even if our relationship isn't. I love you for all that you are and all that you will be. Now it's time for you to do the same. Learn to love yourself, Kass."

Kassidy pulled Lynn into a hug. She held on tightly, as if letting her go would undo all of creation.

"It's time to go, Lynn," said a familiar voice from behind.

"No!" Kassidy said.

"I'm sorry, Kassidy. I truly am," Jacen said.

Kassidy held strong.

"It's okay, sweetheart," Lynn said. "I've learned that there's a shit ton more to life than I could ever imagine. It doesn't seem unreasonable to think that we'll see each other again."

Kassidy loosened her hold and took a half step back.

There were no tears this time. She was no longer shaking. As if a switch had flipped, Kassidy was calm and secure and filled with love. But it wasn't her—it was Lynn. She felt everything and absorbed it. Her body drank in the comfort to intoxication.

"I'm going to the good place," Lynn said.

"The Beyond," Kassidy said.

"Yeah. Can you visit?" Lynn asked.

"No," Kassidy replied. "But one day, I'll see you there."

She kissed Lynn one last time, then watched as she faded slowly into nothing.

Taking a deep breath, Kassidy turned to face Jacen. He had the flat affect of a man who felt nothing, but somehow, Kassidy knew better. She couldn't feel anything from him, which only gave her pause. Somehow she knew he was not soulless.

"Thank you for that," Kassidy said.

"You're welcome. I suppose it was the least I could do."

"Yeah, considering you've not really been that helpful otherwise."

Jacen smirked. "I have. You just haven't listened."

Kassidy sat with that for a moment, confused. Part of her wanted to lash out, but she was filled with a different energy.

"Yeah, I have. I know where it is."

"Good. That's real good. Then I'll leave you with this," Jacen said. "When it comes to the scythe, think less 'quest for the fleece' and more 'Thor.'"

I don't even know how to respond to that.

"Got it. Thor all the way," Kassidy said, perplexed. "Hey, you never told me what you are."

"No," Jacen said. "I suppose I didn't."

With that, he shimmered out of existence. Kassidy didn't know if she'd see him again. A part of her suspected they'd cross paths again one day, but in the end, it was irrelevant. She had work to do.

Closing her eyes, Kassidy tapped into the feelings she'd absorbed from Lynn. The warmth found a home in her soul. When she opened her eyes, the sensation of her power excited her.

Kassidy smiled as she coalesced into vapor and took to the skies.

CHAPTER FORTY-FOUR

KASSIDY MATERIALIZED AT THE GRAVE OF MARLENE SIMMONS, HER adoptive mother and quite possibly one of the sweetest women she'd ever known. Kassidy had been gone from home for about fifteen years when Marlene died. She might not have even known of Marlene's passing had she not been working a missing persons case for a Chicago-based client. As was her practice, she often called hospitals first when someone had gone missing. It was rare, but every once in a while, someone would get admitted with no identification, or they'd be treated and discharged just as quickly as they'd come in. She'd also grown accustomed to contacting county morgues. It was morbid, sure, but she left no stone unturned. One day she'd called and found out about Marlene.

Kassidy put her case aside and dug into the details. Marlene had been shot and robbed by a young gangbanger trying to make his bones. The police arrested him within seventy-two hours. Once she found out his name, Kassidy was standing in front of him within seventy-two minutes.

She traveled to his jail cell through the Nexus and summarily dispatched him. She'd spoken her piece. She'd scared him, hurt him a bit, and in the end, she ingested his life force and ended him. Immediately afterward she traveled to Marlene's grave, cried, and told her adoptive mother that she'd dispensed justice. Deep down, Kassidy hoped that it would be enough to make up for ghosting the family all those years ago. Kassidy bent down and kissed the black granite grave marker, elegantly designed to memorialize Marlene. It was as flawless as she had been in life.

Now, it was less so.

The marker was shattered into pieces. Most of it on the grass, some of it in the six-foot-deep hole where Marlene's casket lay . . . open and empty. Someone had destroyed the lovely remembrance of Kassidy's mother. Someone had desecrated her grave.

Just as she had, someone figured out where Dan had hidden the Scythe of Cronus—and liberated it.

CHAPTER FORTY-FIVE

"I HATE THIS FUCKING PARK." SENAYA SAID SOFTLY AFTER MATERIALIZING in Potter's Field. It wasn't that she had a natural aversion to nice things. Despite the stereotypes of all things associated with death, despite being a Wraith, she liked nice things. She loved beautiful mountains, running lakes, and sunsets. She loved rain and snowfall—she was herself as much a part of the natural order as all those things were. Nevertheless, she hated this place.

Because *she* had been born there.

This was where he'd found Kassidy Simmons, bloody, beaten, and ready to die. This was the spot where he'd felt the first wave of her power, a power that he could not comprehend but knew he had to have. It was here that she came into existence as a Reaper, where she got her first taste of true power, only to later use it against the Primus. It was here the seeds were sown that made Kassidy Simmons the greatest threat to Senaya's plan to make Azra-El all hers.

And it was here that Kassidy Simmons would meet her end.

Senaya walked through the park. In the distance she saw Azra-El on his knees. Was he preparing? Praying? Was he strong enough to even face Simmons tonight? The thoughts ran through Senaya's mind at the speed of light.

Senaya entered the Nexus, approaching him on that plane so as not to incur his wrath. As she neared him, though, she heard him speaking. Yet no one was there. Maybe he was praying after all. But to whom? The only entity he considered worthy of his prayer was Thanatos—and he was actively trying to destroy him. Also, Senaya and two Wraiths had orchestrated the capture and imprisonment of Thanatos. Even if Azra-El was praying to him, those words would fall like butter on a hot skillet.

Curiosity pushed her over the edge, and she crept forward, silently stalking even though she was in the Nexus, a place where he wouldn't hear her as long as he stayed in the real world.

"I promised you I would live a good life, a life of service, of worth. A life such that when I left it, the gods would be pleased to reunite us as reward."

Who is he talking to?

"I tried, my love. I tried so hard. In many ways I succeeded, because when my time came, the gods offered me something else. As Primus, I thought I could find a loophole to you. I served. I did everything Thanatos ever asked of me. Yet he denied my one request—to be with you."

Confusion was Senaya's only ally. Was he talking *to* someone or *about* someone? Was he talking about *her*? Was he in love with Kassidy Simmons?

"It was here though that I found a way, my love. I found a way to reunite us. I found a way to have you by my side forever. Me as a god and you as my goddess. By the end of the night, Thanatos will be no more, and the natural order will be mine to command."

Senaya watched as Azra-El stood and bowed his head.

"Tonight, my beloved Allesandra, my wife, tonight I will bring you back."

As he spoke, he lifted a large scythe to the sky above.

He found it!

Senaya dropped to a knee. She'd known his plan. As his

second in command, she knew he wanted to overthrow Thanatos. She knew he wanted to absorb Kassidy's power because that, added to his own, would somehow, someway, give him everything he needed. All this time, she thought it was about Kassidy. But it was about his wife.

His wife?

What did that mean for her? Would he simply discard her? She had hoped she would become the Primus and his one and only love. In her mind, once he had the power, he would see just how important she was, how important she had been to his ascension. She had stuck by him through everything. Helped him heal. Orchestrated the release of those souls so they could kill and increase the number of souls from which he could feed. She had done all of this for him.

But he'd done nothing for her.

And he'd likely do nothing for her.

His wife?

Senaya felt as if she'd been kicked in the gut. If it had been possible for her die, she might have done so then and there. She was not prone to crying. But her vision blurred as tears formed, ready to fall to the mist-covered ground of the Nexus.

They were interrupted by a sound in the distance. Swirling winds and the resulting blast of snow pulled her attention. Clearing her vision, Senaya watched as Kassidy Simmons stood in the middle of what appeared to be a dissipating snowstorm. She was dressed in all black, much like all Reapers, but there was something . . . more. She seemed determined, full of purpose. Senaya could sense that, even in the Nexus, but she didn't care. Despite what she'd heard Azra-El say, Kassidy Simmons was the cause of it all. If he'd never laid eyes upon that damned girl, he never would have thought to overthrow Thanatos. If not for that damned girl, he never would have thought to pursue the Scythe of Cronus. Without that damned girl, Azra-El would belong to her by now.

She had to go.

Senaya materialized into the real world and marched past Azra-El straight toward Kassidy. She heard her name called. She heard Azra-El demand that she come back. She heard it several times and ignored it.

An arm's length away, Senaya stopped, sizing up the woman who'd caused her so much angst. Her silver eyes glinted with purpose. Power or no power, she was still just a Reaper.

"Well, well, well. Look at . . ."

Senaya stopped midsentence, her eyes locked on Kassidy's, her mouth agape as Kassidy's fist phased through Senaya's chest while her eyes turned from silver to black.

"That's . . . not . . . poss . . ."

Senaya's voice trailed again as Kassidy pulled her hand back to reveal a glowing purple orb. Staring down at it, Senaya reached for her chest but found no wound, no sign that she'd been impaled. She peered into the eyes of Kassidy Simmons.

Eyes that now glowed red.

"No. No. No!"

Kassidy took the purple orb extracted from Senaya, placed it in her mouth, and swallowed. The intensity of her stare increased, as did the brightness. In disbelief, Senaya dropped to her knees.

Her immortality was gone.

"You killed my father," Kassidy said as her right hand transitioned into a large onyx sickle. "You killed my father, and you helped Azra-El kill my love." Kassidy's left hand transitioned into a second large onyx sickle.

"No! No! Wait! I can . . . I can give you—"

"There's nothing you can give me, Senaya. I want nothing from you but your life."

Senaya's life flashed before her eyes as the sickles crossed through her neck.

Her life had not been a good one.

CHAPTER FORTY-SIX

THE KILL ENERGIZED KASSIDY, JUST AS IT HAD THE NIGHT SHE THOUGHT she'd killed Jeremy Reins. There was a time when the satisfaction from reaping made her sick to her stomach. Particularly when she realized that she was being used to further Azra-El's own agenda.

She felt none of that now.

For the first time Kassidy Simmons understood her purpose. She was not a Reaper. She was not a Wraith. She was the daughter of Thanatos, heir to the power of the Death god—his legacy.

Tonight, Azra-El would learn what that meant.

CHAPTER FORTY-SEVEN

KASSIDY STALKED TOWARD AZRA-EL. HER EYES NEVER LEAVING HIS. She sized him up, as she always did, only this time with confidence. She was not the vengeful child full of rage. Her rage was present, to be sure, but focused and purposeful.

"Have you done something different with your hair?" Azra-El asked.

"Not yet," Kassidy said. "Thinking of dying it red though. You know, to match my eyes."

"Well played," Azra-El said, nodding to acknowledge her unprecedented ascension. "I must say, I wasn't expecting this."

"And just what were you expecting? That I'd bow down, fall to the ground, and roll over like a dog?"

"Well . . . yes."

Azra-El had always been cocky. Kassidy had often wondered if he'd been the same way in life. Had he been charismatic and persuasive? Thoughtful and kind? Or had he simply been the same manipulative, abusive, and sarcastic prick he was now? Albeit with much less power. It didn't matter. She hadn't known him then, and in the end it had absolutely no bearing on the fact that he was going to die at her hands.

"Sorry to disappoint. Though when you think about it, this is all your fault. If you'd just let me die . . ." Kassidy let her voice trail off.

"If I'd allowed that, then I'd never get what I want."

"Power?"

"Ultimate power, my dear. The power selfishly monopolized by the gods."

Kassidy's focus shifting toward the scythe in his hand. "How did you find it?"

The ancient weapon seemed to hum with power. It had a long hand-carved wooden handle with a slight curve. Attached to the handle was a large, sharp, curved onyx blade. Kassidy could feel it. There was a slight glow in the blade. She could hear the faint sound of the wooden handle crackle in Azra-El's hand. It was as if the Scythe of Cronus was sentient. No, it *was* sentient. She could sense it.

It was fighting for its life.

"Funny story," he said. "Right before your daddy died, he hotfooted it over to the graveyard. He went to your mother's marker and started digging like a hound dog. He was unflappable. You'd never know he had been in a car accident just an hour before."

Kassidy knew he was trying to rattle her. She kept her mind on the task at hand—killing him.

"Anyhow, once I saw what he was after, I understood. The scythe was there, cradled in the arms of your adoptive mother like a newborn. It began to glow when he reached for it. His wounds were starting to heal. So I swept in, grabbed it . . . and took his head."

It was almost enough to make her pounce. A volcano built inside her, ready to erupt, to destroy everything in her path. To her credit, she held her ground.

Azra-El ground his jaw, and for the first time she felt his emotions. Raw, irrational, primal, and urgent—a contrast to what he presented on the outside. She'd picked up on his occasional bouts of rage, but even those were controlled, more an exercise in power. And she hadn't felt those as an empath as much as she experienced it as one of his Reapers. But this, this was something altogether different. He wanted the power she was manifesting. He wanted it more than anything.

"Your envy is showing," Kassidy said.

Azra-El gave her that cold grin he usually reserved for when he knew something others did not. She probed. She wasn't sure if he'd sense it, but she had to take advantage of the opportunity.

Nothing duplicitous. Nothing to indicate he had a proverbial trick up his sleeve. Was it false confidence? Had that been what it was all this time?

"You think you know so much now, don't you?" he asked with bite. "You think the power of the Primus gives you some type of insight into me? Dominion over all I have commanded for centuries? You dare think you can end me so easily, little girl?"

She hated it when he called her that. It was what he said when he wanted to put her in her place, to get into her head. He was desperate to rattle her newfound confidence.

And still, she nibbled at the bait.

Lunging forward, Kassidy threw an unexpected punch that knocked Azra-El off balance. As he staggered to regain footing, Kassidy followed with a kick to the head, then spun, returning with a foot to the abdomen, before a side kick to the head, knocking him to the ground, the scythe falling from his hand. Kassidy pounced, straddling his chest, and punched over and over. Left, right, left, right, a barrage to the face, turning Azra-El's head from side to side with each blow.

"You ruined everything! You ruined my life! You took people I loved! And for that I'm going to fucking end you!"

Kassidy formed two sickles, each onyx glowing with an intensity they had never before possessed. She plunged them both into Azra-El's chest. The shock on his face, the loud exhale, the feel of his body's response to being impaled, infused her with pleasure. Her satisfaction intensified. She didn't need the Scythe of Cronus.

The only thing she needed was confidence in her abilities.

In herself.

"Your reign ends here, Primus," Kassidy said.

That worry she'd once experienced when she felt satisfaction from a kill was again nonexistent. She'd hoped it didn't mean she would become like him. She hoped it didn't mean that she would simply kill indiscriminately, as he had. As those thoughts flashed in her mind, she had a new hope. She hoped the sound rumbling from his chest wasn't the beginning of a laugh.

But it was.

Azra-El's once pained face morphed into one of amusement and joy. His mouth opened wide, and he threw his head back as he laughed at her, mocking her. She dug and twisted her sickles into him.

"Are you done, little girl?" he asked. "Because it's my turn."

Kassidy felt herself lifted from the ground, enveloped in cold as she sailed through the air from a punch to the face that came out of nowhere. She landed twenty yards away, the ground meeting her body with extreme prejudice. Dazed, she tried to get her bearings and prepare for another attack.

Azra-El stood and retrieved the ancient weapon that had fallen from his grip. Within a second he shimmered and reappeared directly in front of her. He grabbed her by the throat and lifted her off the ground, her feet dangling, kicking out in desperation.

He lifted the Scythe of Cronus to her face, rubbing it against her cheek. Power emanated from the blade. That tingle she'd felt when she'd touched those celestial onyx blades was nothing compared to the electric current front this weapon. It called to her. It wanted her.

"You weren't made for this power, little girl. This power wasn't made for you. I don't know how you managed to ascend, but your time is done."

Kassidy gripped his arm with both hands. She struggled to position herself against him, tried to kick off and backward, but she found no weakness, no point of resistance. Her power, her newfound confidence, slipped away.

"Well, no more red. Look at those lovely black eyes," Azra-El said with a sneer. "Oh, wait. My mistake. I meant to say silver. Must have been a temporary thing . . . Reaper!"

Kassidy felt her control slipping.

Azra-el threw the scythe into the ground, then pushed his hand inside her chest to remove her essence.

CHAPTER FORTY-EIGHT

"KASSIDY!"

She heard her name, but no one was there. There was . . . nothing.

"Kassidy!"

She couldn't see herself. There was only the unmistakable feel . . . of nothing. No light, no darkness, no hot or cold, it was simply . . . nothing.

As a child, Kassidy had been both fascinated and terrified by the prospect of death. Her ability to see Reapers did nothing to ease those fears. She had no idea what came next after this life. Eight-year-old girls simply didn't sit on park benches and talk to beings who ushered souls into the afterlife. Even when Kassidy became a Reaper, her knowledge of the afterlife was limited. People went to the Beyond or to the Void. She had no say in the matter, as far as she knew. There was never an opportunity to slip into one plane of existence or the other to check them out. For the folks headed to the Beyond, all she could do was wish them well and assure them they'd be in a wonderful place. Those who went to the Void, she usually said nothing—unless she was certain they were deserving, like the son of a bitch who'd killed Marlene. Even then, though, she never really knew what it meant to be in the Void.

Until now.

"Holy shit," she whispered. "I'm . . . in the Void."

"Kassidy!"

"Who's there?"

She thought she recognized the voice. It was deep, strong, and seemed to get closer. There was no sense of a presence though.

This place, this Void, was just that—a dark, empty, lonely, cold hollow. It was as if a section of time and space had gone unfinished. It reminded her of the time she went just a little too far into Lake Michigan during a family trip to the Indiana dunes. She and her sister had dared each other, as siblings did, to see who could go out farther into the water. For a kid, there was no greater thrill than that sense of dread when you could no longer feel the floor of the lake. Your mind raced, wondering how far down the bottom truly was. Was it only a foot below? Three feet? Fifty? Were you floating over an abyss that was going to suck you under where you'd be devoured by hungry fish and creatures? Was Jaws lurking beneath?

Kassidy wasn't treading unknown water now though. She was treading a different plane of existence. In water, there was resistance. In this place, there was nothing. In water your body could get warm from your movement, making the liquid world bearable, comfortable. In this place, there was no comfort.

When Kassidy stretched out her hand, hoping to grasp something—anything—there was nothing. Nothing to brace her. Nothing to lean against or sit on. There was just the dark, lonely, cold feel of nothing.

Is this what it's like for the souls that transition here?

Is it just an emptiness with sound coming from everywhere and nowhere at the same time?

How could this be anything less than hell?

"Kassidy!" the disembodied voice said again. "You must return. You must defeat Azra-El."

"I . . . I can't. I thought I could, but I can't. He's too powerful."

"No! Kassidy, you are the child of a god, the child of Death himself. The power he has rightfully belongs to you."

"Who the hell are you?" Kassidy asked, bathed in fear and anger.

"The Primus is a position, not a person. It is an extension of power granted by the god of Death. Azra-El and those who came before him, they did not earn that power. It was given to them. But you, and others like you, are different."

This must be the point where madness sets in.

There was nothingness in the Void. Kassidy could feel her body. She could touch her legs, her arms, her face, but she could see nothing, smell nothing.

Was she even breathing?

She was hearing voices. Well, she was hearing a voice. One she knew, or so she thought. It wasn't a warm and friendly voice. It was deep, rich, almost—regal. Kassidy didn't so much hear the voice as feel it. Throughout her entire being. The hairs on her arms stood up. Her heart raced, even though she wasn't certain it was even beating. The voice filled her. It didn't make her feel safe, but it didn't scare her either. It simply . . . was.

"What is this? Why am I here?"

How many people have I done this to?

Kassidy didn't feel guilt. She was certain that the souls she'd dispatched to this plane were deserving. Unless . . . they weren't. Unless Azra-El somehow had the power to manipulate the will of the universe.

Is that how I got here?

Did he do this?

"Kassidy, you must listen," the voice said again.

"I can't go back, damn you! I don't have the power! I don't . . . have . . . anything . . ."

Anger, sadness, and pity swallowed Kassidy whole. It was as if a large plastic bag covered her, sliding up the length of her before fully enveloping her. She tried to breathe . . . and couldn't. She tore at her encasement, to no avail. She was suffocating. The plastic sheath was shrinking, tightening around her.

This was death.

But just that quickly, it was over.

She was free and breathing, sucking in air as if she'd been held under water for an eternity.

"Kassidy, you have to leave this place. That was just the beginning."

"The beginning? Of what?"

"Of an eternity of torture. You must leave. You must defeat Azra-El."

"Damn you!" she screamed. "I can't!"

Kassidy wanted to cry, but she was over it. Over all of it. She didn't even want a drink. She just wanted it all to end. But not in this place. She couldn't endure an eternity here.

"You can leave this place," the voice said. "The power is within you. More than Azra-El or any Primus, the power is within you. You are a child of Death. You are an extension of him and his power. What belonged to your father belongs to you."

My father?

"Earlier tonight you understood that. Accepted it. But you let Azra-El's manipulations control you."

The voice was right. She'd played right into his hands. Her confidence had been there, fueled and strengthened by Lynn's love, but it had faltered when she'd let the seeds of doubt grow. He preyed upon that.

And that brought her here.

Not him.

Her.

"What do I do? He has the scythe."

"Like his power and yours, the Scythe of Cronus is also an extension of the god of Death. Unlike him though, your power is within. It always has been, just waiting for you to claim it. The power, the scythe, they are tools of death. You are Death's legacy. So—"

"The Scythe belongs to me," Kassidy finished softly.

"Yes . . ." said the voice, dragging out the word like a proud teacher.

"That's why it's fighting against him."

"Yes."

Kassidy thought back to the words Jacen Lucas had spoken when she'd seen him in the Nexus. He'd said to think less "quest for the fleece" and more "Thor."

Guess it's time to see if I'm worthy.

"How do I get back?" she asked.

"You are the Mistress of Death, Kassidy Simmons. Simply will it into being."

As titles went, it wasn't the greatest, but it was better than "Kassidy Simmons, Corpse." It was difficult to fathom that the key to her happiness, to normalcy, was simply embracing who she was. Of course, in her defense, she hadn't known who she was until recently. But there was a difference between knowing it, feeling it, and accepting it.

"Who are you?" she asked again.

"You know who I am, Kassidy. After you return, after you've finished, come find me."

Awareness flooded through her. Awareness, longing, and,

strength. It filled her, just as Lynn's love had earlier. She felt . . . everything. Anger, sadness, guilt, pity, and love.

A father's love.

Thanatos!

"I will . . . Father."

CHAPTER FORTY-NINE

KASSIDY'S EYES OPENED.

Azra-El's hand was within her chest as he prepared to take her essence. She again grasped his arm with both hands, only instead of trying to pull herself from his grasp, she squeezed.

"How cute," Azra-El began, "using your little muscles on me. Aren't you just precious."

His chuckle lingered too long for her liking, and she relished when it stopped and his mouth contorted. As she squeezed, she felt herself being lowered, then heard the first bone crack. In his eyes, she saw her own as they changed from silver to black. When her feet reached the ground, more bones snapped. As Azra-El's mouth opened to scream, this time she felt her eyes as they changed from black to red. When his hand slid from her chest, the bones in his arm grated against one another as her grip became a fist. Staring into his eyes, she felt power run through her that she'd never felt before. She knew, without question, that her eyes had turned from red to gold—the mark of the gods.

Holding his arm up, Kassidy flipped to the side and delivered a side kick to his chest. Azra-El coasted through the air, hitting a tree with such force that the trunk split. With a simple thought, a request of her own will and power, Kassidy shimmered out of view, reappearing directly in front of a stunned Azra-El.

"How . . . is this . . . possible?" he managed to get out in his shock.

Kassidy said nothing. Recalling Jacen's words and her father's voice, Kassidy focused on what she'd learned about herself. She accepted everything she was, and within that, she found courage.

She stretched out her arm. Light illuminated her hand, and as it dissipated, she held the Scythe of Cronus.

"No!" Azra-El exclaimed. "Give that back! It belongs to me!"

Kassidy positioned the scythe in both hands.

"No. Actually, it belongs to my father. But since he's not here right now, I'm going to keep an eye on it."

Bewilderment settled on Azra-El's face, then his eyes widened as realization set in.

"Your . . . father? Thanatos is . . . your father?"

Kassidy answered him with only a grin.

As he sat against the tree holding his crushed arm, Azra-El's eyes flared bright red. He shot up and lunged at Kassidy. Without hesitation, she spun and swung the scythe in a fluid arc.

For several moments, Azra-El's body stood at attention as his head tumbled to the ground and rolled forward in the snow. Before long, his body followed, tumbling down the slight incline, coming to a stop several feet away.

Kassidy studied the scythe in her hand, feeling the weight of its grip. She recalled what they said about this weapon. It could rip a hole in time and space. She could go back and save everyone. She could go back and stop any of this before it began.

She could see her mother.

A crackle of purple energy erupted from the scythe, as if responding to her thoughts. Instinctively, she raised the weapon and tore a line in the air, opening a rift in time and space. Kassidy focused on what she wanted—to travel back, to save everyone she could by stopping Azra-El from becoming the Angel of Death.

She heard one word.

"Balance."

It was soft, like a whisper, but it flowed through her brain like a stream through the mountains.

"Balance."

Kassidy wasn't sure if she heard it in her memory or if someone spoke it into her mind. But it gave her pause. The deaths that had happened were the result of Azra-El—killing people before their time, making Kassidy a Reaper, holding souls hostage as leverage. He had caused the imbalance. He had changed her in a way that she'd been almost unable to recover from. If she continued on this path, if she stepped into that rift, she would again change everything, and someone else's life could be irrevocably altered.

She could not allow that.

She was now the mistress of Death—Death's legacy. It was her destiny to restore what had been damaged.

With a heavy sigh, Kassidy lifted the scythe, traced the rift with the tip of the blade, and watched it close. She scanned for Azra-El's head and body as they lay in the snow. With an outstretched hand, she ignited them in purple flame and watched them dissipate.

Satisfied, Kassidy took a final look at Potter's Field, then shimmered out of view.

EPILOGUE

†RACI LEEDS SAT ON HER COUCH, STARING AT THE TEXT MESSAGE from Kassidy. It was short, but it was sweet and thoughtful. Hey. *Just wanted to say hi and see how you're doing. Maybe we can meet for a drink soon? We should really talk.* It had been days since Kassidy had left her apartment to check on her lover and her friend.

She thought back to the first time she'd seen Kassidy. She hadn't really changed that much in twenty years. Traci had recognized Kassidy almost immediately when she'd come out of the bookstore on Main Street. Traci had been sitting at the coffee shop across the street, cancelling yet another appointment with her psychiatrist, when she happened to glance up from her phone. When realization set in, the scenes flooded back. The kidnapping. The abuse. The fear. The fight.

The girl with the black eyes who'd saved them all.

She'd found her. After all this time, she'd found the woman who'd given her a second chance at life. The woman who'd shown her that even though monsters existed, they could be beaten. The one who'd shown her that there was true magic in the world.

Magic that she'd then sought out.

Magic that she'd studied.

Magic that she'd mastered.

Traci didn't know if she'd have a chance at a long life with Kassidy, or any type of life with her, but she was willing to take what she could get.

Traci stretched out her hand and willed the drink she'd left on her desk to float to her. She took a sip, smiled wide, and texted a reply.

•   •   •

On the observation deck of the Willis Tower, Jacen Lucas stood, staring out at the city he loved. At night, nothing was more beautiful than the lights and energy of downtown Chicago. He gazed at Soldier Field, illuminated and packed with people, bundled up in multiple layers of shirts and socks, desperate for another Chicago Bears win. At one time, he'd been one of those faithful. He'd have braved the cold on a whim just to join his fellow fans for tailgating and sports fun.

That was then.

Jacen had a new job now. A job that kept him busy. A job that would make any one of the fans in that stadium wet themselves. He was an Advocate. Whether he was a force for good or a force for something else rested solely on the needs of the world at large—though sometimes things happened simply because he wanted them to.

Like the coin toss in tonight's game.

But there were new things looming in the universe. Threats, dangerous elements that could threaten a delicate balance. He was powerful enough to intervene, but that wasn't exactly his job. Jacen moved people around like chess pieces, and for someone who'd never actually learned the game, he played it like a master.

He walked from his view of Soldier Field to the eastern view of the city, an illuminated Navy Pier in the distance. Next to him stood a woman with long dark hair, haunting hazel eyes, and finely sculpted Mediterranean features.

"Kassidy has ascended," Jacen said. "She did well."

The woman smiled and nodded.

"And the next steps are in place?" she asked.

"They are," Jacen said.

"The girl?"

"Traci? She's in play."

"Mr. Burke?"

"Yes. Jaxon has been found. We start with him tomorrow."

"Good." She turned to face him. "Thank you, Jacen. I am in your debt."

"Oh, yes you are. And I promise you, I'll be calling in that marker."

"I'd expect nothing less from an Advocate," the woman said.

Jacen bowed and shimmered out of view.

Seconds later, the woman put on her overcoat and walked toward the exit. Her hazel eyes transitioned to an ethereal blue.

"I'll see you soon, Kassidy," she whispered.

ACKNOWLEDGMENTS

Writing is a solitary art. On any given day, the author's only companions are a pen and a pad—or a keyboard. But there are many people behind the scenes that offer support and breathe hope into the artist—and that support helps the words flow.

To my mother, Azizza, my biggest champion, your love and support carried me through the years and helped me get to this point. I cannot possibly thank you enough for all you've done. Loveness!

My father, Robert, and my son, Derek, have both taught me the importance of finishing what you start. I'm an awful student, admittedly, but their work ethic is an excellent example for anyone and it's something that's been inspiring to me over the years. Hopefully, when I grow up, I can be just as tenacious as the two of you. The son becomes the father, and the father becomes the son. I love you both!

This book would not be happening if not for the many people I've met in the San Diego writing community. But I wouldn't know the people in this community had I not been encouraged to transition here from Chicago. For that, I must thank my cousins, Hassan, and Vanessa Davis. Thank you for opening your home to me to allow me to fly. Much love Cobruh and Sisco!

Somewhere along my journey I managed to obtain a Master of Fine Arts degree in Creative Writing. Many thanks to National University, but a special thanks to my advisor and mentor, Amina Cain. You helped me shape the wet clay that was my thesis into a workable manuscript. I will be forever grateful.

And to the writing community of San Diego—what can I say? I have learned so much about the craft of writing and the business of publishing from sitting with you, talking with you, and listening to you. The support is heartwarming, and it keeps me motivated to do my absolute best. Thank you to San Diego Writers Ink for the wonderful workshops, Mysterious Galaxy Bookstore for hosting events featuring amazing writers, Jonathan Maberry and the Writers Coffeehouse, and the staff and workshop facilitators of the Southern California Writers' Conference.

Watching the journey of several local writers was inspiring. Their experiences helped push me to work harder. One of those authors, Indy Quillen, encouraged me to attend my first writers conference, and it was there that I met the people I'd eventually partner with to publish Death's Legacy. So, thank you for that, Indy. I'd likely not be here at this time, without you!

I've worked with two amazing editors on this journey. Thank you, Dori Harrel for taking my manuscript and helping me chip away at the rough edges, while working hard to fine tune my voice. And thank you, Molly Lewis for asking those tough questions and shining a light on some shadows within the story.

And to Holly Kammier and Jessica Therrien . . . I warned you I'd be thanking you on a regular basis, and I'm warning you now that it will likely continue well beyond this book. I am so very thankful to have met you both, and so incredibly grateful that you took a chance on me. Being a part of Acorn Publishing has been a dream come true. I look forward to a continued partnership with the Acorn Family!

ABOUT THE AUTHOR

Dennis Crosby grew up in Oak Park, IL and completed his undergraduate work at the University of Illinois in Chicago. With a degree in Criminal Justice, he spent six years working as a Private Investigator and during that time developed an affinity for writing poetry. While working on a master's degree in Forensic Psychology, Dennis transitioned into social service. Dennis has spent the last twelve years working with men and women experiencing challenges with mental health and addiction. He currently serves as Clinic Director for an Opioid Treatment Program.

With a lifelong passion for writing, Dennis wrote dozens of short stories, tapping into his creative side, but did not pursue the finer points of the craft until later in life. After leaving Chicago and moving to San Diego, Dennis had the opportunity to get more involved in the writing community where he strengthened his talents and understanding of the craft. To further augment his writing skills, Dennis completed an MFA program at National University.

A self-proclaimed geek and lover of pop culture, Dennis still lives and writes in San Diego, CA.

Made in the USA
Coppell, TX
11 December 2020